Death
at the
Devil's Hands

by

Miriam Winthrop

CaliPress

2020 CaliPress© Paperback Edition
Copyright © 2020 by Miriam Winthrop
All rights reserved, including the right of reproduction in
whole or in part in any form.

Cover art photo credit:
Reynisdranger/https://flickr.com/photos/37996646802@N01/3054059656
by cogdogblog 2008, modified
All other art is the sole property of Miriam Winthrop.

Published in the United States by CaliPress©.
CaliPress@comcast.net

ISBN-13: 9798561951589

1 Literary Fiction/International Mystery and Crime
2 Literary Fiction Themes/Friendship
3 Mystery Characters/Amateur Sleuth
4 Mystery Settings/Islands

Death at the Devil's Hands

1

The morning it started, Frau Meickle woke late. Why, she couldn't say. Even when on vacation, she rose early. What made her take the binoculars to the patio, she didn't know. She had never done that before, either. And what prompted her to focus on the cove below, she had no idea. But that was what she had done.

Perched a quarter of a mile above the ocean, the house had quite a view. The water in the cove below was as turquoise as any tropical sea but icy cold, Frau Meickle knew. To the west, she saw the yacht that had been anchored offshore since her arrival, blazing white in a bright sun. The mid-Atlantic location of the Azores archipelago attracted many such luxury vessels. A repurposed fishing boat hugged the coastline. She had seen it twice before, bringing divers who wanted to see the rich underwater life. A small ferry headed to open water with tourists watching for pods of whales. She saw whales and dolphins from the patio every day, but they held no interest for her.

That morning, her attention was claimed by a patch of water at the center of the cove, where a basalt arch rose through the surface of the Atlantic. Broken at its top, it looked like the fingers of some undersea giant rising from the depths. Near its base, a stain was darkening the crystalline blue water to some muddy shade. Close by, the fisherman who she usually saw earlier in the day was silhouetted black against the strong sunlight reflecting off the water. He entered the shadow of the giant's fingers, where he prepared to set the first of his traps. She followed him until he disappeared from view behind the stony outcrop, and squeezed her eyes shut to clear her vision.

She returned her attention to the yacht. Through the twin lenses of the binoculars, she saw a woman bundled against the brisk air in a long hooded robe, shuffling back and forth across a small stretch of deck, and a stroller being pushed round and round an equally small space further aft. Nothing of interest to Frau Meickle.

The divers were already underwater, but the divemaster remained on board. For the first time, she saw him up close. Magnificently built, he stood at the bow wearing only a pair of shorts despite the early morning chill. Deeply tanned skin slid over muscle as he lifted his arms and pointed his own pair of binoculars in her direction. She pulled the binoculars away from her eyes and moved out of sight behind a potted tree. It crossed her mind that the divemaster might have been watching the fishing boat, which had come dangerously close to the spiky rocks, but she thought nothing more about that.

She peeked at the scene between large glossy leaves. The patch of discolored water at the base of the ragged pillar had become a streak that reached from the rocks to the beach below her. Through the binoculars she followed it back to its origin, where a ring of pink foam had formed around the giant's finger. She adjusted the focus. A clump of black strands she had taken for seaweed of some sort resolved into strands of hair. She had just made out two eyes, open in surprise, when something in her peripheral vision drew her attention. It was a shark.

It was a lovely evening to fly.

Through one of the grimy terminal windows, Lori saw Carlos Bettencourt running through his pre-flight checklist. After nearly a hundred flights together, it was a familiar sight. His tall, trim figure carried a clipboard around the Cessna, checking the movement of the rudder, inspecting the flaps, kicking the tires, looking into the fuel tank.

The man was as well groomed as ever. The neatly pressed black pants and white shirt he usually wore when on the job had been replaced by navy pants—neatly pressed—and a white shirt of only a slightly more relaxed nature. Even at a distance, his dark good looks stood out.

The terminal wasn't a place for travelers to line up for outgoing flights or to wait for luggage from incoming flights. It was one small room where pilots and their passengers took refuge during the downpours that could hit the island without warning. There were five plastic chairs and a folding table with a deck of playing cards that had been there so long no one could remember who had left it. The calendar on the wall showed a picture of dogs and a summer month three years in the past. Two stained glass ashtrays spoke of the habit that still had a strong hold on islanders, old and young. An 1960s refrigerator held an assortment of soft drinks, a couple of bottles of local wine, and the last piece of a cake that a pilot's daughter had made for his birthday. The new golf clubs his friends had chipped in to get him were propped up in a corner. No one would take them. This was Santa Maria, and here everyone was a neighbor and everyone was family of one sort or another.

There were no scheduled flights. Arrangements were made informally, by email or text, over the phone or over the fence. *Could you get me to my cousin's wedding party on Terceira next Saturday? I want to show my relatives from Canada what our islands look like from the air. I need to go into Ponta Delgada tomorrow for a day of shopping.* Packages were brought in and dropped off, even mail could make its way to the airfield when the larger airport was socked in with fog or too busy with tourist flights carrying descendants of the diasporas that had depopulated the archipelago of nine islands.

Carlos spotted Lori the moment she opened the door to the tarmac. He lifted his trademark dark glasses to the top of his head and waved. He no longer lost his train of thought or dropped things when he saw her, but he was no less smitten with the statuesque blond than he'd been at first sight.

Halfway between the terminal and the Cessna, they kissed once. The nature of their relationship now called for more than the casual three kisses with which he had greeted her when they first met, one on each of her cheeks and a third traditionally meant to wish an unmarried woman luck in finding a husband.

She clambered in through a door under the wing and settled herself for a flight that at twenty minutes would be half the time it had taken her to commute from her Manhattan co-op to her office on Madison Avenue.

After Carlos had checked the instrument dashboard to his satisfaction, he tucked a lock of Lori's long hair behind her shoulder and fastened her harness.

"Are you worried we'll crash?" she asked. Her lighthearted tone told only part of the story. She may have trusted his piloting skills as much as anyone's, but she still felt the nerves of a first-time passenger whenever she flew in such a small plane.

"I just like taking care of you." He didn't share her nerves. He was a good pilot, skilled in dealing with the sudden updrafts and storms above their islands, and he knew he'd bought a good little plane. It had cost him his inheritance, every single euro of his inheritance.

There was no air traffic control to clear takeoff. No flight plans had been filed. Carlos would be flying *visual flight rules*, watching the skies for other planes. He pushed the throttle forward, released the brakes, and turned the key to set the propeller spinning.

The din was barely muted by the headsets they wore, and she heard his voice only indistinctly. "Ready?"

Their arms touched in the small cabin. She leaned against his and gave him a thumbs-up.

He flashed a smile, bright white against his olive complexion, and the soft-spoken, formal man gave way to the adventurer with a whoop. Past the terminal, down the runway, and they were airborne over the Atlantic Ocean.

From the air, Lori saw the brilliant green fields and valleys of what had become her home, the island of Santa Maria—or to be more specific, Casa do Mar, the struggling rural hotel of Anton, Catarina, and their children. That there was no blood relation was irrelevant. That they had met only sixteen months earlier made no difference. They were her family. Since the evening she'd told the ocean *I'm staying here*, she'd been the happiest she'd ever been in life.

Carlos was confident enough to flip through the local newspaper while the plane forged ahead, level and steady and on course. He'd been known to do more than that, alarming Lori by cutting the noisy single engine to float quietly above the ocean. "If we run out of gas, my *aviãozinho*—my little plane—can glide like this for miles," he soothed her. "We can be like birds and set down beside the cows in a pasture."

He pointed to a notice for the sale of a house near Casa do Mar. His friends thought they knew exactly why he was interested in replacing his tiny bachelor apartment on São Miguel with a house close to Lori on Santa Maria. But there was more to it than they realized. Anton and Catarina's family had drawn him into its orbit, just as it had Lori. He was fond of the Sunday dinners, the football games with the children, the peaceful evenings watching the sun set over the ocean, the nights of music and dancing with what seemed to be the entire village.

He raised his eyebrows twice in rapid succession to ask to what she thought of the little stone house, at one time where the village cooper had made casks for local wines.

Her gold-green eyes straight ahead—and a bit wider than usual—she jabbed her hand at the cockpit window, through which the São Miguel airport had suddenly emerged through a light haze and was growing larger by the second.

Humor flickered in his eyes. "I'm going to have to teach you to fly my aviãozinho, so you do not worry so much." He twisted around to grab the pilot's cap he almost never wore, and he put it on her head. "One day, in a year or two or three, you may want to take it out yourself."

He saw a long future for them.

Air traffic control made itself known through sizzling static. Near-total immersion had improved Lori's Portuguese quickly, but she could only make out that something unexpected had happened.

"We must circle while another plane lands," Carlos filled her in.

"The pilot beloved by all doesn't have priority?" she teased. It was only partly in jest. Despite his reserved demeanor, he was popular.

"The runway is being held open for a plane carrying a sick man."

"Do you want to call Martim?" One of Carlos's closest friends was introducing his fiancée to them over drinks at the marina.

He banked sharply left and took them into a 360° turn over São Miguel. "It will probably be about twenty minutes."

"What if it's longer?"

He knew this side of her—the obsession with time that plagued most Americans—and he handed her his phone with a grin.

It was a short conversation. Martim was as unconcerned as Carlos. He said Natalia was probably going to be late by about half an hour, and he was content to take pictures of what was shaping up to be a beautiful sunset while he waited for everyone. Island time. *Probably. About.* Lori still couldn't shake a lifetime where 7p.m. meant 7p.m. and not some undefined time after that.

The light was waning when Carlos gently set down on the runway to start their evening, Lori saw the reason for their delay. A gurney rattled its wheels as it was pushed across the tarmac by an attendant whose pace was close to running. The lack of forethought was also something that Lori found difficult to accept. No ambulance waited. Instead, the patient, frail and small in a blanket cocoon, was lifted into a large SUV that sped off down the highway.

I hope they make it, she thought.

Each of the nine islands of the Azores archipelago has its own character. They range from pastoral to urbanized, from temperate climates to Mediterranean climates, from the fine sandy beaches of

Santa Maria to rugged Ponta do Pico, from tiny Corvo with fewer than five hundred residents to São Miguel, the most populous of the islands.

São Miguel is also the most modern of the islands. Its capital, Ponta Delgado, seems almost busy with the occasional bleat of a taxi horn, clusters of tourists taking pictures, and planes carrying fresh seafood to all parts of the world.

A procession of boats was converging on the harbor. Some were pleasure craft or had been converted to service tourism, but the majority were the boats that brought up crustacea and fish from the fertile waters and ferried produce between the islands. During the day, this was at its heart a working marina.

At night, the waterfront became a place where islanders spent a few relaxed hours, fishermen complained or boasted about the day's catch, old men re-lived memories, families celebrated occasions, and couples shared a romantic evening. The colorful lights of shops, cafés, and newer buildings—one as tall as twelve stories—were reflected on the shiny white hulls of yachts and the wine glasses of diners.

Lori and Carlos swung clasped hands gently back and forth as they walked. They bypassed most other islanders, who strolled at a more leisurely pace, and along the way they caught snippets of conversations.

"I think she likes me," one young boy confided in another.

"No dessert for me tonight," a portly man patted his stomach, and Lori smiled at the thought of Anton's recurring resolutions to eat less.

A couple of girls at that age between childhood and adolescence, overtook them, each talking on her cell phone.

"It will be alright," someone reassured a friend.

Two women, intent on unwrapping candies, nearly bumped into them. "We have to sell the farm," one quavered. It wasn't the first time Lori or Carlos had heard that from strangers and from friends. It was a problem. Modern lifestyle and the distance of the islands from the rest of the world were taking their toll.

Lori had been keeping an eye out for Martim. "Do you think we should call again?"

Carlos shrugged. For him, an hour's delay wasn't the same cause for alarm that it was for the former New Yorker whose life had run on schedules before moving to the Azores. He chuckled and passed her his phone.

Martim's phone went to voice mail. She sent a text. *Lori here. Making sure you're okay.* No response. She handed the phone back to Carlos. "Wouldn't he answer if he were just delayed."

He kissed her. "Maybe he and Natalia are occupied," he said suggestively. "He will let us know if he still wants to meet."

They had reached the far end of the marina. As commercial waterfronts go, it was as close to seedy as one got in the Azores—which wasn't very. Fights occasionally broke out. Drugs were sold but not much. Liquor was smuggled in duty-free. A pickpocket—not native—had been arrested by police two months ago. A prostitute—also not native—had been seen milling around when a cruise ship docked last summer and had been promptly deported.

About 9:30, they headed to a restaurant at the end of a wharf, where diners could look out the windows by their tables and directly into the black water below. As in many European cities, it was a reasonable time for islanders to eat, so there was a line outside the front door.

"What do you think of the house?" Carlos asked.

"It's close to Anton and Catarina."

He could barely wait for her response before adding, "It's a thirty-minute walk to Casa do Mar!"

It wasn't clear whether he meant that was how long it would take him to walk the distance or that was how close to her family Lori would be if she lived in the house with him. "Are you thinking seriously of moving?"

In his excitement, he skipped over answering her question. "The owner left the house as a child sixty years ago. He returned twice, but the last time he told the estate agent that he's too old to make the trip again."

The businesswoman in Lori stepped in with a reality check. "Aviãozinho was a big expense. Are you ready to take on more?"

"You know we have few buyers for houses on our islands, so the price is good. And I can rent it for two years, while I work on the house."

He was so happy. She hated to burst his bubble, but her radar was on alert. "Work?"

"The outside is in good shape. The inside needs some attention."

With his optimistic life view, that meant the inside was in ruins. Actually, the place sounded remarkably like the buildings of Casa do Mar when Anton and Catarina bought the old dairy.

"That means potential but..." She was about to say something about being cautious when a group of German tourists came up behind them, bringing with them a strong smell of beer and a weaker one of vomit, and called for a table.

Carlos covered his nose and drew Lori closer. A waiter caught his eye and lifted his eyebrows in the direction of a table with the bill and a stack of euros at the center.

Lori felt Carlos's rising tension when the Germans, laughing loud and hard, crowded them from behind. "I'm sorry," he said, and he put a protective arm around her. "Shall we go somewhere else?"

"I'm fine." She knew *he* wasn't fine. In fact, she'd never seen him uncomfortable in quite this way.

The large table the waiter had alerted Carlos to was vacated and quickly pulled apart into four smaller tables. Reserved signs were placed on each, and the waiters exchanged small smiles. One of the tourists pushed his way inside and had angry words with a waiter, in German not Portuguese.

Carlos turned his back on the scene and put himself between Lori and the group.

"We'll be seated soon, and all this will be forgotten," she soothed.

The confrontation ended in a stalemate, and the drunken group stormed off to try their luck elsewhere.

Lori unwrapped her shawl. "I'm glad that's over with."

Carlos forced a smile.

"What's wrong?" she asked as he pulled out a chair and held it for her, one of the old-fashioned courtesies that had taken her by surprise—and that she had initially resisted when she first arrived—but now one of the things she treasured as simply a Carlos-thing.

He gritted his teeth. "I am familiar with such behavior. I know those voices. I know those smells."

"Your father?"

"My father. My grandfather. My uncles and cousins." The story of his life before he learned to fly had been limited to sketchy descriptions of a childhood as a quiet boy in a home with a hard-working mother and a father who liked to drink and was often at sea.

Two hours later, they were feeding each other the last bites of the pastry they had shared. She held herself still and allowed herself to be drawn into his warm brown eyes and gentle smile. He marveled at her poreless skin—now tanned by year-round exposure to sun—her perfect mouth, and her very white, very regular teeth, as favored by Americans.

By the time he lifted his finger for the check, it was after midnight. Outside, the marina was winding down for the night. Ropes creaked and rowboats thudded peacefully against wood pilings with every swell from the open sea. Palm fronds sculled the air. Seagulls swooped in to feast on fishermen's leavings and the oysters exposed by low tide.

Arms wrapped around each other's waists, they walked slowly along the shore, ankles tickled by foam, feet slipping into silky sand. The air had cooled, but walking warmed her and Lori slipped off her shawl. Carlos hadn't been used to seeing such muscular arms on a woman when they first met, but now he found himself proud when she wore sleeveless dresses, as she had tonight.

When the last rectangles of light from houses along the shore blinked out, she reached for his wrist and turned it to see the dial of his watch. "It's late even for the islands." And by the time they'd worked their way through warrens of deserted roads to Carlos's apartment, a tinge of light had appeared in the eastern sky.

It would get busy again in this next hour after dawn. The aromas of baking bread would waft from bakeries. Cow bells would sound in the distance. Bicycles would spin on cobblestones. Church bells would ring for morning Mass. And of course, fishermen would set out to sea again.

Under the outside stairs to his small bachelor apartment above a grocery, they stopped in a shadowy niche to kiss. She tasted wine and chocolate and smelled the cedar of his cologne. She looked into his eyes and felt the possibilities of a new day—with Carlos.

One of Anton's three phones was ringing. Eyes closed, he reached in the direction of the offending sound but, disoriented by the time of day, he swiped everything off the night table. With one very large hand—at the end of one very long arm—he patted the rug beside the bed. The first phone he touched was reserved for Casa do Mar business. It didn't tremble as the ring-ring went on. The next one his hand found was his lifeline to family and friends, also perfectly still despite the insistent trilling. His eyes popped open and with great effort he held them open. The third phone had been issued by the Central Government, by the president himself, to be specific. Anton wriggled the top half of his body off the mattress and scanned the upside down view under his bed. Polished wood but nothing more.

The ringing didn't stop. He managed to swing his legs over the side of the bed and stand, all the while searching for the phone. One stumble was enough to take him nearly halfway across the small room; one more step was enough to nearly crush the phone under his foot.

"It's Luis," a voice informed him. Luis Gomes was head of the Judicial Police, which had authority over more serious criminal activities on the islands—not that there were many. "I'm sorry about the hour."

The hour was midmorning but anyone who knew Anton also knew that for him, it was the middle of the night. Luis wouldn't be calling just to chat.

"A man was found dead near Ponta Delgada yesterday morning." Hearing nothing but heavy breathing from Anton, he went on, "We think it might be a visitor."

In addition to being Minister of Heritage for the islands, Anton had special responsibilities for the vast majority of visitors to the islands: the descendants of emigrants who had been forced to leave their homes by waves of misfortune: earthquakes and volcanoes; the potato blight; diseases that wiped out thriving vineyards and citrus groves; an end to whale hunting.

"A visitor?" The two words were as much as Anton could manage.

"There's a tattoo."

Anton shook his head to clear the cobwebs. "A tattoo? Many people have tattoos."

"It's not the sort of tattoo. You will see."

"I take it the death is suspicious in some way."

"It might have been an accident or homicide…" He continued a couple of seconds later, "…or a shark attack." Luis let that sink in. A shark attack would affect tourism, and the islands depended on tourism for economic survival.

This was another factor that put Anton squarely in the middle of a visitor's death. He had more experience with the international press than most others on the islands, having dealt with well-known billionaires, missing tourists, and foreigners who'd tried to use the islands for everything from drug trafficking to establishing communities that were on the cusp of being cults. Although it wasn't likely the death of a single visitor would attract the same attention; the Azores were usually off the radar of most of the world. "What information is to be released?" he asked.

"That's up to you, Anton."

"I'll work up a press release and send it for approval to…"

"Yes. To the president." Neither had worked closely with the newly elected president before; this would be a test of what to expect from him in the future.

"I've arranged for a car in Ponta Delgada and some assistance…although I know you'll have the help of your own team." By Anton's team, he meant Catarina and Lori.

"And you have the authority to do as you wish," Luis said meaningfully.

For a while after he'd said his goodbyes, Anton thought about the delicious possibility of returning to sleep. He could imagine stretching out in bed. He could imagine pulling the puffy comforter up over his face and shutting out the gray morning light. He could imagine letting his eyelids slowly close. It was, after all, still before ten.

But the urge to share what Luis had told him grew until he gave the hair on his head a rough scrubbing, stretched his fingertips to touch the ceiling, and went to find the person he always had in mind when it came to sharing.

He poked his head in the kitchen. The room was empty, but in the sweet-honey, warm-butter smell of the rolls she'd baked and the bright splashes of pinks and oranges from the cosmos she'd cut, it held a trace of the woman he loved.

The kitchen was his favorite room. He loved the creaking of the floor underfoot, the chips in the woodwork that revealed paint of a dozen different colors, the Dutch door that was usually left open to a view of the Casa do Mar hillside. It was where he pictured his family when he couldn't be with them. It was where they shared meals and worked, where the children did their homework, at the dented and scratched oak table previous owners had left in the barn because it was too heavy for them to move. It was where he and Catarina started their day and ended their day, together.

Sombra sprang to her feet when he opened the door. It wasn't because the dog was his. She'd actually been his gift to Catarina. It wasn't because he was more affectionate with her than others; that distinction would have to go to his daughter, Liliana. It wasn't because he played with her more than others did; that claim belonged to his son, Toni. It was because he could never deny her food when she looked up with hungry, Eeyore-like eyes. Never mind that Sombra romped around Casa do Mar all day, the dog was becoming very well padded. Anton bent at the waist to give her a scratch, and she rewarded him with an affectionate lick.

Tendrils of overnight fog still hung over the island, so thick that it had collected on leaves and dripped on the stone patio outside like a feeble rainfall. He didn't see his wife until she materialized in the doorway, more beautiful to him than even on that first day he had seen her, a tall Dutch girl of sixteen with flaming red hair. Still long and thick but now a rich auburn, the fog had misted it with a silvery cap that he patted off with a dishtowel.

"You are up early," she said, and she poured his strong, black brew into the cup painted *Papa* in a child's hand.

As the fragrant steam slowly rose from his cup and disappeared into the air, he told her about the call from the Luis.

"You are certain the man was dead by yesterday morning?"

"That's what Luis said. Why?"

"Lori texted that the friend they were to have met last night never showed up, but she did speak with him before they landed."

"So…she is…" Even in these more relaxed times, his conservative nature made it hard for him to say the words, "…staying with Carlos in Ponta Delgada?"

A boy's laughter came from just outside the Dutch door. "I bet Carlos is happy about that," quipped Toni—ten years old and the image of his father in face and temperament.

Anton poked his head out and lifted a scolding finger to Toni, who was already nowhere to be seen in the fog.

He was, however, quite pleased at the turn of events with Lori. Finding a husband for her was high on his wish list, much because his own marriage to Catarina made him grateful every day of his life, and he wanted same for the young woman he saw as his younger sister. He'd given the matter a lot of thought—far more than Lori had herself—and had narrowed her choice to Carlos and his own American nephew, Ethan.

He took his first sip with an audible sigh, opened his laptop, and read aloud from the Judicial Police file Luis had sent. "A young man was reported drowned early yesterday morning by Hanna Meickle, a German visitor renting a house above Breakwater Cove. The local police responded within half an hour and found the man on some rocks just offshore. He didn't appear to have been in the water a long time. Both the body and the surrounding area had been washed cleaned by high tide."

He scanned as he scrolled down. "Apparent shark bites. No identification. Possible visitor. No one local reported missing. Body taken to coroner. A few pictures of the scene—wet rocks and seaweed. There isn't much more."

He opened another file and looked at a list of names. "Luis has assigned two officers to the case. I'll have them go around the neighborhood to see if anyone noticed something." He pursed his lips. "They're with the local police." Conflicts between the local police, which had jurisdiction over minor crimes, and the Judicial Police were not unknown. Anton had had a territorial dispute with the São Miguel local police chief in the past. Luis, whose authority trumped that of the local police chief, was making clear just who was in charge.

Catarina put a plate of linguiça in front of him.

"What's the occasion?" He loved the garlicky sausage, but recently she'd been making gentle efforts to improve his diet.

"You have to go to São Miguel," she stated the obvious.

While she made herself a second mug of the milky coffee she preferred, he slipped Sombra a sliver of linguiça, which the dog took to a far corner with a swishing tail. She would return—but only if Catarina's back was turned.

"Would you come with me?" She was as essential to his investigations as she was to his life, but that wasn't the only reason he asked. He thought it would be good for her to get away for a couple of days. In one month, she would be starting as the principal of the Santa Maria lower school. It was her dream job, the direction she'd wanted her life to take before her choice to marry Anton led to her parents disinheriting her. Anton and Catarina had been rather old souls even then, accepting that carefree times and some ambitions would have to wait, as they had.

Anton knew that even a dream job would come with some stress. A generation ago, a child commonly had four, five, even ten siblings. Today, many families had just two or three children and with fewer children, parents had more time to fret about them. There would be worries about progress, complaints about unfair teachers, anger over disputes in sports matches, bad feelings about the casting of school plays.

After the dishes had disappeared into the old cast iron sink, they walked hand in hand through the derelict barn that connected the two spaces the family had made livable for themselves when they moved into Casa do Mar, a kitchen and bathroom at one end and three tiny bedrooms and Catarina's cherished bathtub at the other end.

Now filled with defunct tools, stacks of milking stools, and wheelbarrows that had collapsed to their sides when one wheel rotted, the barn was much like all the buildings of the old dairy before Anton and Catarina began to restore them. Smoky wisps of fog had worked their way through broken windows, where they dribbled down the glass panes and wet the wallboards. Mice scurried in milking stalls; dead insects, their exoskeletons sucked empty by spiders, gathered in corners; husks of caterpillars, vacated for a short life in the sunlight, climbed posts. With a century of dust and cobwebs obscuring every window, it was dimly lit even during the day. At night, it could be pitch black without the flashlights they kept in baskets at either end of the barn.

But they loved every part of their island home.

2

It was a day of sparkling sunshine and Gulf Stream warmth, one of the many moods of the islands. Overhead, birds floated silently on gentle thermals. At the shore, children splashed and built sand castles. Outside cafés, people sipped espressos and sodas.

Returning to his home island always made Anton a little sad. He knew he must have walked the roads cut into its hills with his mother before cancer took her from him. He knew he must have fished off the pier with his father before grief claimed the life of the widower. But Anton didn't remember. What he did remember was doing those things with Catarina.

As arranged by Luis, an unmarked car from the Judicial Police pool was waiting at the airport, keys in the ignition and a printed copy of the file they had reviewed on the passenger seat. Catarina wedged it into the door pocket. They would look through it carefully that evening. For now, they wanted to get to Hanna Meickle before her memories became clouded by time or by the stories that all witnesses can't help but create from what they actually saw, some quickly, some very quickly.

The house Frau Meickle was renting was on a less settled part of the island, not along the coast or in the easily accessible valleys that had been claimed by the first whalers, fishermen, and farmers who settled the Azores. Here and there, driveways cut into the steep cliffs, none marked by street numbers or signs of any sort. With the only directions being *between two large laurels about 6 kilometers from the center of the village*, it took a while to find the entrance.

Anton parked the Fiat at the bottom of the narrow driveway and, Catarina by his side, made his way uphill. He'd been trying to walk more—as directed by Maria Rosa, their island's nurse practitioner and nearest neighbor, and urged by his wife—but his failure to do so consistently was making itself known. He heard his pulse thrumming faster and harder in his ears, and he worked to take in deep lungsful of air.

They left behind the tangles of unpruned trees at the bottom of the driveway, where weeds choked the gravel, for a world different from any they had seen on the islands. Semi-tropical by climate, plants of all sorts could grow lushly in the native soil, but here stark vegetation was set symmetrically, trimmed into unlikely shapes, bracketed by sleek white walls. Shiny metal cones held outsized lightbulbs that at night would illuminate not the path but the modern sculpture set randomly among spikey plants.

Catarina's eyes fixed on a giant bronze sphere as they walked. "Not the most attractive landscaping," she observed.

"Damn hideous," said Anton.

On an island of small stone buildings built two and three hundred years before, the house at the top of the rocky promontory stood out. For one, it was many times larger than virtually any home on São Miguel—or on any of the islands. For another, it was a modern glass-and-steel construction, with a roof of two steeply pitched plates that faced the same direction. Sunlight glanced off the shiny manmade materials. Windows reflected sky and the tips of the tallest trees.

Anton shook his head once with regret that such a monstrosity could be found on his islands. Then he shook it a second and third time to try to dislodge the image from his brain. He was a tolerant man in most matters, but he felt a strong responsibility to protect the land and the culture he loved from being replaced.

The house seemed to grow taller with every step toward it. Watching a line of birds enjoying the view from the roof peak, Catarina tipped her head further and further back until just before they reached the door, she was thrown off balance a little. She instinctively grabbed for Anton's arm, and he instinctively held her tight.

Still panting from the climb, he asked, "Ready?" and he took a half-step behind her. She wasn't there just to keep him company. It went without saying that she would take the lead in the interview. His participation would be decided after they met Frau Meickle.

She lifted a sleek steel door knocker the size of a dinner plate. The sound of footsteps grew as someone approached the door, followed by the unusual sound of not one but two locks being turned. They had never even received a key to the front door of Casa do Mar when they bought it two years ago, and they had never felt the need to have one made.

"Who is there?" The question was asked in a voice one might expect of an attorney arguing a case in court or a political candidate debating an opponent, and it was asked in German, which settled the issue of Anton's participation, unless the woman spoke Portuguese or some of the English Anton had been working hard to learn.

Catarina, who was fluent in four languages, answered in German. "This is Catarina Vanderhye. I am here with Anton Cardosa, Minister of Heritage for the Central Government.

The door remained shut. "What is it that you want?"

"We are here to talk about the report you made to the police on Tuesday morning."

Apparently that wasn't enough information. "What does the Minister of Heritage have to do with a police report?"

Her procrastination wasn't in vain. Their exchange gave Catarina time to form an impression of the woman behind the door and to decide on the best way to deal with her. "Minister Cardosa's responsibilities include matters that deal with visitors to our islands."

The door was opened decisively. Backlit by strong sunlight coming through floor-to-ceiling windows stood a woman in her forties, trim, tan, and dressed in turquoise Spandex shorts and an orange tank top. She gave the impression of being very fit.

Catarina extended her hand with a small smile and slightly lowered eyes. It would be best to assume a subordinate role, she had decided. "Frau Meickle, the minister and I both extend our apologies for the incident that has disturbed your time on our islands."

The short curls on her head gave a single bounce when she nodded, "Come in." Even when speaking, her face remained as rigid as her muscled arms.

Inside, an air conditioner hummed—not common but probably necessary in a house where large windows couldn't be thrown open. Catarina preferred fresh air scented with sea brine and garden flowers, even if it was a bit too warm on some days and a bit too cool on others.

"Would this be a convenient time to ask a few questions?"

"I don't see how I have anything more to contribute."

"Your skill in observation might be essential to discovering the truth."

She liked that. "Yes. Of course. Come this way."

She turned 180° and headed to a glass wall that overlooked the cove where the body had been found.

Had Anton's face reflected the thoughts running through his mind as he walked through the open plan house, it would have been very sour. With sharp lines and hard surfaces, it was not a welcoming space to him. It was a room washed of all color—carpets, walls, sectional sofas, flat expanses unadorned walls and a marble coffee table large enough for two grown men to stretch out on, all in some shade close to gray. There were none of Casa do Mar's homey touches, no proudly framed crayon drawings, no pitchers or bowls with cracks from fiascos now remembered with a chuckle, no flowers from the garden or crumbs from the rolls that had been baked that morning. No, this was not Casa do Mar.

"The government appreciates your help," Catarina emphasized as they settled on white leather chairs.

"One must do one's part."

Catarina could see Frau Meickle fighting with herself over which persona to adopt: cooperative or inconvenienced. "Clearly, you are someone who does her part—and more."

That settled it. "I am, of course, happy to help."

Before asking a single question, Catarina gave Frau Meickle an opportunity to define her position in their relationship—and Frau Meickle was happy to avail herself of that opportunity. The first thing she told her was that she was a director at an investment bank headquartered in Zurich. She had rented the property for the one week she took every spring to re-energize before returning to her demanding job. She took a tangent to explain that her research had indicated such re-energizing was best accomplished by going to, as she put it, "some out-of-the-way spot where there is nothing to do." The brief account had told Catarina quite a bit about how to best approach the woman.

"Could you tell me what you remember of that morning?" Catarina had learned that with most people, it was best to ask open-ended questions and wait to hear what they said. It told her what was uppermost in someone's mind.

"For some reason, I woke rather late, about 8:30, and went directly to the patio." She pointed through the towering windows to a whitewashed expanse with a lap pool. "The owner keeps a pair of binoculars in the drawer there, and I took them with me."

The last thing Catarina wanted to do was interrupt Frau Meickle's train of thought but in this case, she thought it would help bring to mind more of what they were there to find out. "Would it be possible to see where you were standing?"

She sprang up. This was not a woman who enjoyed sitting still.

Anton, on the other hand, struggled to get out of his low-slung chair. When he joined them, Frau Meickle was pointing to the two halves of a basalt arch that had split at some time in the distant geologic past and now loomed over the ocean's surface close to the shore. Islanders called it the Devil's Hands not just for its shape—like knobby fingers—but for the reddish hue it took on at sunset. Anton, who'd grown up on São Miguel, had been warned to steer clear of it since the first time he rowed away from the shore on his own. The Azores were after all the tops of jagged undersea mountains, and just below its surface, the ocean hid numerous peaks that could snag boats small and large.

The waters surrounding the Devil's Hands were death traps.

Coruscations twinkled off water drops that sprinklers had left on the quartz floor and on a steel railing that ran along a deck larger than all of Casa do Mar's living spaces put together. Not a place where he could relax, thought Anton.

"It was there, caught in the rocks between the two formations," Frau Meickle was pointing out to Catarina.

Anton looked at the place where it looked like the Devil was reaching down to grab an unfortunate soul between his forefingers and thumbs.

When Frau Meickle caught sight of the large man's shadow on the water-beaded floor, she gave Anton a narrow-eyed look.

He was oblivious. Catarina was not. Although he lacked his wife's talents in the area of nonverbal communication, he was always attuned to her. Their eyes met, and he knew his presence was not appreciated. He stepped away.

"Can you recall any details about the body?" she asked.

"He was naked and his abdomen was open to the water."

"So he was bleeding?"

"I noticed a change in the water color first, darker in the area near the body. I thought I saw a ring of pink around the pillar, but I wasn't sure until approximately one minute later. I looked at where the waves receded around the base. The foam they left behind was pink at first, and it deepened to bright red."

"How long did that take?"

"Approximately three minutes."

She was a good witness, detailed and decisive. "What did you do then?"

"I went directly to the phone to call the police, but there was a delay while I was connected to two people before reaching the correct department." Criticism of police procedure was clearly implied.

Naturally, the sight of a dead body would claim most of a person's attention. But it is often what doesn't claim one's attention that is important—the oil slick a hundred yards from a crash scene, the shift in sound before an airplane plummets to the ground, the headache before the stroke. "Are you able to remember anything about the area around the body?" Catarina challenged the competitive woman's memory.

Staring at the cove, she tightened her lips in concentration. "There was a yacht not far from shore, just there," she pointed to two o'clock, "and a smaller boat with divers not too far from it." She moved her arm to the left and adjusted it until she was satisfied. "The morning whale watching boat, a blue and red one, was heading out from Ponta Delgada," she moved her arm even further south.

Catarina said nothing. It was at times like this, when people were thinking aloud, that they said what was sometimes lost to the more focused mind. She did what she knew her husband was doing, fixing the scene in her mind, to be sketched out and labeled as soon as they returned to the car.

"And the fisherman," Frau Meickle said, as though she had surprised herself with the memory. "There a was a fisherman in a rowboat on the other side of the basalt pillar, very close to the body. I see him there every day, after my morning swim in the pool. I believe in staying active," she gave an aside. "That morning I slept late," she said slowly as though it puzzled her, "yet he was still there."

"He may be an important witness." *Or suspect.* "Did you notice anything that might identify him?"

She thought.

Catarina waited patiently.

"The side of the boat was painted with an anchor with an X over it, gold over green."

"How much longer was it before someone arrived to talk to you?"

"Less than half an hour, about the same time the Coast Guard boat entered the cove."

"What did you do while you waited?"

"I had coffee."

Frau Meickle had reached the end of her time as a cooperative witness. "If there is nothing more," she said, walking quickly to the front door.

As they followed her, Anton whispered one word to Catarina. It was enough. They understood each other well.

"You are the type of person who might notice such things, Frau Meickle. Did you happen to notice any sharks in the water that morning?"

"Yes. There were several."

Anton understood, and his heart sank.

She turned her patrician profile to the door and opened it wide. "But they came later, just before the Coast Guard boat arrived to remove the body."

Anton felt a sourness in his mouth on the way down the stairs. It was unusual in a man with the responsibilities he held, but he disliked even admitting to the existence of evil, let alone seeing it manifested as a violent death. He had insisted on coming alone, not because Catarina wouldn't be able to handle what he was about to deal with but because he loved her and wanted to spare her.

Rather than relying on a makeshift basement space—as they did on the smaller islands—São Miguel had a morgue. Anton had to bend at the waist to see through the window set in a metal door at the end of a long hall. He'd never seen so much tile in one room—the floor, the counters, and the walls to a height of six feet, all of it white. Against the far wall, he could see a single stainless steel gurney and two stainless steel shelves, which looked more like bunk beds stripped of mattresses than places to accommodate the dead. To the right were two large sinks and cabinets fitted with locks, and to the left, under the narrow windows set just below the ceiling, a counter of the sort he remembered from high school science classes held balances, a few amber-tinted glass bottles, and a microscope.

Also unlike the smaller islands, São Miguel had a coroner. True, the position was filled only on an as-needed basis, but it was filled by someone who had special training in gathering evidence left by the dead.

Anton jumped when a face suddenly filled the other side of the glass, staring directly at him with black eyes bulging behind thick glasses. It was Guilherme Nunes. They'd worked together before, and Anton appreciated how, when a child's life was in danger, the doctor had overcome his aversion to reaching conclusions quickly and had provided crucial evidence.

The young man pulled the door open. "It was not made for the likes of us," he tipped his chin at the door's window.

"Indeed, it was not." Anton extended his hand to Nunes who, although probably half Anton's weight, matched his height.

Nunes wiggled gloved fingers in front of Anton. "Later," he said. He was a man of few words.

Thanks more to the air conditioning unit whirring in the background than to its below ground location, it was cool in the morgue. The temperature did little to mask the butcher-shop smell of violent death that Anton had sadly become familiar with. The disinfectant and whatever they used to mask the odors only added a faintly sweet but still nauseating smell to the air.

"You are now on São Miguel?" Anton asked, more to compose himself than to socialize.

"Yes." That was as much of an answer as he would give. The man was all business.

Nunes walked around him and took two long strides to the wall.

Anton hadn't noticed a second gurney tucked in a corner. The top of that one held a dark gray body bag, and he could see the twin peaks made by someone's feet and the rounded shape of a head, with depressions where the eye sockets were and a small knob in the center made by the nose.

Nunes swung the gurney into the center of the room and under the low-hanging fluorescent lights. He wheeled over a small stainless steel cart with metal instruments neatly lined up on its top: scissors, scalpels, retractors, and other things Anton couldn't name.

Anton closed his eyes, in part a respectful prayer for the person whose life had ended, in part his inclination to distance himself from the dead body.

When he heard the soft growl of a zipper opening, he forced himself to look. He saw the head first, black hair dried into stiff spikes and a complexion the color of tea. It wasn't at all what he'd expected. The man Luis said had been caught by the Devil's Hands was not really a man. He was more a boy.

Anton felt a stab of grief for a young life lost.

He broke out in a cold sweat when he saw the torso. To quell rising nausea, he tried focusing anywhere but on the gaping hole in the middle of the abdomen. His eyes lingered on a scar that scraped into the hairline from the middle of the boy's forehead and left a C-shaped area of scalp without any hair. He was slender, his flesh sunk into the intercostal spaces between his ribs, making him look emaciated. Scratches, washed clean into thin lines and tiny punctures, covered his extremities. "What can you tell me?" he asked, and he heard the tremble in his voice.

Nunes was known for his meticulous work, and he started with a long-winded explanation of the measurements he had taken to determine the boy's origin. "I cannot confirm anything," he said—not unexpectedly from the man who resisted equivocality. "There was nothing to identify him, and I mean nothing. He was naked. I've taken swabs for DNA. I can send those in, with your permission for the additional expense."

"Yes. Do that, please."

"Comparison to standard growth indices gives an age of fourteen or fifteen, but he is smaller and shorter than one would expect at his actual age."

"Why is that?" He immediately regretted asking. Nunes liked to proceed in his own orderly fashion—and without interruption.

Nunes looked over the rim of his tortoiseshell glasses. "This body shows signs of malnutrition. That probably interfered with growth, so I am putting the age at closer to sixteen or seventeen."

The child must have been terribly hungry, Anton thought.

"I can confirm a history of abuse. There are multiple chipped teeth and fractures, caused and healed over a period of fifteen or so years. The right radius and humerus alone show four rotation fractures, which result from the twisting of a young arm, and two bucket fractures, which result from pulling the arm of a child."

Anton's fist came down on the edge of the steel cart, and the instruments jumped out of their orderly rows.

Nunes carried on, but Anton had seen his face soften for a moment, and he realized that this was not someone without heart, just someone trying to cope with realities most people can avoid thinking about. "Other fractures on both arms are commonly found when a person tries to break a fall by extending an arm."

He pulled down the plastic wrap nesting the boy's head, which was flattened at the top. "Here you can see a perimortem injury to the skull." Again he looked at Anton over the top of his glasses. "It is at the top of cranium."

Nunes walked across the room and with a knuckle, he jabbed at the transparent plastic shield covering the keyboard of an open laptop. An X-ray appeared on the screen. At the center of the mottled white bone, there was a network of fine black lines. "Come," he motioned to Anton. "These thin radiating cracks on the cranium indicate contact with heavy object at high speed."

Anton couldn't help himself. "The death wound?"

Nunes didn't answer. "Now that we have assessed the skeleton, we can move on to the internal organs and body exterior." He returned to the gurney and the body of an unknown boy.

"The vital organs also show scarring that is consistent with beatings over many years. The stomach is, of course, missing, so its contents could not be analyzed for information on the last meal; however, I have sent the intestinal contents to the lab, and that should tell us something about what he ate a day or day before his death."

Anton was about to ask when he could expect the results, but he caught his words and made them into an indecipherable mutter.

The tiniest of smiles appeared on Nunes's face. "Thursday, if the plane made it to Lisbon in time to get the sample to the lab before it closed."

Again, Anton's brain stopped his mouth. He only nodded.

"Here on the wrists and ankles, we find extreme trauma to the skin and underlying tissues, consistent with being restrained, more likely by manacles than by rope." He took a breath. "Those injuries were ongoing over the past three to four weeks."

In his mind, Anton was writing the sad story of a boy. *He was starved and beaten for most or all of his life, and then manacled until his death.*

"There are several small circular bruises on the cubital fossa," he pointed to the inside of both elbows. "I cannot be certain about most of the bruises but at the center of the most recent one, there was a puncture." He spoke in past tense because he had already excised the area.

Anton peered at the raw patch of grayish-pink flesh. "Drugs?" He had done battle to keep drugs away from his islands and their population of young people who were bored with its quiet lifestyle.

Nunes didn't seem to mind that interruption. "I will say that the puncture was likely made by a hypodermic needle." But he couldn't let it go without a qualification. "The toxicology report is still to come, however."

He gave two pieces of disappointing news. Interpol had no matches for the fingerprints, and saltwater had left nothing in nail scrapings. "I will say that the nails were unusually long for a male, at least a month's growth."

Anton looked at the childlike hand on the gurney and wrote another sentence into his story of the boy's life. *He was held captive for a month.*

Nunes knew what Anton was thinking—and feeling—and he gave him a few moments before saying softly, "I do have what may be helpful evidence. There is a tattoo on the upper arm." He shifted the body onto its side and slightly rotated the right arm.

This was the tattoo Luis had referred to, in color or design not what was usually seen. Anton squinted. The dark red ink was hard to see on the boy's wrinkled brown skin.

"I've taken enhanced photographs. Those are included in your copy of the forensic jacket."

"It looks like a number below lines and letters." *SHP? SNP?*

"SNP, and the lines look like a cross of some sort. The number is 3-1-1. This is not the type of cheap ink transfers young people sometimes use. He was tattooed when a younger boy, and the skin has stretched since then."

"How old?"

Nunes was about to decline answering but relented. "Five. Six. Seven. It is more difficult to calculate because of the malnutrition. We cannot know when that began or how acute it was."

A child was tattooed, starved, beaten and—at least for the past month—held captive. Anton added fierce anger to the emotions he was feeling.

"We move on to his death."

Anton finally looked directly at the boy's midsection. It looked exactly like what he had feared, like a large bite had been torn out. His heart sunk further. To know a child had suffered was excruciating to consider. To know his life had ended so violently made it even worse.

"Death occurred at approximately 8:00 on Tuesday morning."

Anton's eyebrows shot up. "You can pinpoint it that closely?"

"Everything worked in our favor. The body was taken from the water thirty minutes after the police were phoned. I was alerted immediately and prepared to take essential measurements—body temperature, water temperature, body size—and samples." He looked over his glasses and at Anton. "There was no hypostasis."

Anton peaked an eyebrow.

"There was no opportunity for blood to settle in the body after death. Post-mortem lividity was compromised by the body's location in water." He checked Anton's face for understanding and added, "Because hydrostatic pressure was approximately equal on all areas of the body, blood did not settle in limited areas. Despite that restriction, given the amount of water in the lungs and the O_2 saturation of tissues, I can say that death occurred within seconds of the victim entering the water."

Anton drew in a sharp breath. He hadn't missed the importance of what Nunes had said. "He died immediately after he went into the water?"

"Initially, it looked like a case of death by either shark attack or drowning, followed by sharks eating the fresh body, but now there is the possibility that he was dying before entering the water."

"How...?" Anton stopped himself.

Nunes returned the expected look of exasperation. He held up a warning finger. "I cannot say anything definitively; however, look here." He pointed to an area on the side of the gaping hole in the boy's abdomen.

Anton saw nothing but the same ruffled flesh the bordered the rest of the wound.

"This is the end of a clean-cut wound, almost an incision. He may have been stabbed by a sharp, thin-bladed knife. The shark bite came afterwards, perhaps minutes before the body was removed from the water."

Nunes stripped off his gloves and dropped them into a tall waste bin that opened with a wave of his hand. He handed Anton a folder. "This is preliminary. My report final report will be posted shortly and updated as results from the laboratory in Lisbon come in. The assigned investigator did her best to photograph the scene before the tide came in, but it was pretty much underwater by the time the Coast Guard boat got there."

"Could you also send a photo of the boy's face, as..." Anton searched for a word, "as unintimidating as possible." He would have to show it to ordinary people, grandmothers and schoolteachers and shopkeepers, who were to be protected from being confronted with what they knew was there but could turn a blind eye to.

"It is already there, along with a picture of the tattoo."

Anton felt a familiar mix of emotions: shame that such a crime had happened on his islands; anxiety over what that would mean to the tourism so many—including his own family—depended on; determination to find the person who had intruded on his peaceful community; and profound sadness.

He was relieved when Nunes finally turned away with a curt, "That's it for now."

Anton left the mortuary feeling very glad he hadn't brought Catarina.

Anton had skipped lunch to interview Frau Meickle, and the meeting with Dr. Nunes had robbed him of any desire for his usual afternoon snacks. It was now one of his favorite times of the day: dinner time. And he was very hungry.

He had hoped to avoid the more built up commercial marina near the center of town with its smell of diesel and cigarettes and its buzz of conversation and bursts of loud laughter. He wanted to share a quiet dinner with his beloved Catarina, and one of his many contacts on São Miguel had recommended a nice restaurant a few miles from Ponta Delgada.

The area reminded Anton of what had become of the neighborhood where he had grown up. A short generation ago, it had been a cluster of small farms and family-owned shops, and everyone had taken pride in keeping them close to picture perfect. Squat apartment buildings and a chain store had replaced them. Around him, a crumpled napkin skittered on the sidewalk, and weeds pushed their way up between the cobbles. No one in his parent's generation would have tolerated such a sight. They would have taken on themselves to pull them. Anton bent over and did just that, depositing the tuft of weeds in a trashcan he passed.

Times were changing on the islands—at least in some parts of some islands.

Removed from the vigilant eyes of adults, the area had also become a place where teens hung out. Anton's head turned as they passed a knot of them. He'd seen girls with more than one piercing in their ear lobes before. He'd even seen a young man wearing earrings—although he had been a tourist. But he'd never seen a girl with a stud in her lip. He slowed to a near stop.

Catarina tugged on his arm. "Let them be. They are not bad kids."

He knew most weren't bad kids. Most still showed respect for adults, especially their parents and always priests and the law. Teen pregnancies were virtually unheard of without marriage following soon afterwards. Although shoplifting and boasting about it to friends happened from time to time, he could acknowledge that had been true in his day, as well.

Anton hadn't stared because he disapproved. He had stared because he'd seen himself in them and the future he would have almost certainly had if not for Catarina. Before meeting his redhaired girl, he had spent the greater part of his free time as one of a group of restless boys. Although all were older than fifteen-year-old Anton, they had followed his lead, roughhousing and trying to outdo one another in cursing, drinking, and whistling at girls—to torment them rather than to attract them.

What disturbed him was the future he saw for them. Distance from urban centers meant few of the activities favored by the young and even fewer jobs. Many of them, then and now, left by the route he and Catarina had taken—attending university and getting jobs in other countries. Most of them never returned.

Among those who stayed, the specter of drug use loomed. A little after Anton met Catarina, a ton of cocaine that smugglers had intended for European markets washed ashore on the beaches of São Miguel. Some of it was taken and sold by residents, leading to addiction and death among the island's unemployed, unoccupied youth. It was one reason why Anton wanted to balance his desire to preserve the archipelago's heritage with the tourism that would bring employment.

The restaurant had once been where boats badly damaged by storms were dry docked for repairs. The sign above the front door still read *Alves Marine Mechanics* and on either side of it, twenty-foot rollup doors were open to the mild night air. It was a small place, with about ten wood tables, their tops marked by interlocking rings left by wine glasses and coffee cups. Grappling hooks and heavy chains dangled overhead, but the lower half of the cavernous space was cozy with potted trees and candlelight.

The smells of garlic and baking bread and fresh fish pushed their way to Anton's nose, and his mouth watered. He spotted an empty table at the back and worked his way past diners, greeting them as old friends. Such was the nature of the man. Along the way, he spotted the soup one couple was having and the pie two friends were sharing, and he made the first two decisions about his meal.

The waitress was happy when their accents let her know they were fellow islanders. She handed them two menus—small pieces of paper probably printed at home—with a few selections. She pulled a pencil from her gray hair and asked if they would like wine. Catarina smiled to herself. She suspected the simple question would lead to a genial conversation between her husband and the woman. (It did.)

Ten minutes later, they had learned that the restaurant was a family business. The waitress took care of the diners; her husband cooked the food; her children brought in the fresh produce and wines. They settled on tuna that one son had caught that morning and greens that one daughter had grown in her garden. And, of course, a bottle of local wine made from the grapes they grew behind their house.

Anton had switched out his suit jacket for a cardigan, and Catarina had wrapped a shawl around her shoulders. Each looked relaxed to the other. The sun was putting on an extravagant evening show of pastel clouds and shimmery water. The sand had a pink glow, as did Catarina's alabaster skin. Thirty years later, her beauty could still make him tremble with love.

Anton kept what he had learned from the medical examiner to himself. Catarina rarely had the chance for a night on the town—such as it was—and he didn't want to ruin it for her. He even turned off the text alerts on his phone, which had been known to chime repeatedly throughout dinner.

They took a few minutes to write postcards to Liliana and Toni. Now such an old-fashioned gesture, children of their generation were thrilled with the novelty. No street number or even street name was needed for them. Just *Casa do Mar* and the post office would know where to take them, not because it was a particularly well-known address but because people knew in each in their community.

Their talk was exclusively about family.

"Have you heard from Lori?" he asked.

"She's somewhere nearby."

"Still with Carlos!" He gave a double wink. "Did they ever get in touch with Carlos's friend?"

"Lori says they still can't reach him."

"He's probably somewhere having fun before the wedding."

Catarina told Anton about the house Carlos wanted to buy.

"It would be a good investment," he said, taking a celebratory drink of a very good *vinho verde*.

He couldn't fool her. "We both know why he wants to buy it. I do think Carlos is ready to ask Lori to marry him."

"You look concerned."

"I am concerned that Lori may hold back and that may hurt Carlos."

The children were never far from their minds. With Lori also away, Toni and Liliana were staying with Maria Rosa across a narrow road from Casa do Mar. Just before they left their hotel room, Anton and Catarina had made their usual call to say goodnight to them.

"They're growing up." Anton was only just catching on. Catarina had noticed it months before.

"At least Toni's interest in video games still takes a back seat to football," said the father who was also a coach for one of Santa Maria's youth teams. Toni was typical of most boys his age; he loved sports and wandering the island. One thing distinguished him from his friends: a determination to become a doctor that he'd shown since the age of six.

While Toni took after his father and socialized freely and often, twelve-year-old Liliana took after her mother. She had always been the quieter of the two children, preferring time with her books to other play. Although she'd played with dolls, she'd never passed through that phase of obsessive role playing, dressing her dolls for all occasions and giving them starring roles as actresses, rock singers, and brides. Her dolls hadn't dated or gotten married. They hadn't fought with girlfriends over clothes or boys. Perhaps she just hadn't seen enough of that to have a template.

She'd always been as open with her parents as Toni was, but recently Catarina had seen her exquisite eyes—her entire body—take on a private look that said she now had an inner life her parents were not privy to.

Anton twirled greens around his fork. "We'll bring them the usual gifts?"

Catarina nodded. "I have already called the bookshop. They have set aside a children's book on genetics and another on coding." Recently, the daughter who had always loved history and literature best had shown an interest in learning to code.

Family issues discussed, Anton speared a bite of pie. He was lifting it to his mouth, when Catarina asked him what he had learned from Guilherme Nunes. Before he opened his mouth to answer, she saw a wave of distress wash over him, and she said, "Perhaps we should wait until tomorrow. Tonight should be for us."

And so it was.

They were spending the night in Ponta Delgado, without the responsibilities of children and goats and guests and everyone else on Santa Maria. So they walked along the shore, they took off their shoes and wiggled their toes in the cold water, they hugged and they kissed just as they had since they were sixteen.

3

Anton knew who owned the red and blue whale watching boat: the Vieira family whose son had married a cousin of his friend, Matias Costa. That was the most recognized form of identification on the islands; you were who you were related to—and everyone was related in one way or another.

He had recommended the Vieira whale watching excursions to his guests at Casa do Mar. They always returned thrilled with the experience. The Azores were along the migration routes of four species of whales. His people had manned and captained ships that supplied whale oil for lighting and bones for corsets in the nineteenth century, and they'd been known as the best of whale hunters.

In the way of many cultures, every Vieira family member had a role. Mama Ema and Papa Vitor were well into their seventies but between them, they sold tickets, welcomed passengers, and gave out the cookies that were made at home twice a week. One son captained the boat, the other managed the business and could call attention to whales, dolphins, and sea turtles in barely intelligible versions of six languages. Everyone pitched in.

The marina was quiet. Fishermen had long since come and gone out to sea. Visitors were resting between morning and afternoon activities. Locals were working in downtown offices and shops. Tied up at the newest of the docks was a former trawler, now brightly painted red and blue and outfitted with cushioned benches.

"Olá, Vitor!" Anton called out to a man who was sound asleep on the deck of the *Santa Cruz.*

A menacing growl came from a shady nook at the stern. Anton knew it was only Mano, an extraordinarily smelly mongrel who was never far from his master.

Vitor lifted a well-worn straw hat from his face, pulling up some of the few remaining strands of white hair on his head. "Eh?" He looked around and spotted Anton waving from the dock.

Every time Anton saw Vitor, he found him a little more wrinkled and a little grumpier. This time was no exception. "Do you have time to talk, Vitor?"

"I'm taking my nap." An age-blotched hand was returning the hat to his head when he spotted Catarina, shielding her eyes from the high sun with one hand and waving to him with the other. "But I will always have time to talk to the beautiful senhora Vanderhye," he said with undisguised delight.

The delight vanished when he added, "You can come with her, if you want." Anton's interruption of his nap was only to be tolerated if it brought Catarina.

Vitor's chair wasn't what anyone would expect on the deck of an old fishing boat—or any boat, for that matter. It was a recliner upholstered in burgundy velvet and upgraded with a cup holder and a side pocket that held the day's newspaper. He pulled a lever at the side and popped into a seated position to wave them aboard.

Before they were at the top of the gangplank, Mano came over to assure himself of their good intentions, and then he returned to the nook he had claimed for himself when he was a puppy.

Impatient as always, Anton had his first question out of his mouth before they were halfway across the deck.

Catarina put a hand on his arm. That was enough of a reminder. It was a lesson he had to relearn regularly. His wife—a genius in human relations—firmly believed in the value of starting with a friendly chat.

Vitor patted his sagging belly. "Big lunch," he told Catarina after she'd kissed him on both cheeks, "so I was sleeping like a baby after the bottle." After throwing Anton a sour expression, he hooked his suspenders with his thumbs, pulled them into place over his shoulders, and reclined again.

Anton was a sociable man—at times, a very sociable man—but the next twenty minutes were a misery for him. Catarina congratulated Vitor on the birth of his first great-grandchild. Vitor congratulated Catarina on her appointment as principal of the Santa Maria elementary school. Catarina reminisced about the time when Liliana won the prize for best sweet rolls. Vitor reminisced about the time when Ema won the prize for best fruit tarts. And Anton sat there, opening his mouth and then closing it when his self-control chased away his impatience.

At long last, there was a lull in the conversation, and he jumped into it. "You had the boat out three days ago?"

"Same as always." He scratched at a hairy forearm.

Anton wondered whether Vitor's change in tone was because he wasn't as fond of the topic or the person who was talking. "What time did you leave the marina?"

"Same as always, when the bells ring for morning Mass."

"So you would have crossed Breakwater Cove about 8:30?" He took Vitor's milky stare as affirmation. "Did you have customers on board?"

Vitor lifted both of the bushiest white eyebrows Anton had ever seen, as if to say *What do you think?"*

Anton drew a deep breath. "How many came to see the whales?"

Vitor thought. "Fifteen."

"All visitors?"

"All tourists." Mano underlined Vitor's intent was a short bark. His choice of word was intended as a pejorative. One of the most difficult parts of Anton's government job was helping his fellow islanders to see tourism as more than just an evil to be tolerated for the economy's sake; it was an extension of their own ingrained hospitality that allowed them to share their culture with the rest of the world.

Catarina stepped in. "I am sure you explained our expectations when you sold the tickets."

"Of course. Nothing goes into our water." He put a forefinger behind one ear and drew it across his neck to the other ear. "And if I see anything, I'll deal with it like that," he cackled.

"We are lucky to have you looking out for our islands, Vitor."

With that, Vitor gave up everything he knew about the tourists who had gone out looking for whales on the morning a boy was found dead in Breakwater Cove. They were all, as far as he could tell, part of a group from an English-speaking country, Australia if their tee-shirts and caps were to be believed. Most were in their sixties but "didn't look as good as Ema," he said loudly.

Ema had just come aboard. Always comfortably rounded, she looked like she'd lost a lot of weight, and Catarina wondered about her health. The stroke she'd had a few years ago seemed to have affected her speech but nothing else.

Ema smiled and waved but would not be joining them just yet. Walking a few feet behind her was their youngest grandchild, a teenage boy who walked mechanically while swinging a pair of binoculars in front of his face. Catarina knew Zezé would have to be fed and settled before Ema could relax. She had studied child development as part of her education degree and suspected there had been some neurological damage at birth.

Anton interrupted Catarina's laugh over some small joke of Vitor's, "The tour operator doesn't need a ticket, correct?"

He delivered his answer with a scowl, "Of course not."

"Did you see whales that day?" Catarina abruptly changed the subject.

The scowl was replaced by a gap-toothed grin. "We have an almost perfect record, dear lady. Remember, my ancestors hunted whales in these waters. I know them well. Tuesday was an especially good morning. We were accompanied by two pods of dolphins and a whale came up to scrape the barnacles off its fin on our hull." He leaned sideways to pick up a fragment of mollusk shell from the deck and showed it to Catarina, slapping his leg hard. "You should have seen them!" he hooted. "Screaming and running. They didn't know whether to hide in the pilothouse or take pictures with their little phones."

Catarina took a few moments to laugh with him before moving on. "And the tour operator?" she brought the conversation around to Anton's question.

"She's a cute young thing. Ana or Dora, something like that." He turned to Anton. "And yes, she got on and she got off."

"Are you sure every one of the fifteen tourists got off the boat with the tour operator?" Anton persisted.

"Tomas!" he bellowed. "Bring your book!"

The Vieiras' second son came out of the small pilothouse carrying an old-fashioned ledger. He verified that Vitor had sold fifteen tickets, which were showed as passengers boarded and collected as they left.

"Could anyone else have been on board without your knowledge?" Anton's mind considered every possibility.

"Below decks is locked and with a captain the size of my son, there's no place to hide in the pilothouse." Vitor laughed loudly.

"Did either of you notice anything that seemed wrong in the area of Breakwater Cove?"

Vitor was happy to be brought in on a search for wrongdoers. He thought. "That fisherman was there, setting his traps by the Devil's Hands. He's all wrong. Never miss a chance to send my wake his way."

Catarina had taught her husband well; he held his tongue.

"I never used to see him in our waters," Vitor went on, "but now he's always around. It's not like it used to be, more fish than anyone knew what to do with. It's getting harder and harder for a man to bring in a good catch. Locals got to watch out for each other, or we won't have anything left."

He thought some more. "Some damn yacht, mostly hidden by the Devil's Hands. Those white monsters have been all over our waters since Ema's sister came from Terceira, spitting fuel, dumping trash." He leaned toward Catarina and grumbled, "She's been here for five weeks."

Catarina nodded sympathetically. Anton waited.

"I only saw the bow, dear lady, so I can't say more."

"Maybe one more," Tomas recalled. "One of those tourists asked me if the sharks were a danger to divers. I think there was a diving boat."

"It was a Costa diving boat but without the Costas," Vitor said, proud of his memory. "It was captained by a pretty boy, who likes showing off his body to anyone who'll look his way."

"Your memory is faultless, Vitor. What would Anton do without you?"

He beamed.

"Do you know anything about the—" she cleared her throat, "—pretty boy?"

"I know he was very close to the Devil's Hands when the man was found dead there."

It wasn't even mildly surprising that he already knew why they were there. The island grapevine was high speed and comprehensive.

"But I don't see him as capable of harming anyone."

How many times had she heard that? Yet even those who committed murder had friends, and presumably few people thought their friends capable of doing such a thing.

Anton was almost whimpering with questions.

At long last, Catarina said, "Do you think you could help my husband a little more?"

He looked at Anton and then back to Catarina. "In exchange for some of your sweet rolls, yes."

The deal was struck, and Anton rushed out the questions he had refrained from asking, in the back of his mind a fear that Vitor's cooperation could be cut short at any time.

Anton learned that the fisherman kept to himself, reluctantly exchanging cursory waves when others came close to him. His boat was the *São Pedro*, out every day, gone by noon, and rarely docked in the marina. In itself, that wasn't unusual. On the islands, many fishermen pulled into the marina only to offload their catches to the larger boats that crossed open water to sell them at premium prices.

Vitor could offer no clues on the identity of the yacht, other than that its bow was big and white and "looked ridiculous." He did remember that it had moved on by Tuesday afternoon, though.

Anton shifted from the boats that were near Breakwater Cove to something that still troubled him: the sharks.

"Sharks follow the dolphins," Vitor informed him. "And the dolphins were far from land that morning." He turned to Catarina, "It's true what they say about the whole world getting warmer these days, you know. Dolphin cows never took their new calves to the valleys when I was younger." He really did mean *valleys*, the frigid valleys of those undersea mountains, one of whose peaks was the island on which they stood.

"You saw sharks there on Tuesday morning..." Catarina prompted.

"Now that I think of it, just as we spotted a whale, three sharks broke away from the pod where they were hoping to feed on vulnerable calves and headed toward shore."

"And that was near..."

He pursed his lips trying to remember. "The Devil's Hands. They headed toward the Devil's Hands."

"I'll let you get back to the nap we interrupted, Vitor."

"Secret to a long life, dear lady: naps."

With one eyebrow lifted, Mano watched them leave. Near the gangplank, they saw Ema and Zezé. He had lined up grapes in three orderly rows on one of the cushioned benches and was eating them one by one with his eyes glued to his binoculars.

While Catarina and Ema talked, Anton watched the boy as he followed the comings and goings at the marina. How lucky we have been with our children, he thought, how very lucky.

The afternoon started well enough, with the accumulation of those small, seemingly irrelevant bits of information that eventually knit themselves together to write the story you are trying to hear. Frau Meickle's neighbors had been canvassed, the Australian tour group had been located, and Dr. Nunes's report had been posted.

Anton, who possessed the manners of a generation that was passing, held the door open for his wife, running his fingertips over the large brass bell mounted beside it. Now used to alert the marina that a nearby vessel was in danger of sinking, it was once an old ship's bell that had in fact been salvaged from one of those sunken ships.

The man in the small harbormaster's office had made himself comfortable on a chair with his legs stretched out and propped up on his desktop. Beside his blackened sneakers was a hand-lettered sign: *Gosto Branco, Capitão do Porto.* He didn't look up when they came in.

Anton took in a cluttered little office that hadn't seen a cleaning in many years. An overflowing wastebasket. A pen that had rolled into a corner so long ago that it was veiled in cobwebs. A yellowed and torn poster stating the marina regulations.

He cleared his throat.

A forty-something man with thinning hair pulled into a pony tail—a look uncommon on the islands—glanced up from his newspaper. His sweat-stained shirt looked like it hadn't been washed recently.

Unlike the early days, Anton no longer had to fake his legitimacy to investigate. It was a good thing, too. For the first time since he was dragged into such matters, he was not only asked for his identification, the harbormaster studied it carefully and looked from him to his picture twice, before reluctantly grunting something that might have been, "What do you want?"

"I want to know which large vessels—something that would be classified as a yacht, might have been in the area of the Devil's Hands the day before yesterday."

"Why?"

Anton knew enough not to give away any information he didn't have to.

The harbormaster sensed he wouldn't get an answer from Anton, so he turned to Catarina with hopefully raised eyebrows. He wouldn't get anything from her either.

Anton stated his business again, this time more firmly and with a touch of superiority to let Branco know that he could make a harbormaster's job more demanding than this harbormaster's job currently was.

Branco looked at a cheap watch held to his boney wrist by a plastic strap. "How long is this going to take?"

"It could take a while. Quite a while…depending on how soon I get the information I want."

"It's my lunchtime." He stared at Anton. Anton stared back. "I don't start at a normal hour. I start early, seven, sometimes six." He was unconvincing. Catarina would wager he started later than that and spent much of the morning catching up on sleep.

Anton ignored him and joined Catarina at the window that overlooked the marina. In its reflection, he saw Branco slowly lower his legs to the floor and swivel around to start up his computer, an older desktop model grimy with fingerprints and dried spills. Anton turned and looked closely. The man seemed to be touching too many keys to simply be looking at information.

Branco looked up and shifted the screen away from Anton. He said, "There were two large vessels, the *Sirena* and the *Iaso*."

Anton was at his side too quickly for the man to react. "What about this one, the *Doura?*" The ship had occupied A-1, the largest slip in the marina.

He held Anton's gaze. "That came in unexpectedly." He scrolled up. "It's been here before."

Anton pointed at the spreadsheet on the screen. "Why are so many of fields left blank?"

"A lot of them put into port for a few hours, so—"

"So there isn't enough time to do your job?"

"We've got a busy marina here. I've got other responsibilities!"

"You are going to give me the information I want. You are going to give me *all* the information I want."

Branco stood, masking nerves with a confrontational stance. "Three large vessels were in the area last Tuesday." He repeated the names slowly. "*Sirena. Iaso. Doura.*"

He was still dragging his feet. Innocently, Catarina asked, "Do you want me to send copies of your report to the president's office, Minister Cardosa, or just to the head of the Judicial Police?"

They quickly learned that the owner of *Sirena* was a quirky man, a Norwegian who knew English quite well but seldom said more than ten words when he came by once a week to pay his fees. Other than meeting occasional guests and picking up supplies, he spent his time aboard his boat.

"When did the *Sirena* dock?"

Branco looked baffled.

"When?"

"It's always here. I mean, it's been here a long time. It goes out for short excursions and returns."

"Where is it berthed?"

"Just today, it tied up at the old wharf. " With his chin, Branco gestured to the north end of the marina.

"It was somewhere else before today?"

"Here at the western end, always at the same slip, A-5."

"Why the move?"

It was the laugh of a man taking pleasure in someone else's pain. "It's the only one he can afford now."

"Now the *Iaso*."

Branco opened his mouth to protest but quickly closed it. "It's registered in the Bahamas. Everything by the book with those people."

Apparently, going by the book was unusual enough to mention. Anton made a mental note to have Branco's records checked by the Coast Guard. "Go on."

"Captain comes in for the registration, but someone else does the business. Both dressed up and smelling of cologne."

Catarina heard something in Branco's phrasing. "How often does the *Iaso* dock here?"

He set his jaw and ignored her.

"Answer!" Anton spat out.

On an edge between defiance and capitulation, Branco said slowly, "It's come in many times over the past few years. Stays two or three weeks and leaves like clockwork. Prefers a berth closer to the restaurants and shops, A-1 or A-2."

"What is listed as the reason for coming in our islands?"

Branco consulted his spreadsheet. "Pleasure. Always pleasure. It cruises the Central Atlantic and Mediterranean."

"Do they bring visitors in?"

He shrugged.

"Check. Your. Log."

"None registered. None actually. Sometimes passengers arrive in a shiny new car, and then the *Iaso* goes to open water with them."

"And the *Doura*?"

Branco swallowed. "As I said, it was only in the area for a few hours. A lot of them do that. They put into port for supplies and leave. I don't know anything about them."

Catarina saw his carotids pulse a little faster. And she'd heard how he slipped into talking in generalities. *A few. They. Them.*

Anton didn't trust Gosto Branco, either. "What were your hours on Tuesday?"

"I don't know exactly."

"Try approximately."

He was thinking fast. "I have to adjust my schedule depending on needs. Responsibilities, you know." He checked their faces. "I get here a lot earlier than I actually open the office, you know."

"What time did you arrive?"

"About nine," he said defensively.

They suspected he was rounding down from closer to ten, over an hour after the boy's body was seen at the Devil's Hands.

"And all three boats would have been moored at that hour?"

"Like I said, the *Sirena* is usually here. Could've left. Can't say." He tightened his lips. "I can't keep my eyes on everything, you know."

"The *Iaso*?"

"That I remember," he brightened a bit. "The captain was waiting... The captain arrived to register his return just after I finished my morning rounds."

"What times was that?"

Dark red crept up his cheeks. "Maybe eleven. Because I was busy with those morning rounds I told you about."

"The *Doura*?"

"It..." he shifted through his thoughts, "It...I'm not sure."

"Did you see or hear anything unusual that day?"

He started to fall back on his usual disclaimer about knowing nothing when he stopped himself. "Funny you should ask…a crewman—maybe I'm supposed to say crewwoman these days—off the last ferry claimed she was nearly run over by a black car racing into the parking lot."

"Did you look into it?"

"I was in a rush to get home. Tuesday's the night my mother makes *couves* for dinner. Anyway, the marina itself may be well lit but not the parking lot. What could I see if I went over there?"

"Is there CCTV?" Even on the smallest of the islands, that type of surveillance had become commonplace.

"My budget is limited."

He turned to Catarina. "Please remind me to look into the harbormaster's budget." To Branco, he said, "Do you track vessels before they arrive or after they leave?"

"Me? No. I usually know when they're a day out or if they've got special requests. I also have to deal with special requests, you know," he gave Catarina the look of someone who had suffered greatly.

"So you get no reports of the movement of boats in our waters?" Anton knew that wasn't true.

"That's not what I said. Reports are sent to the Coast Guard from marinas all over the islands, in case of loss of communication or sudden storms, you know."

"And those reports are posted for all harbormasters. Right?" He was letting Branco know he'd caught him, if not in an outward lie then in trying to mislead him.

Eyes on Anton, Branco slowly shut off his computer.

"I want a complete report on all boats that have registered in this marina in the past year, and I want it emailed by tomorrow morning. That means *everything* you have in *every* record." He snapped a business card on counter.

"Tomorrow?" he whined.

"Make that by midnight today."

He opened his mouth to protest but closed it.

"Now clean up this place up and yourself," Anton ordered. "You don't reflect well on who we are."

At the dive shop, Anton renewed acquaintance with the Costa brothers, Alberto and Júlio, both of whom had attended the same school he had, fellow mischief makers of a slightly older generation. He saw in Alberto, the older and smaller of the brothers, the discontented boy he had been in the body of a discontented man. When Alberto made an unpleasant joke about the trials of married life in a way that Anton would never do, he and Catarina looked at each other and shared the same private thought: It was not that way for them. And they felt sorry for Alberto.

Alberto confirmed that their diving boat had taken a Canadian couple to Breakwater Cove on the morning the boy had been found dead. The "pretty boy" Vitor had seen was Fabiano Deníz, but he hadn't heard from him in two days. "It's not what it was for us, Anton," he said with some bitterness. "These young men don't know the meaning of hard work. Fabi comes. Fabi goes."

Júlio, always the more mellow of the Costa brothers, stepped in. "We rely on two local boys when a divemaster is needed, and one of them usually shows up."

"You heard the *usually*, right?" countered his brother.

"It's true that Fabi isn't always available when needed but most of the time, he lets us know in advance."

"*Most of the time*," Alberto emphasized.

"He's called at the last minute a few times," explained Júlio. "I think he has other commitments."

"Another job?" Anton asked.

"He's a waiter. But that's at night," he shot a look at his brother, "when the boat doesn't go out."

"What makes you think he has other commitments?" Anton may have asked but he knew full well that on the small island, word about people—their travels, their health, their jobs—got around.

"Look, all you need to know is that Fabi is well liked and good at his job. He comes from a good family. They keep to themselves. His father has some health problem. The mother is a maid for Henrique de la Rosa."

Anton remembered that man.

"He gave her a job after his wife died and he needed someone to take care of the house and raise the children."

"From what I hear…" Alberto stopped and cleared his throat, "it's a well-paying job."

It was often that way on the islands. If not a blood relative, the person you passed on the street was likely to be a neighbor or go to the same church or teach your child or have married your second cousin once removed. People felt a responsibility to one another. They knew about misfortunes and stepped in to help. That cultural mindset had allowed the people of the Azores to survive the challenges of living in such an isolated and challenging environment.

So, the offer of a well-paying job to someone in need didn't surprise Anton; the person who had made the offer did surprise him. He remembered de la Rosa, and it piqued his interest to hear of any generosity on his part. Perhaps the man had changed, but Catarina often said that although the years—in this case twenty of them—could change a person, that person's character tended to remain unchanged. De la Rosa had been a stingy and arrogant younger man and was likely to be a stingy and arrogant older man. He couldn't picture him having the heart to offer Fabi's mother any more money than the least he could get away with paying her.

"That was good of him." said Catarina, who was unaware of de la Rosa's reputation.

"Good?" Júlio snorted. "I wouldn't use that word in connection with Henrique de la Rosa. The man thinks he's better than the rest of us. From what I hear, it was his son, only twelve or thirteen himself at the time, who stood up to the old man right on the church steps. He told his father that his little sister needed a woman to raise her. De la Rosa laughed hard at his son, but the next day Fabi's mother started work."

"She has stayed all these years?" Catarina asked him.

"I think her relationship with the children protects her job, and she needs the money enough to put up with de la Rosa. Her younger boy's retarded. Never went to school. Stays at home."

Surprising to Anton, Alberto sounded sympathetic. Catarina wasn't surprised. She knew that many people fall into playing a certain role early in life; Alberto's was the curmudgeon of the Costa family, so that was the face he showed the world.

"That's why Júlio gives Fabi such leeway, working the hours he want, blowing off commitments."

"Rarely," Júlio felt necessary to interject. "Rarely."

Anton left with Fabi's phone number—for all the good it did him. As the rest of the day unfolded in a way Anton did not want it to, he called many times, but the phone rang without an answer and without going to voice mail.

Had she lived in any of hundreds of fishing communities around the world, Frau Meickle would have recognized the X painted over an anchor that she had seen on the hull of the fishing boat in Breakwater Cove. It was the cross of St. Peter, the patron saint of fishermen. And had she lived in the Azores, she would have known that its gold and green colors were associated with certain villages on the islands.

Anton and Catarina spent over an hour walking up and down the commercial wharves looking for the *São Pedro*. Here, too, they were thwarted. They couldn't find the boat that had been in Breakwater Cove at the same time as the boy whose ghost had followed Anton ever since he left the morgue.

When they spotted a harbor patrolwoman, they picked up their steps. She did remember seeing the boat, but not much more. "There used to be two of us in the marina for the day shift and two of us for the night shift. Now there is only me, and I leave by three," she apologized.

Anton knew harbor patrol was shorthanded these days, challenged by an uptick in tourism, large commercial fishing vessels that were edging closer and closer to the Azores' fertile waters, and the yachting season that had transatlantic cruises making a stop midway between the Americas and Europe.

Catarina glanced at her nametag. "Elena, by any chance do you remember where the boat was moored when you first saw it?" It was a simple question, asked without pressure, but Catarina knew one memory often led to related ones if not blocked by expectations.

Elena furrowed her brow and looked up and down the waterfront. "I do," she said slowly. "It first caught my attention because it was docked so long after the rest of the fleet set out."

Catarina nodded but said nothing.

"Then I saw the owner...I don't know his name...a fat man coming fast...He was followed by one of the kids who work at the tackle shop. They were carrying...What were they carrying? Lines and netting. You know the sort used to repair the traps?"

Catarina nodded.

"I asked to see his license, just because he'd bought so much. You know we can't be too careful these days or outsiders will fish out our waters. He didn't have one and said he had no need for one, since he was bringing in lobsters and crayfish just for his family."

When Elena's gaze turned from her memories and back to them, Catarina asked, "Have you seen him since then?"

"He comes in for supplies from time to time and, yes, I've walked by, but I've never seen a catch—let alone one that's over the limit."

Elena directed them to a group of men sharing sundown beers on dock pilings. "Matias and his friends are always around. You could try talking to them."

Matias had been watching them, and he waited, smiling a welcome as they walked over. He had seen the *São Pedro* on Tuesday morning, but in a marina where time was told by when the fishing fleet set out and returned, all he could say was that it set out "late," by which he meant after seven. Apparently, its captain wasn't a commercial fisherman; he never seemed to have a catch to offload on the docks where fishmongers, restaurant chefs, housewives, and the large processing ships bid on the day's catch.

The *Iaso* was also well known to Matias and his fishermen friends. The first comment Anton and Catarina heard about the yacht was long low whistle, like one that might have followed a particularly attractive woman walking past a New York construction site. Other reactions were as favorable and not only for the size and beauty of the vessel. The captain and crew were known to be generous with locals, handing over rolls of bills for restaurant deliveries and transport to and from the airport. They kept to themselves, didn't dump in the harbor, didn't intrude with loud music or bright lights. The *Iaso* was pretty much everything the locals could want in a visiting yacht.

They confirmed what the harbormaster had said. The *Iaso* had been coming to the island several times a year for the past two or three years. Visitors usually flew in to join them before they left to anchor offshore, usually in the calm waters of a nearby cove.

"The schedule's the same. In port a few days, out a few days, and back. You just missed her."

"So it will be back?"

"In three or four days. Guaranteed."

Anton moved to another of the larger boats that Branco's records showed were in nearby waters three days ago. "What can you tell me about the *Sirena*?"

Catarina saw smirks.

"She used to tie up right here. Now she's getting closer to the local atmosphere," one of the men waved his hand towards the northern end of the marina.

Anton could see the boat moored not too far away, and he felt a glimmer of hope that a visit would lead to some progress in the investigation.

"That ship used to grow roots into the sea bed for weeks," Matias said, "then break loose for a day or two when tourists arrived for their," his voice took on a mocking grand tone, "*grand tour of the island*."

"The captain doesn't have many paying guests?" asked Catarina.

"Captain Lars Karlsson welcomes only dupes."

"What's he like?"

The question was met with heartfelt laughter that left tears on more than one cheek. One said, "He's not what he claims to be."

"We'll be talking to him soon," Anton told them.

"He's in town," said one.

"Getting his uniform shined," said another. That led to more laughter.

"Tell us about him," Catarina asked gently but seriously enough to quiet them.

"His pomp matches his splendid uniform."

"He belongs in a children's movie—"

"—about Napoleon."

Catarina was just forming a picture of a Modern Major General when Anton's phone sounded with a message alert.

That's when the day really went downhill.

"It's Luis Gomes. The president wants to see us," he said, tapping his screen. "This can't be good."

It was not good. Luis and Anton had been called into the office of the new president, Rafael Borges, not with a friendly phone call that asked if they were free but with his assistant's demand that they be there within the hour. Word had already gotten around that Borges was different from his predecessor in many ways. This was clearly one of them.

Anton shared the sensibilities and laid-back personality of the former president, João Moniz, the man who had pledged support for Anton's proposal to create a living heritage trust, the man who had appointed him Minister of Cultural Heritage, a title that usually shortened itself to Minister of Culture or Minister of Heritage.

Moniz had edged their dream closer to reality by giving a large tract of land on Santa Maria the designation of a living heritage trust, to be protected environmentally and culturally. Everything from mills to vineyards to communal ovens would be used as they had been at various times in the island's past, a living model of the Azores's history that preserved their heritage and allowed a more traditional way of life for those who were sustained by it—if enough money could be raised with private grants.

The heritage site would undoubtedly attract tourism that would generate desperately needed employment and fund modern medical care and good schools. But Anton and Catarina, and now Lori, were determined not to do that at the expense of wiping out what they cherished. They didn't want cruise ships dominating the harbors. They didn't want lines outside cafés and crowds in the terraced vineyards and on the pristine beaches. They didn't want the noise or trash or crime that the rest of Europe was now contending with.

All that—not to mention the future of Casa do Mar and his role as minister—now lay in the hands of a man who hadn't given a single indication that he appreciated any of it.

On the steps of the presidential palace, Luis extended his hand to Anton and kissed Catarina on both cheeks. "I am sorry to take you away from an evening with your husband, senhora. We shouldn't be long." He shared a look with Anton. The new president had a reputation for ushering people in and out of his office with great speed. "Perhaps you would enjoy a walk while we talk?"

The presidential palace was a two-story colonial-style building. At one time, it had been the home of a banker who had become wealthy lending money to the merchants who carried goods to and from the New World. The grounds were now a peaceful park with a pond and palm trees, and Catarina was happy to spend her time gathering ideas for her own Casa do Mar gardens.

The interior of the presidential palace was a legacy of grander times. It was built when many islanders were suffering under a Portuguese king whose interest in them was mainly as cannon fodder and revenue for foreign wars. What the architecture was designed to glorify was not what Anton found reason to celebrate about his islands, he thought on his way to the second floor.

He'd been in the president's office many times before as a guest of its previous occupant. The only physical change he noticed was the addition of a grandfather clock, but he felt a different atmosphere the moment he crossed the threshold, almost as though the weather had taken a sudden turn for the worse.

When they went in, the president was walking toward an oversize window, his back to them. The phone conversation they overheard gave the impression of a difficult man, but Anton was one who was optimistic about finding the best in others, so he waited with hope that another, better side of the man would soon show itself. There was an abrupt goodbye, and Borges turned and walked to them with his first demand. "Cardosa, I expect a full report on the body found in Breakwater Cove on my desk by noon tomorrow. Until then, I will make do with the basic information from you two."

After being on a friendly, first name basis with the man's predecessor, the words were a slap to Anton. For the next ten minutes, the grandfather clock ticked loudly in the silence between the president's questions.

"Have you talked to Immigration?"

"Yes," they said at the same time.

"Have asked at the hotels?"

"Yes."

"Have you talked to the harbormaster?"

"Yes."

"Have you checked with Interpol?"

"Yes."

President Borges didn't stop pacing while he asked and they answered, everything from who had conducted the autopsy to how many harbor patrolmen had responded to the initial call about the body. In fact, he didn't stop pacing the entire time they were there.

What Anton had heard was true: Rafael Borges was a micromanager. Nothing to hold against the new man, he said to himself. He tried to convince himself that the interrogation was simply because the president wanted the best for the people he served, that he wasn't familiar with the thorough approach he and Luis always took, that somehow news of their successes hadn't reached him.

He stopped trying to think the best of Borges when the president raised eyebrows grown bushy with age and yelled, "And you still don't know the name of the person who died? How hard can it be? We're on an island, for God's sake!"

Anton kept his temper by focusing on the rain-streaked window behind the president and hoping Catarina was staying dry.

The clock ticked away the seconds while the president found a Lisbon newspaper on his desk. "There have been two reports of this in the mainland press, and they didn't come from my office." As though mirroring the president's temper, the raindrops pelting the windows grew larger and gained energy. "Gomes, get your department in order or we'll talk about someone else to do it!"

The president's eyes bored into Luis. "I don't have to tell you that our survival now depends on tourism, and tourists will not come if they read words like *possible shark attack* and *safety concerns*. You're going to have to issue a statement."

An actual press briefing wasn't necessary. None of the international media had offices or even stringers on the Azores, and the local press usually got information with a call or over a beer with a friend. Luis would simply send out a reassuring statement to people he knew well.

"As for you, Cardosa, I know about your arrangement with my predecessor, but this is a new administration with a new focus. I'm concerned you might be doing too many things to do any one of them effectively. I want you to consider your priority. Is it your ministerial duties, this cultural preserve idea, or your rural hotel?"

The words stung. In the instant that followed, Anton saw everything he and Catarina and Lori had built crumble. No longer Minister of Heritage. The heritage preserve just a scatterbrained idea someone once had. Casa do Mar ruined.

Luis and Anton each let out a long, deep breath when they were dismissed. They took the stairs slowly, two veterans of a system that left them subordinate to politics, happy to find solace in each other. By the time they stepped back into the gardens, clouds were breaking up to a starry night.

"We will survive this, my friend," Anton said to lessen the blow he knew Luis had taken.

"Three-and-a-half years is a long time to survive such uncertainty."

After they said their goodnights, Anton found Catarina on a bench in the gazebo, dry and content.

"He isn't João," was all he could muster saying before he wrapped a long arm around her shoulder, for his own comfort more than for hers.

They strolled in silence for a while. Catarina picked up a fallen blossom and handed it to him. He drew her closer, again because he desperately needed her, and he told her about Borges's parting remarks. Neither had to name their greatest concern. It wasn't that Borges would remove Anton from his post as Minister of Heritage; from the start, they'd known the appointment could end at any time. It wasn't even having to leave Santa Maria if Anton lost that appointment and Casa do Mar failed; rootless until they'd found each other, they now carried their roots—their family—with them. It was the threat of losing what they wanted for the people of the Azores.

4

It happened sometimes. The archipelago that reaps the benefit of being planted in the path of the Gulf Stream experienced the occasional tropical storm, the rare hurricane, the unexpected frosty morning.

It was such a morning on Santa Maria. Catarina could feel it on her face and burrowed further under the covers and closer to the big bear of a man who never seemed to feel the cold. Anton wrapped his arms around her and both remained in one of those dozy states for the next half hour.

Catarina reached for a sweater and put it on over her nightgown.

Anton sneezed, and Catarina blessed him. "I hope you're not getting sick." She pulled the quilt up around his neck and kissed him. "Stay in bed. Lori and I will get everything ready."

Being the middle of his night, he was already back asleep.

Catarina was usually the first one up at Casa do Mar, so she was surprised to smell coffee brewing before she reached the kitchen. "You are awake early," she greeted Lori. "Do you have something on your mind?"

Catarina always knew.

Lori pulled the paper top off the bottle of milk that had been left outside the kitchen door before she woke up. "Let's talk over coffee."

Catarina understood. Whatever was on Lori's mind—and she had an idea what that might be—would need time to talk over thoughtfully. While they made breakfast for the children, she filled Lori in on what they had learned on São Miguel. "Just a boy," she said with a sadness she felt.

Lori shared that feeling, but her mind was also on how the death would affect travel to the islands. The survival of Casa do Mar had become very personal to her, and that survival depended on visitors who valued the safety and peace of the islands.

Catarina looked at the old cabinet clock on the wall, a flea market find from her student days with Anton. "We have time to talk. Shall I heat the milk?" She took her oversize cup and Lori's mug from the shelf.

But they didn't have time. Before they could sit down, Toni came through the door an hour early for football practice, followed soon afterward by Liliana, who was excited to start her classes in first aid. All thought of romantic conundrums or the death on São Miguel or pouring a cup of coffee were lost in the rush that followed.

Maria Rosa arrived with dark circles under her eyes. "I can drop Toni off at the football field on my way to the first-aid class." She didn't wait for a response, just waved the children through the door. "There are many days coming when you can take everyone to school." Her words were what Catarina would have expected to hear but not in such a weary voice.

Five minutes after they left, Lori and Catarina were working to the sounds of Casa do Mar. Beto's crew, restoring what was to be the third of Casa do Mar's guest cottages, was hammering and sawing and occasionally breaking out into song. Jardineiro and Jardineira, tending to the grounds, gave an occasional caprine bleat of satisfaction. And as always, waves rolled onto the beach below the cliff.

Catarina covered a corner of the old oak table with an orderly row of the papers slowly making their way through the tired printer. She worked best with hardcopies. She started with notes on what they had learned from Frau Meickle, Vitor Vieira, the Costa brothers, and the people they had talked to at the marina. The email from the harbormaster, sent at precisely 11:59 last night, went on top. She had asked Anton for the police report from Luis Gomes. She had not asked for the folder with the autopsy findings. She had seen how he tucked it away under his laptop.

Beto's work on the guest cottages had meant no time to bring the Casa do Mar living quarters into the twenty-first-century, leaving the kitchen with only a single electrical outlet and no wireless capability. Lori's workarounds had turned the kitchen floor into a mass of snaking wires that linked devices, power sources, routers, modems, and a landline.

Her fingers tapped the keyboard of her laptop at a speed that seemed almost superhuman. She took a picture of the map Catarina had marked with a red X where the victim had been caught in the Devil's Hands. She determined the GPS coordinates. She downloaded a Coast Guard chart showing water currents around Breakwater Cove the day he died.

A little after nine, Anton walked into the kitchen without the expected bounce in his steps, without the cheery grin his face usually wore without effort. His large brown eyes looked at Catarina and then at Lori, each time pursing his lips to acknowledge they were about to embark on sad but necessary business.

He put his cup, twice emptied of espresso, into the sink and stared out the window. The beginnings of an investigation were not easy for him. A sense of forward motion was too easily lost to the frustrations of false leads and information that seemed just out of reach. But Anton was a born leader, now the de facto leader of his community. He understood his responsibility.

He pulled back his chair and started. "For a number of reasons, we can accept what Vitor told us and what Frau Meickle told us as the best of their recollections. We know Vitor well, and the times both gave jibe with the call made to the police station and when the body was found by harbor patrol."

"What if their recollections are faulty?" Lori was the one who challenged Anton most vigorously, and he appreciated that.

"They corroborate each other's stories. Also, Luis sent a couple of officers to follow up with the Australians who were watching for whales; they may not have added anything, but nothing they said contradicts what Vitor and Frau Meickle told us."

He raised one finger. "The *São Pedro* was in Breakwater Cove that morning. According to Vitor and others in the marina, the fisherman's a relative newcomer. He told harbor patrol he only fishes for pleasure, but he's been seen out a lot recently."

He raised a second finger. "Fabiano Deníz took the Costa diving boat to the cove, which he does once or twice a week. When Frau Meickle saw him, the divers were underwater. He was alone."

Catarina reached for a folder. "Harbor patrol reports that the Costa boat was still in the cove when they arrived. The divers were on board by then. They said they had not seen anything."

"They could have been involved, themselves." Anton wasn't the only one Lori challenged.

Catarina acknowledged that but added, "They were visitors, though, so perhaps it is less likely that they would conspire with Deníz to lie."

Anton lifted his head. "What sort of boat is it?"

Lori had followed his unspoken thought. A moment later, she turned her laptop around to show the homepage for Costa Diving—a homepage so basic it looked like it was a classroom assignment from the 1990s. "It's a repurposed fishing boat—with a large hold, I imagine." A hold large enough to hide someone the divers never saw.

Anton nodded thoughtfully. He held up his hand again, this time adding a third finger. "Both Frau Meickle and Vitor mentioned a yacht in Breakwater Cove, but it wasn't there when harbor patrol arrived."

"Exactly where in the cove did they see these boats?" Lori asked, fingers poised over her keyboard. Anton and Catarina hovered over the paper map and showed her. "I'll add that to the file with the victim's location and currents. The Coast Guard might be able to make something of it."

She stopped and thought. "Couldn't the victim have been in the water for days—when other boats were in the area?"

Catarina told her about how Frau Meickle had remembered seeing the foam on the waves darkening from pink to red in the five to ten minutes she watched.

"Perhaps that was only because he was closer to the shore?" It was a delicate way to suggest what would have happened to a fragile human body trapped between sharp rocks and powerful waves.

Anton's finger went to the folder under his laptop. "No. He died shortly before the police boat arrived." A transparent image of the boy appeared in his mind, and it could only be put aside by his determination to discover who had mistreated him. "Our next task is to identify which of the three yachts known to be in the area was the one near the Devil's Hands that morning."

Catarina consulted her own laptop. "I did not print what Branco attached to his email. There were forty documents with over five hundred pages of information." She paused. "He could be trying to distract us from what he does not want us to know or he is the type who doesn't like to answer to anyone. It is probably both."

Lori had an idea. "Could you forward what he sent?" In the minute after her laptop sounded with the arriving files, her eyes quickly tracked back and forth, her brows knit, her lips pursed. Then a gotcha smile appeared on her face. "Just six files have been modified since they were created. One shows the thirty-seven boats berthed at the marina last Tuesday." She opened a browser window, and her fingers flashed over the keyboard, looking for information. She toggled between the new tab and the spreadsheet Branco had sent. "Only three of these could be classified as yachts, the *Iaso*, the *Sirena*, and the *Doura*." She turned her laptop so Anton and Catarina could see the entries.

Catarina pointed at the screen. "Most information has been entered carelessly. Look at the abbreviations and misspellings. Look at the missing information."

All the blank fields and sloppy entries hadn't been lost on Anton when he first saw the marina log. "Trust Branco to take the easy way," he grumbled.

"That is not the telling point. The information on the *Doura* is complete and carefully worded." Catarina scrolled and pointed again. "See here...and here." Every field from the name of the captain to the number of crew and passengers was filled out.

What Catarina was saying dawned on him. "He filled that in yesterday."

Anton asked Lori, "What about the other files that were modified?"

"In the other five, the *Doura* is registered at the marina overnight, once with the *Iaso*, four times with the *Sirena*."

"Are there any registrations for the *Sirena* and the *Iaso* on days when the *Doura* is not at the marina?"

"Several. In fact, the *Sirena* seems to have been berthed in the marina long-term for the past year. It leaves for short periods every month or so. The *Iaso* only started coming to Ponta Delgado two years ago. It registers when it arrives, anchors somewhere offshore for a few days at a time, and leaves two or three weeks later."

Silence took over. No one could figure out if all that was even relevant. Lori got up and stretched. Catarina made fresh coffee. Anton sent a text to Luis asking for more information on all three yachts and, reluctant to confront the next task, four more texts that were anything but urgent.

He was relieved when Beto appeared at the Dutch door. That usually meant ten minutes on updates about the restoration and double that on updates to community news. But Beto was only looking for a missing tool and some commiseration. "Some of these guys don't have the respect for tools that we were taught. Last week, I found a hammer left out overnight and in our climate, that can doom it," he grumbled on the way out.

As reluctant as Anton was to share the medical examiner's exam with them, when they gathered again he slipped the folder Dr. Nunes had put together from under his laptop, opened it halfway, and with a thumb and forefinger extracted a picture before closing it again. "There's one more thing before we return to São Miguel."

A closeup showed the enhanced closeup of the tattoo Dr. Nunes had found on the boy's right arm.

Catarina squinted over the picture. "Red ink. And it looks like it has been stretched."

"The boy was tattooed with this when he was very young."

Lori tapped her keyboard. "It looks like S...N...P." She scanned lines of possibilities. "It could be anything from a nature conservancy group to an organization that promotes the use of seat belts."

"Nothing tied to children?"

"Several but nothing that jumps out as a reason to tattoo a child."

"You should also know that part of the wound caused by a sharp, thin-bladed knife."

"Part?"

"A shark bite came afterwards."

Catarina reached out to Anton. "Is there more?"

The child was beaten and starved and probably held captive for the past month.

He steeled himself and told them everything he knew. The toxicology report had come in. Trace elements, indicative of good nutrition, were within normal levels in recently formed tissues, such as skin and blood, but woefully inadequate otherwise. After a short lifetime of malnutrition, he had eaten well in recent weeks. His stomach contents were missing, but his intestines showed a curious progression of having eaten several large meals in the two or three days before his death to not having eaten at all the day before death.

That was where the drugs were found—not the recreational drugs teens might use but several expensive, prescription-only drugs in a combination that mystified Dr. Nunes.

"Pedophiles?" Catarina could only manage the one word, and the other two could only manage shrugs. Although they knew such things could be hidden around them, there had not been a single case reported since a scandal involving the Church thirty years before.

"The boy came from somewhere," Anton blew his words out on a wave of frustration.

Lori wished she could say something to reassure him that it was just a matter of time. She couldn't. "I've tried missing persons' reports, but the truth is that it would be the longest of shots without narrowing the field. We don't have a clue where he came from, and no one is missing on the islands—except Carlos's friend, Martim. Still."

"I wish we could help with that, but right now we have enough to deal with. I...we?" he looked to Catarina, who nodded. "We will return to São Miguel tomorrow morning to talk with Fabiano Deníz of the Costas' diving shop and the magnificent

Captain Karlsson of the *Sirena*. I'll also ask Luis to have the *São Pedro* tracked down."

"I'd like to hitch a ride with you," Lori cut in. "Carlos needs my support. Martim's father may think it's a case of cold feet before the wedding, but his mother is worried that he's at the bottom of a ravine with a broken leg." The latter scenario wasn't fanciful. Every year, people—usually visitors unfamiliar with the landscape—fell into one of the fissures created by the powerful geologic forces still at work on the islands.

As they cleared the kitchen table and went outside to clear their minds, they all had the same thought: there's so much we still don't know.

They started their day in *Convento Real*, a convent that had been restored as a pousada, or historical hotel. The cloister now served as a restaurant and at a table surrounded by mounds of salvia and clouds of the colorful butterflies they attracted, Catarina sipped her sweet milky brew, Anton downed his series of strong espressos, and Lori drank what was called café americano but somehow never equaled the black American coffee she preferred.

A little before eleven, Anton and Catarina set out to talk to the first person they hoped to eliminate from a growing list of suspects, and Lori left to meet Carlos. All vowed to return home for the night.

Lori stood back when Carlos knocked on the door. There was no sound of a lock turning; that would be unusual even on São Miguel. The door swung open quickly. A look of anticipation was followed immediately by disappointment when the woman saw their faces.

Short and heavyset, she had the fair skin and almost black hair seen in many of Portuguese ancestry. "You are a kind friend to come, Carlos."

He kissed her on both cheeks and took her into a long, close hug. "Soon you'll have the pleasure of scolding Martim for worrying his mother like this." His tone was lighthearted but Lori heard the tension in his voice. "This is my friend, Lori."

The woman introduced herself to Lori as Alicia and gave her the traditional two kisses. "Carlos said you helped Minister Cardosa to find the child who was missing on Terceira." In the small and isolated archipelago, that had become front page news on all the islands—literal front page news not the lead in an online newspaper.

She invited them into her small house, which looked much as it had when it was inherited from Martim's grandparents. The skirted sofa was worn but comfortable, the drapes were faded, and there were scratches on the bare oak floorboards and water rings on every tabletop. Theirs wasn't a wealthy family, but everything was tidy and very clean. A faint smell of melting candle wax was still in the air from the votive that had burned down in front of a statue of the Virgin Mary on the mantle. Next to the statue was a picture of Martim. Despite the changes of the past few decades, these were still very Catholic and very conservative people.

Alicia would not be dissuaded from bringing them coffee. After she left for the kitchen, Carlos whispered, "It will take only a few minutes. They need reassurance."

They turned out to be Martim's immediate family: his brother Rafe, who seemed to be forcing an air of nonchalance; his sister, who was overtly concerned; and his father, who was embarrassed that so much had been made of the fact that a man in his thirties was late returning home.

"Both sides of his bed were tucked in," Alicia said as she handed Lori a cup of coffee. There was a saying in the Azores: Leave one side of your bed untucked or you may not return home to it. She had said it with a small laugh, to give the impression that she herself thought it was complete nonsense, but Lori knew islanders were a superstitious lot. *If you drop a knife, a man will visit soon. If you forget to bless the fish at dinner, the next catch will be poor.* She had learned to keep her thoughts about such irrationality to herself—and never to wave with her left hand, which could be taken as wishing someone an early death.

Everyone avoided the reason they had gathered with small talk until Rafe took a deep breath and said, "Mama is worried about Martim."

Martim's father harrumphed.

Alicia addressed Lori, "We understand he is a grown man and occasionally does not return home at night. I don't pry. But this is different. He always tells us when he won't be home—even if it's only a short call."

Another harrumph.

"I know something is wrong, Joca. I just know."

Joca tightened his lips and sat back in his chair.

"He could be waiting for us to come and help him."

Rafe looked at Carlos. "I talked to Távo down at the police station. He didn't seem to think there was any cause for alarm."

Carlos was thinking of the reason Anton and Catarina were on the island when he said, "Things may be different now." He regretted those words before they left his mouth.

"Why?" Alicia tensed.

Lori jumped in. "Because now I will tell Minister Cardosa about Martim's absence."

A grateful mother moved even closer to Lori and quietly thanked her.

She took out her phone and started tapping with both thumbs. Her rudimentary Portuguese had grown fluent and colloquial since she moved to the islands. "Let me get some information…" she saw the worried look that crossed Alicia's face, "…so we can find Martim more quickly. Has he ever been away this long?"

"Sometimes for work," Rafe said. "He flies a plane, like Carlos, and sometimes weather will ground him on another island or a tourist will be delayed."

Alicia was quick to say, "I called his work. They have no idea where he is."

"Martim has a plane of his own now," Rafe gently offered his mother as an explanation.

Far from helping, she now looked stricken. "If he took it up and something happened, no one would know where he was."

"Let's try to figure out where he was last and work forward from there. When I spoke to him, he said Natalia was also going to be late, and he was happy to take pictures of the sunset until we all met up at the marina. That was about seven on Tuesday night. Did anyone hear from him after that?"

They looked at each other and then at her and shook their heads *no*.

"Since it was seven, he was probably…" she corrected herself, "he may have already been at the marina. Would he have driven there?"

Alicia answered, "In the afternoon, he had a tourist flight, his last one for someone else's company." Tears filled her eyes.

"He would have driven his own car from the airport to the marina," Rafe said. He gave Lori the name and location of Martim's employer, which Lori entered in her phone.

"Have you been in touch with Natalia?"

None of them met her eyes. Martim's sister, Beatriz, parted her lips just a bit and delivered a cold, clipped answer, "I called many times. Natalia doesn't answer her phone. Her father says she's in bed with a cold. He says he hasn't seen Martim."

"What about the rest of her family?"

"There's only Natalia, the father, and a brother."

"Names?"

"They won't talk to you."

"They'll talk to Minister Cardosa." Her assurance was rewarded with a pat on the hand from Alicia and the offer of a cookie.

Lori continued the entry in her phone. "So there is Natalia…the rest of her name?" She knew surnames were a relatively new concept on the islands and in some of the rest of Europe for that matter. Since the first settlers in the fifteenth century, Azoreans commonly had two given names. As a third name, one child could be given his mother's third name, another could take his father's, and another could have a third name that had never been in the family before. A single family could have a Maria Clara Simas, a Maria Rita Fontes, and a Maria Emelia Moniz. Even today, a child can be baptized with a second name—a surname—neither parent has but a distant ancestor carried.

Apparently, Beatriz was in charge of information on Natalia's family. "De la Rosa. She is Natalia Anamaria de la Rosa. The father is Henrique." She feigned a haughty tone. "Senhor Henrique Pedro Gustavo de la Rosa."

Joca interrupted with another harrumph, which was perhaps a more positive assessment of Henrique de la Rosa than the scowl that appeared on Rafe's face and the tightened lips of Beatriz and Alicia.

"And the brother?"

"Gustavo."

Rafe nodded slowly to himself. His mother reached over the coffee table to squeeze his hand. There was some history there that wasn't being shared.

"How long have you known the de la Rosas?"

"The children have known each other since childhood," Alicia said. "Rafe and Natalia were in the same class at school.

"And Gustavo?"

Again, they exchanged glances. But no one spoke.

"Do you still socialize?"

All three said no at the same time. Then Alicia added, "Gustavo wasn't as devoted a friend as my children were."

"Did the families get together with the de la Rosas to plan the wedding?" she probed.

"No. We invited them but…"

"You'd think he would want the marriage," Joca exploded. "He's desperate for grandchildren."

"His son isn't married?"

"He's not the sort to marry."

Beatriz put her cup down. "All we know is that Martim's marriage to Natalia is set for next month, and not one person in the de la Rosa family seems concerned that he is missing. Not one person at the police station seems concerned that he is missing."

Joca waved off her concern. "He's somewhere, celebrating or recovering from celebrating. Leave it be. He's a grown man for God's sake!"

Lori finished by taking information about Martim's other friends, his car and new plane, and the places where he liked to go, especially to take pictures.

Alicia pulled away from a long hug at the front door to look into Lori's eyes. "You will find my boy?"

She didn't want take away a mother's hope—or to give her false hope—so in the end, she hugged her back and said, "I'm going to look for him right now."

After they left, Carlos made sense of all the uncomfortable glances and stilted responses in the Sousa living room. "You know islanders are related in many ways."

Lori nodded, thinking about the familial intermarriages that took place on the isolated and sparsely populated islands.

That wasn't what Carlos meant. "Villagers go to the same churches, shop in the same stores, attend the same schools. We know each other very well. We keep each other's secrets very well, especially from outsiders."

"I don't have Catarina's gift, but even I knew they were holding back."

"In the days—not too long ago, actually—when there were clear class distinctions, the de la Rosas were one of the few wealthy families. They have lost much of that wealth, or rather many of those who had less then have more now. Senhor de la Rosa still has power, though. Some of it is simply because people have held on to the belief that he has control over their lives. Some of it is actual power from favors owed by those in authority and by the financial interests he has. To this day he dominates his own family."

"What happened to the mother?"

"She died when we were all in our teens. I remember a night soon afterwards, one of those rare nights when Natalia was allowed out of the house. She and her brother had joined Martim, Beatriz, and me on the beach, and we were drinking wine and talking about plans for our lives. Natalia said she wanted to leave the islands, to go away to school, but her father would never allow it. He said she was needed at home."

"He could stop her?"

"Partly, it was his mental control of her, but he had also made sure that neither of his children had a euro of their own. And they knew he could make it hard for them to work anywhere on the island if he wanted."

"I wouldn't be surprised if he expects her to care for him in his old age."

Carlos nodded in agreement.

"So he's not in favor of her getting married?"

"I don't think it's getting married. I think it's marrying Martim. She was engaged to another man a couple of years ago. Senhor de la Rosa was crowing about it all over town, how they would move in with him, how the grandchildren would be coming soon. Then she fell in love, and that was that." He gave her a kiss.

"What could he have possibly had against Martim?"

"Gustavo and the Sousa children were best friends for many years."

"Alicia said Gustavo wasn't as good a friend as her children were. What do you suppose she meant by that?"

"Martim was in training for the Air Force when he was caught drunk at the helm of a boat he'd taken without the owner's permission. There had been some property damage. It was considered a small infraction but because a child was injured, it went to trial."

"Gustavo didn't stick by his friend?"

"He did not. He refused to testify about Martim's character when, as a de la Rosa, his words would have made a difference."

"Could that have been at his father's urging?" The word that had first come to mind was *demand*.

"Probably. Regardless, Martim went to jail. His career was over. Ever since, Gustavo has stuck close to home and father."

"So he can provide the grandchildren Senhor de la Rosa wants so badly."

Martim made sense of Joca's remark about Natalia's brother not being the sort to marry. Homosexuality was still an awkward subject for some, especially the older generation, to discuss openly.

Carlos paused before starting the car. "I thought we'd find him on a friend's couch, a little hungover and very sorry he'd worried his mother." He looked at Lori, "Now I'm not so sure. He could be lying at the bottom of a cliff or crashed in a ravine."

From what Carlos had said, talking with the de la Rosas was going to take more than simply requesting few minutes of their time, so Lori had made a last minute call for Catarina's help. That way, even if they said nothing to her, Catarina might still glean useful information.

The house was the largest colonial home on São Miguel that had not been converted to a government building or a museum or a hotel. Built in the sixteenth century, when the Portuguese Empire was the largest and wealthiest of all European countries, it may have been intended to rival the governor's mansion closer to the busy port. This house, however, was located on two acres of land overlooking that mansion—one might say looking *down* at that mansion.

From the other side of the front door, they heard male voices—one tyrannical, the other tyrannized. The curtain in a front window moved before Lori pulled the bell. Then there was silence, and the door was opened by a worn-looking woman wearing a black shirtwaist dress with a white apron. Looking past the brow furrows and downturned mouth of a seventy-year-old, she was the right age to be the mother of Fabi, the divemaster.

The woman couldn't decide how to respond when Lori explained they were representing Anton Cardosa, minister of the Central Government, and introduced Catarina as his colleague. She opened her eyes wide and turned around, as if looking for someone to tell her what to do. She asked them to wait, started to close the door, then changed her mind and showed them into a sitting room.

Heavy, dark, and deeply carved, the furniture ranged from Renaissance to Victorian but nothing more recent. Gilt-framed oil paintings covered every wall, and silver pieces covered every table top. It looked like everything in its place, and its place hadn't changed in centuries. The room smelled of the same lavender wood wax Lori's mother had used before her parents cleared out the contents of the house she'd grown up in and replaced everything with clean-lined pieces that looked like they'd come from IKEA. It brought back a flood of memories, a few good, most not.

Two men made a joint appearance, son standing in back of his father, literally and figuratively. The family resemblance was startling. With the exception of a slight softening of the flesh that had come with age, Henrique de la Rosa looked very much like his son. That is, until the conversation began. The exchange of pleasantries that brought a smile to the younger face did nothing to change the set jaw of Henrique de la Rosa. His eyes kept the cool look that men who are assured of their importance have.

Catarina began with words that could be taken as an apology for Anton's absence or a reminder that cooperation was to Henrique's advantage. "Minister Cardosa would have liked to meet you, but he is at the Presidential Palace." Naturally, she did not explain that Anton was only there to meet Luis for a working lunch.

Henrique de la Rosa asserted his own position with a posture of superiority and, "The Palace is much like my own home in style although, as you might expect, I have a greater fondness for my own since it has been in the family since it was built."

"We are here on behalf of the Sousa family. They are concerned that Martim has not been in touch since Tuesday night."

Apparently, he had expected that they were there for a completely different reason, perhaps political fund raising or to request his presence at some local government event. Catarina's statement took him by such surprise that it took a moment before he shrugged and said, "We know nothing of that."

He turned his attention to his maid. "Bring coffee and the almond cake, sliced thin, on the Doccia china." He was used to being in control of every detail.

"I understand that he is engaged to your daughter."

He had no comment on that.

"Do you have any idea why he might not be in touch with his family?"

"It is not my place to comment on how people behave, whether as young men or as adults." He left it at that.

Catarina knew his response was in island code. *There were certain things— indelicate things—that it would not be proper for him to talk about. After all, he was not one to speak ill of others.* The question was whether he truly wanted to respect Martim's privacy or he only wanted an excuse to let slip Martim's failings. "Many young men carry a reckless mistake or two into adulthood with them," she tested him.

He didn't move on. He appeared to consider her comment carefully and, sounding reluctant, he said, "There are reckless mistakes, and there are criminal acts," he swallowed the last two words as if unwilling to utter them.

"What do you mean by criminal acts?" She saw the momentary satisfaction that washed his face when he was given the opening to inch closer to what he wanted to say.

"There are such things as girls and drinking, such things as Gustavo and I, too, have indulged in," he gave her a conspiratorial chuckle. Then he arranged his face to look solemn. "Then there are such things as theft and endangering the public. For those acts, it is quite right to pay the price." He had said what he wanted without actually saying it: Martim had committed a crime and had paid the price.

Catarina's interest in this was not what Martim had done; Lori had already told her about the boat theft and its aftermath. Initially, she had been trying to form an impression of the man, but soon her attention had been drawn to his son. Others would not have noticed the single-second waves of anger that washed Gustavo's face, tightening his lips and jutting his jaw before he masked his feelings again.

The maid returned with coffee and the cake—sliced thinly, as demanded. When she set everything down on a table between the father and the son, her hands trembled a bit. Her eyes immediately darted to Henrique de la Rosa and the frown of disapproval that had appeared on his face.

Following the civilities of thanking Henrique and complimenting the cake, Catarina turned to his son.

"Have you seen Martim recently?"

She may have asked Gustavo, but Henrique answered, "They are no longer friends. Why would he see him?"

"I haven't seen him since I picked up Natalia at the Sousa home a couple of weeks ago," Gustavo mumbled. He checked his father's face and quickly looked away.

Henrique took a lump of sugar from a silver bowl and replaced the tongs somewhat more firmly than was needed. "I have learned that it is best to steer clear of some people, senhora Vanderhye. In prison, even a good man can become a bad man. And a bad man can become worse. Maybe that is what happened to Martim."

Some electric emotion was coming off Gustavo—Catarina thought hatred, but whether of her questions or of his father's responses was unclear.

"Do you have any ideas about where he might be, Gustavo?"

Gustavo checked his father's face again and kept checking it as he gave a list of places on the island that any local would think to look for someone.

"Minister Cardosa would like us to ask Natalia, as well."

The elder de la Rosa drilled into her with his tiny black pupils, showing dominance. "Natalia is lying down. She hasn't been well. But I can answer for her. She has not heard from the man since Sunday. Maybe he changed his mind about marrying her."

Lori had heard the creak of floorboards overhead. Unless there was a second maid upstairs, Natalia wasn't lying down. She put down her plate and asked to use the bathroom. Thankfully, Henrique didn't ask the maid to escort her. She bypassed the hall she was directed to and went upstairs. *I can always blame my less-than-perfect Portuguese for misunderstanding the directions,* she reassured herself, and she took a turn for the part of the house above the sitting room.

It wasn't hard to find Natalia. Martim's fiancée stood in the open doorway to a room darkened by drawn drapes. She looked older than in the picture of her and Martim on the wall of his parents' living room, petite and fairer than her father and brother. She had reddish hair, and sprays of freckles decorated her shoulders and the bridge of her nose, not an uncommon look among Azoreans of Flemish descent.

"Natalia?" She'd been lost in thought, and Lori's voice startled her. "I'm a friend of the Sousas. Martim hasn't been home since Tuesday night." Natalia backed into her room. "They're worried, you understand."

She took a breath. "I was worried, too. I was supposed to meet him at the marina. He didn't answer his phone. So I got worried."

Her train of thought was odd. First, she was worried. Then, she got worried. "You were worried before you were supposed to meet Martim?"

She stared at Lori, deciding what to say, which in the end didn't answer the question. "There's a good reason he isn't answering his phone. Probably." She clasped her hands.

"What could that reason be?"

She looked down the hall. "I don't know. My father thinks... My father says there's a reason."

"What reason?"

"He says that there is always the possibility that someone from Martim's past returned to harm him."

It seemed an odd reason to explain why a young man hadn't returned his fiancée's calls.

Natalia blurted out, "Martim is a good man now."

When footsteps sounded in the downstairs hall, she said, "I must go," and she closed the door behind herself.

When Lori returned, the maid was still standing by, eyes sharply on the master of the house. Catarina had worked her magic. She was handing Henrique one of Anton's business cards, on the back of which she'd written *Convento Real*. "If you cannot reach Minister Cardosa at the number on the front, please feel free to leave a message here."

He thanked her warmly. "I will be certain to if I hear anything that could help him."

He leaned forward and spoke as though to a confidante. "You can understand my feelings. The Sousas were not the right family for my daughter to marry into."

In his mind, the possibility of a marriage was now in the past.

5

When Anton and Catarina arrived at the marina, a blanket of clouds was clearing to reveal a faded blue sky, but the ocean still pulsed dark gray and darker green. Seabirds, shrieking and crying, were following the early fishing boats back in. Some gulls saved themselves the effort; they squatted on the pier, waiting to eat any fish that wasn't secured.

Branco spotted them from a distance and scooted into the harbormaster's office.

"It may be a good sign that he was not inside reading the newspaper." Catarina tried to look on the optimistic side of things.

"I've asked the Coast Guard to look into him." Once Anton lost faith in someone, it was hard to restore.

He walked slowly past the window of the harbormaster's office, caught Branco's eye, and doubled back to look through the glass again. He didn't need anything. He was letting the man know he was being held accountable.

"Is he looking a bit spiffier?" Catarina asked.

"Perhaps," was all he said.

On the way to interview the captain of the *Sirena*, they stopped to say hello to the Vieiras. Catarina brought Vitor a box of pastries, which he happily shared with her and grudgingly shared with Anton. "Ema's at the doctor," he told Catarina. It was as close as he could bring himself to admitting he was worried.

She patted his arm. "That is a good way to get healthy." But she remembered how thin Ema had looked the last time she saw her and she, too, was worried.

Anton was anxious to get going. "It must be time for your nap, Vitor."

"No nap today. I'm looking after Zezé." His youngest grandchild was looking at a fishing boat through his binoculars. "As long as he has something to look at, he's not much trouble. And Mano helps me." He reached down and patted the smelly dog.

Catarina hugged Vitor goodbye. "Let us know if we can help."

"I will, dear lady."

She looked at Anton to prompt his goodbye, but Anton was staring at Zezé. "Was Zezé on board last Tuesday morning?" And before Vitor could answer, he asked, "Was he looking through his binoculars?"

"Tuesday? Let me think." A long period of muffled grunts followed, after which Vitor said, "Tuesday, Zezé's mama took him to the doctor." He gave Anton a dismissive wave of his hand. "That means *no*."

And another possible lead evaporated.

The *Sirena* was moored in an odd place for a yacht, at the working end of the marina. Across from the shiny white symbol of wealth and privilege was a warehouse with flaking paint and a tin roof. Blood, fish scales, and seagull droppings were splattered over the cement floor and walls, and it was chaotic with activity. None of that disturbed Anton and Catarina in the least. Places like these, where catches of the day were unloaded and sold to larger distributors, were emblematic of the hardworking fishing communities that had built their islands.

What did disturb Anton—and terribly—was a waterlogged tree trunk that had collected the natural detritus that lapped the shore and along with it, plastic straws, Styrofoam cups, cigarette butts, even medical syringes.

Since neither of them spoke Norwegian, Anton called out to the deck of the *Sirena* in English for permission to come aboard. It took a while and a couple more requests, but eventually Captain Lars Karlsson made an entrance from the pilothouse, still buttoning his jacket. He paused and approached the top of the gangplank, slowly and regally. He was indeed as described, almost a caricature of a yachtsman, in a crisp white uniform with golden braids decorating cuffs, collar, and cap.

His words welcomed them heartily. "How are you enjoying our islands?" Anton had only just opened his mouth to reply, when Karlsson went on, "I know the Azores well. I've sailed these waters for decades on this grand vessel. She's won many awards, you know."

Not only was the *Sirena* one of the most modest yachts he'd seen around the islands, Anton had never heard of Karlsson. Catarina picked up on another anomaly: Karlsson's name and appearance may have been Scandinavian, but his English had an accent she associated with the American South.

Karlsson led them directly to the saloon, dominated by the figurehead of a mermaid. "The *Sirena* is so much better than those larger ships." His tone made Catarina suspect that he really wanted to be the captain of one of those larger ships.

He caressed the mermaid's wooden tail. "The original Sirena. I named my ship for her when I purchased her."

"When was that?" Catarina asked, smiling as she took the seat he offered.

"Can I offer you refreshments? Our staff has gone ashore for supplies, but I think I could rustle up some tea or lemonade." He looked at Anton. "Or perhaps something stronger?"

He seemed relieved when they declined.

"Such a beautiful space," Catarina said.

"It is. As my guests, I could take you around the islands and you could sit here, look at the beautiful scenery, and enjoy the sumptuous meals made by our talented chef."

"There may be some misunderstanding, Captain Karlsson. My husband and I live on Santa Maria." His face fell. "We run a rural hotel—"

"A hotel! Your guests would love excursions aboard the *Sirena!* You can tell them they will be part of a world they couldn't enter otherwise. You can tell them our location at this end of the marina is only temporary."

His face fell again when she introduced Anton and explained why they were there, and wariness filtered everything he said after that.

She returned to the question he hadn't answered. "When did you acquire the *Sirena?*"

His eyes shifted left and right as he considered whether to tell the truth or not, and when he spoke it was to Anton not Catarina. "You understand. In business, appearances are everything. It reassures the customer to hear certain things," he gave a confidential laugh.

Anton's English lessons, given mostly by his own daughter, Liliana, had taught him quite a bit in the past two years. He understood exactly what Karlsson had said, but he remained stone-faced and turned to Catarina.

"Last July," he finally answered her.

"Is that when you first moored in São Miguel?"

"That would have been September."

"You have a business taking visitors on excursions?"

"A business? Goodness, no. Not a real business. I take people I've met to sail around the island, not paying customers, really. Friends, just new friends."

"We are looking for a yacht that was seen in Breakwater Cove last Tuesday morning."

"Tuesday," he said slowly. "Tuesday," he repeated even more slowly. "I might have been passing through those waters, showing friends around." A spot of bright pink bloomed on each of his cheeks.

Anton handed Catarina a folder. Inside were two of the pictures he hadn't wanted to show her. Eyes on Karlsson, she opened it.

He twisted his head to look. "Is he…?"

"Have you ever seen this boy?" she asked. Catarina always chose her words carefully. As many people do, Karlsson might convince himself he wasn't really lying if a question could be interpreted another way. So she hadn't asked if he knew the boy or was familiar with him.

His eyes opened wide. "Why are you involving me in this?"

She needed to see him answer. "Have you ever seen this boy?"

"No. No." But he was nervous.

She slipped the top picture under the other one, a closeup of the tattoo on the boy's arm. "Have you ever seen this?"

He examined it closely before saying no.

"Exactly where in our waters was the *Sirena* last Tuesday morning?"

Karlsson's attitude had changed. He was serious and a little scared. He drew a deep breath. "I took some guests out on Monday afternoon and anchored here and there for the next four days. As I said, we might have been somewhere in the area of Breakwater Cove one of those days."

It was an unusual—and an inept—captain who didn't know where his ship had been anchored. "Are any of your new friends with you now?"

His eyes shifted again. "All four left yesterday."

"We would like their names."

Apparently, to remember the names of people he'd just spent four days with, he had to go to the adjoining pilothouse and slowly leaf through papers on a clipboard. While they waited, Anton and Catarina looked at the mementos that filled the saloon like exhibits in a museum. Open scrapbooks with faded construction paper displayed black-and-white photos of celebrities partying on the yacht's deck. One newspaper clipping from 1983 told of the dry docking of the *Sirena* sixty years after Lady Ann Dorman launched it with a bottle of champagne. Above a detailed model hung a framed announcement of its purchase by American Lars Karlsson, with an account of his plans for a glamourous restoration of the run-down yacht—one that didn't seem to have come to fruition.

"There were four men, fishing, playing cards." Karlsson showed Catarina, and she took a picture of the registry with her phone.

"Who else was on board?"

"I hire local crew when the need arises. They've all gone, too."

"Could any of them have gone missing while you were at sea?"

"Missing? No. Not missing. I paid each one as he left the *Sirena*."

She wrote down what little he remembered about the crew in a small notebook. "And your chef?"

He gave a sheepish look. "Actually, I pick up meals from Gosto's Restaurant on the wharf and the bakery next door if guests are staying overnight."

Anton stared at the *Sirena*'s captain. His expression alone shook the man but when he then spoke quite clearly in English, Karlsson's jaw went slack. "We'll be back. I assume you'll still be here?"

"Well, no. I mean yes. What I mean is… The *Sirena* may be moving on soon." He left it at that.

Anton very much enjoyed his lunch at the restaurant in the marina recommended by Vitor Vieira. Tuna steeped in garlicky olive oil. Crusty bread, baked just hours earlier, of course. Lemon cookies to go with his fourth espresso of the day.

He needed his sustenance, he thought. Fabiano Deníz, aka Fabi, would be returning a trio of divers shortly. Neither Lori nor the local police had been able to add much to what the Costa brothers had told him about the young man. Depending on which of the brothers you listened to, Fabi was either a pretty boy who didn't take his work seriously or a well-liked and competent divemaster. The local police had confirmed that he lived with his parents and that his mother took care of Henrique de la Rosa's house and his children, but the fact that such a miserly man paid her well still pricked Anton's brain.

Catarina joined Anton as he picked up the last crumb of the last lemon cookie with a fingertip and popped it in his mouth. Her shopping bag was filled with things to bring back to Casa do Mar.

They waited while Fabi puttered into a slip at the end of the dock. The origin of the pretty-boy description was obvious. Sun-bronzed, tall, and muscular, he flashed a white smile so often it looked like he was a model at a photo shoot.

Before tying off the boat, he pulled off his undershirt, a skimpy one at that, and wiped his torso down slowly, all the while looking at the three young women who were his passengers. His biceps flexed as he helped them on to dry land. All that muscular effort really didn't seem necessary to Anton. It did, however, capture the women's attention and probably fattened the tips he was handed before they waved sweeping goodbyes.

Once he heard why Anton and Catarina were there, Fabi wasn't quite as attentive. He bunched up his undershirt, tossed it in the hold, and leaned forward.

An aggressive posture, Catarina noted.

"Make it short. I've got to get back to the dive shop, or I'll miss the next load of tourists."

Under other circumstances, Anton would have had some sympathy; more and more, making a living meant relying on visitors to the islands. Given the tone of Fabi's response, however, he took a harder line. "You were in Breakwater Cove last Tuesday morning. What did you see?"

Fabi made himself comfortable on a gas tank precariously tilted against a piling. "Sea. Sky. Boats. People."

Anton's height alone could be intimidating; when he set his jaw and narrowed his eyes, the gentle man could look truly frightening. He walked past Fabi, boarded the Costa boat, and started searching it.

"What do you think you're doing there?"

"Is there a problem?" Catarina asked, atypically firm.

"That man is costing me valuable time and money." He looked angry, but was that the reason or was there something else?

Catarina could have soothed him, but she preferred to see how his temper played out.

"Can he do that, just board and tear things apart?"

"Minister Cardosa has full authority."

He didn't bluff with any claim to contact his lawyer. Not only was that not in the culture, as it was in other countries, but he clearly didn't have the resources to have a lawyer on retainer.

One eye on Anton, he finally answered the question. "I took divers there Tuesday morning. Canadians. Two of them."

"Did you dive with them?"

"No, but I checked all their certifications."

Catarina heard both belligerence and fear in his voice, and she thought she knew where the fear came from. Who said he checked the *all* the certifications of two divers?

"You are certain two entered the water and two returned?"

His breathing picked up. "Yes."

She would let Anton take it from here. "Minister Cardosa," she called out, "S Deníz is starting to remember more about the time he spent in Breakwater Cove."

When Anton joined them, he brought a clipboard with him.

"S Deníz remembers taking two visitors diving on Tuesday morning," she said.

It was the way she emphasized *two* that told him where to begin. He flipped through the pages on the clipboard. "The receipt from Costa's shows you were to pick up William and Marianne Reasoner at the Hotel do Ouvidor at 7:00." He waited for a response that didn't come. "Is that correct?" he said loudly enough to startle Fabi.

"Yes."

"You took them to Wharf D. Correct?"

He chewed the inside of his cheek. "Yes."

Anton shuffled through more receipts. "You got gas that morning?"

Fabi's confirmation was guarded.

"At the Esso on Calle Maritimo?"

Fabi suspected he was being nudged into a trap, but he couldn't figure out what the trap was or how to avoid it.

"Why go so far in the other direction for the gas? There are five stations between the Reasoners' hotel and the wharf."

He shrugged an I-don't-know, but his defiance was all but gone.

Anton scowled. "S Deníz, you are going to cooperate right now." The *or else* went unspoken. "How many divers did you take to Breakwater Cove last Tuesday morning.?"

"Four," he sounded more like a boy caught writing graffiti than a cocky pretty boy.

"Two were the Reasoners. Who were the others?"

"Portuguese. From the mainland. Two men." He explained to Catarina, "I leave a few flyers of my own at cafés in neighborhoods with rental houses. It doesn't bring in much business, but—"

"But when it does, the money doesn't have to be shared with the Costas," Anton stated the obvious.

Fabi faced Anton foursquare, pressed his lips together, and nodded.

"Who were the two men?"

"I don't know. I swear. One of them called me, and I picked them up the next day. They paid in cash."

Fabi claimed to be bad at recognizing faces, and indeed the descriptions he gave could have applied to half the male population of Portugal, and the location of the café where he'd picked them up had a lot of house rentals.

"Minister," Catarina broke in, "S Deníz says the passengers were unaccompanied when they went diving."

"So you were on board the entire time they were in the water?"

"I have to watch the water at all times," he recited like a schoolboy, "in case there's trouble."

That didn't really answer the question. "What did you see?"

"Water?" he said tentatively. Anton's patience was wearing thin and a low, soft growl escaped his lips.

He rushed to add, "I'm serious. I watched the water, and no one surfaced until the end of the dive." He added, "And I took them back, all healthy and happy."

"Did you take any pictures that morning?"

The question perplexed Fabi. "Pictures? Why would I... No, sir, I didn't take pictures."

"What other boats did you see?"

He said he remembered nothing more than a vague impression that other boats were in the cove.

When Anton's questions reached their end, Fabi turned to Catarina. "So, what's going to happen? Are you telling the Costas?"

She looked at Anton, and Anton fixed Fabi in his gaze. "You have until Wednesday to tell them yourself." Fabi flinched.

He started to return to his boat, but Anton called him back. "One last thing." He held out his phone screen and showed him the same two pictures Catarina had showed Karlsson. Fabi stared at the tattoo for a very long time but blankly. But when he saw the picture of the young boy, he pushed the phone away like it was a ball hurtling to his face. "I don't want to see that," he said, and he leapt across the gap between dock and deck, engaged his motor and sped off, slapping an incoming wave and spraying people on the far dock with saltwater.

Those who weren't familiar with the way Anton drove—and a fair number of those who were—were terrified by his seemingly reckless behavior behind the wheel. He plummeted down hills that ended in steep drops to the ocean below. He swerved around hairpin turns. He avoided oncoming cars by a hair's breadth. Much to the distress of his passengers, he'd been known to turn 180° from the direction he was driving to look something that caught his eye. His mind jumped from one thing (for example, the road) to another (for example, what he planned to have for dinner that night.) He never looked like he was concentrating on any one thing. But he was. He was one of those true multi-taskers—able to talk and enjoy the sights and navigate, all while watching out for a rogue cow who didn't respect curfew and wandered across the road.

Still, everyone strapped their seatbelts when Anton was the driver.

He banked left and right on the narrow winding road that followed the cliff facing Casa do Mar. Beside him in the front seat, Catarina took in the nighttime smell of low tide that pushed through the half-open window on the driver's side. In the back, Lori and Carlos sat back and looked out at a sky pricked with stars.

There'd been no discussion about where they wanted to go when they landed back on Santa Maria. It was Water's Edge. When she'd first come to the island, locals had struggled to explain to Lori, the newcomer, exactly what Water's Edge was—a community center? a restaurant? a bar? a clubhouse? Whatever it was called, she now understood: Water's Edge was the heart of the community.

Passed on through generations of two families, the Costas and the Dekkers, for 150 years, Water's Edge was now owned by their friend, Matias Costa, and nine-year-old Paolo Dekker. The boy's mother, Isabella, safeguarded his interests. Just about everyone expected that soon a wedding would officially make the three of them one family.

It was at Water's Edge that Anton, Catarina, and Lori had first thought of themselves as detectives. Talking about the unexpected death of Isabella's husband, they had playfully compared themselves to characters in the British detective shows they liked so much. That was when Catarina made a serious observation. She, Lori, and Anton were each one facet of a good detective. Together, they were one complete and very good detective. Catarina contributed her intuitive understanding of people and her ability to read their true feelings, sometimes when even they weren't aware of them. Lori had an aptitude for ferreting out facts, made easier by her familiarity with technology and her days on Madison Avenue. Anton was a genius at finding the pattern in those facts.

Anton took a sharp right off the main road. Within feet, pavement gave way to crushed basalt, packed down by centuries of cart wheels, carriage wheels, and now car wheels. The old Volvo climbed a steep incline, and soon they heard the rumble of waves. They were close. He barely slowed as he steered the car around a tree that grew in the middle of the road, over a deep depression that extracted a squeal of protest from the rear axle, and into a parking place he made from the corner of a playground.

Patrons no longer brought their own candles to light the fifty meters or so to the patio outside Water's Edge. Instead, fairy lights twinkled in trees, and the warm glow from a patio firepit served as a beacon of good times to come.

The door to the dining room stood open to the night air, but it took a while for them to make their way to it. Anton was

spotted by friends and acquaintances, by colleagues and near-
strangers, and each of them was drawn into his orbit by those
friendly eyes, that puckish smile. He listened to their problems,
shared laughter over the antics of their children, gave wise words
about whether to start a business on Santa Maria or consider
moving away, and brought them up-to-date on the progress of the
living heritage site they all cared so deeply about. It was that way
wherever he went on Santa Maria. The man could have run for
president of the island and walked away with every single vote.

Just when the other three despaired of ever eating, Isabella
appeared on the patio. Stunningly beautiful, she stopped
conversation—at least, male conversation—as she moved
sinuously between chairs and offered to refill wine glasses. She
caught Catarina's eye and said for all to hear, "Your table is ready.
You must come now," and she waved them into the dining room.

They were seated across from two chairs hanging on a wall.
Legend had it that they had been made by the first Costa and the
first Dekker to own Water's Edge, symbols of their importance in
the days when everyone else there was sitting on wine barrels and
boulders. The banquettes were cushy, the lighting was soothing,
the tabletop cheery—all thanks to Isabella's touch.

Matias poured wine, a *vinho verde* from a vineyard on the
south side of their island. There was no wine list, and there would
be no menu. Like most diners, all of whom were locals that night,
they let Matias decide what to bring them. He knew what his
friends and neighbors liked, and his judgement was rarely
questioned. They were left to enjoy what always felt less like a
restaurant meal and more like a special family dinner.

For the next hour, Estela—waitress, mother of Toni's best
friend, and soon-to-be a kindergarten aide for Catarina—refilled
their glasses and brought the evening's small plates. Everyone
focused on crusty bread, sardines caught that morning, olives from
a neighboring orchard, cheese made by Beto's wife, tomatoes from
the Water's Edge garden.

The change in location did little to limit socializing. None
of them minded. It was a welcome break from the depressing
thoughts that had occupied their minds the past few days. Amid
the swells of conversation and laughter, the clatter of plates and

clink of glasses, people called out greetings or waved, and pleasantries were exchanged in passing.

From a nearby table, Felipe Madruga quietly raised a glass to them. Thanks to Anton, he was now the island's very capable chief of police. Also thanks to Anton, the lonely fifty-year-old had found romance for the first time with Gabriela, who'd just relocated to Santa Maria to be with him. That was what Anton was like: he made those around him happier simply by being who he was.

Felipe's job as police chief was more supporting the people he served than fighting crime, which on Santa Maria was generally limited to occasional car accidents, petty theft, and fist fights, as well as drunkenness (which could lead to car accidents, petty theft, and fist fights.) He had the right temperament for community relations, and even the island's rebellious teens, who he'd been known to track down and publicly discipline, gave him the respect he deserved.

In between demands on their time, Matias and Isabella sat with them.

"Have you had time to visit Manuel?" she asked in her soft, almost childlike voice.

Catarina started to reach for her hand, but Matias got there first.

"Not yet," Anton told her. "We will as soon as possible, tomorrow or the next day."

"Any news about his prospects?"

"The high court has acknowledged the reason he did it, but the crime…"

She lowered her eyes and her cheeks colored. The crime had been murdering Isabella's abusive husband, his own brother, to protect her.

To ease the silence, Matias opened a new bottle of wine and poured small glasses for everyone. They tasted together. "What do you think?" he looked to them.

Anton sighed his approval. "One of your recent finds?" Matias travelled to small vineyards on the islands two or three times a year to stock the Water's Edge cellar. And he was always happy when friends appreciated his efforts.

When Estela returned with a platter heaped with the island's own grass-fed beef and homegrown vegetables laced with olive oil and garlic, Anton's empty stomach grumbled loudly enough to attract a glance from her.

By tacit agreement, while they ate there was no talk of sad matters, of a friend whose disappearance was causing his mother grief, of a boy whose life and death had been so cruel. But afterwards, when the four diners were left to finish a second bottle of Matias's latest vinicultural discovery, the conversation inevitably turned to the grim tasks ahead.

"We still have to identify the victim," Lori said with no enthusiasm whatsoever.

Catarina stopped her. "It is a small thing, but could we call the poor boy by some name other than *victim?*"

They looked at each other. What do you call someone you know nothing about?

"Ángelo?" Catarina suggested. It was perfect.

Lori wished she believed there were angels or even some chance of life after death. "Still not a single report of anyone like him reported missing in all the E.U."

Carlos interjected, "The police don't seem to be concerned enough about Martim to report him missing. They asked his brother, Rafe, if he drank too much or took drugs. They asked if he had had a fight with his fiancée. They asked if he could have been involved with something shady. No, no, and no. And in the end they just said that his family should be patient."

"He could be having one last fling before the wedding," Anton suggested what Martim's own father thought.

Carlos was shaking his head no before Anton finished. "Rafe talked to his friends and looked through his room. His passport and suitcases are still in the house."

"Was he…" Catarina chose her words carefully, "…absolutely certain about wanting to marry? There were no other women he was interested in?"

"He was obsessed with Natalia. More than once, he said he couldn't believe his luck when she agreed to marry him or he worried that she would call it off."

"Could there have been an accident?" Anton asked, thinking of the dangers of flying a small plane.

"No." Carlos was surprised at how loud his own voice had been and apologized. "He returned as scheduled from a tourist flight Wednesday afternoon."

"A last-minute flight with another company?"

"One of the things we were to celebrate that night was that he had flown his last flight for someone else. He'd just bought his own plane and was setting himself up in business, *No Céo com Martim*." In Heaven with Martim. He took a large swallow of his wine. "I checked all the companies anyway. No one has seen him."

"And his new plane—"

"Is in its place at the airfield."

Lori added what she knew. "I talked to him as Carlos and I were circling São Miguel about seven Tuesday night. He was waiting for us in or near the marina."

"His brother says no one in his family heard from him after that," said Carlos.

"And Natalia's family say they have not heard from him," said Lori.

They discussed what they'd learned that afternoon, from the strained relationship between the two families to the confrontation on the church steps that had led to Fabi's mother securing a place in the de la Rosa home to the odd explanation for Martim's disappearance given by Henrique de la Rosa.

"Perhaps it calls for another visit." Anton's voice had taken on a different tone, perhaps not angry but cross. Since his childhood on São Miguel, Anton had known about the patriarch of the de la Rosas—a haughty bully who he'd love to put in his place. "Since this doesn't involve visitors, I can't get involved officially, but if you send me a good picture of Martim, I'll take it to the local police in São Miguel tomorrow."

He looked at Carlos and emptied his glass of the last sip of wine. "You and Martim's family should ask the islands' best surveillance agents if they noticed anything."

Carlos didn't understand yet, but Catarina and Lori were already chuckling. It was an old joke of Anton's; he meant the older women who rested their elbows on window sills and watched the comings and goings of their neighborhoods for hours at a time.

Carlos opened his mouth to say more but stopped short. A group of young men was passing their table, ogling Lori on their way out the door. There was no denying she was attractive with her long, long legs and blond hair cascading over her shoulders. But they wouldn't dare so much as say anything in front of Anton.

Matias was at the table quickly. "Every time you come, you distract our customers from their food," he teased Lori.

"Or perhaps you have more customers because they come hoping to see Lori," Anton countered.

Carlos chafed and edged closer to Lori.

"I'm sitting next to the only man here who interests me," she said loyally. In the millisecond between when she'd felt the sentiment and when she'd expressed, her mind had added one word in the interest of complete honesty: *here*.

Even the parsley garnish on Anton's plate had disappeared by the time Isabella put a small caramel cake in front of them and passed out four plates. After the winded walk up Frau Meickle's driveway and the straining of his jacket buttons, Anton had vowed he wouldn't have dessert. He demurred but only for the moment it took him to check Catarina's face. She was smiling at him. Just this once, then. He would be more careful with what he ate starting tomorrow morning.

It wasn't unusual to hear the glassy chime of an incoming text from Anton's government phone. It *was* unusual for him to look at the screen during dinner. This was an unusual time, though, and no one minded when he fished it out of a pocket, along with scraps of paper he'd collected since that morning.

His expression was serious when he read the message. It was a form of communication he was quite comfortable with and, making good use of both thumbs to tap the screen, he replied quickly, a distressed expression solidifying on his face as he did. The dots that meant someone was typing a response appeared, so Anton waited.

Accompanied by the sound he associated with toy gliders diving, a bubble of words appeared. As he opened his mouth to tell them what had happened, a second glider dove in on his phone.

He pushed his dessert plate back. It was Carlos he addressed. "I'm sorry, my friend, but Martim has been found."

Carlos's hand tightened on the edge of the table. "Found?" Anton's words should have been accompanied by a different facial expression, a different tone. "What do you mean *found?*"

"It appears that he died…that he was killed at the marina."

Catarina put her hand lightly Carlos's arm.

"Are they certain it's him? You know, his looks aren't distinctive." His was a typical response. People acknowledge that bad things happen and happen often, but they rarely believe those bad things will happen to them.

"The policeman who was called to the scene," he glanced at his phone, "a Távo Brum, is a friend of Martim's. He identified the body and told the family."

"He had become such a good man," Carlos exhaled the words to himself.

Anton steepled his fingers. It was too much of a coincidence to have two murders so close in time and place on a peaceful island. They had to be connected. And if they were connected, he could officially look into Martim's death.

Gravitating to the children was an impulse that Anton, Catarina, and Lori felt when confronted with the evil that sometimes infiltrates the barriers good people built against it. The first thing they did when they got home was to look at their moonlit faces, sleeping soundly through the creaking wood floors, the whispered goodnights, the kisses on foreheads, as children do.

6

"Twelve hours ago, I was relieved that Martim had gone missing after the other body was found." Carlos was still shaken by last night's news.

Lori walked by his side as he went through his pre-flight checklist, kicking aviãozinho's tires and looking into the fuel tank. "I can remember his voice so clearly. 'I'm content to take pictures of what's going to be a beautiful sunset while I wait...'"

"I still think there must be a mistake. It couldn't be Martim." He tucked his clipboard into the door pocket beside the pilot's seat and waved in the direction of the tiny terminal, where Anton and Catarina were waiting. Neither of them saw him.

Anton was standing at a high point on the road with two visitors who had just arrived from America, pointing here and there at nearby places of interest. Ever-friendly, he'd had struck up a conversation with them and learned they were returning to their home island, as they put it, "two generations after leaving," a common enough statement from Azorean emigrants who never forgot their homeland. Now they returned to vacation, to retire, to resettle and raise new generations.

Catarina was doing as she often did, being a good neighbor. She was inside the terminal with the pilot who had brought the visitors, asking about his family as she tidied the room and sorted packages waiting to be picked up. The father of three wondered if Catarina could keep a close eye on the youngest of his children, who would be starting at her school next month. Of course she would, she reassured him.

Carlos's tall, trim figure reached the terminal at the same time as Anton's tall, not-so-trim figure.

"We are ready for takeoff," the young pilot said wearily.

Anton eyed him closely. "Could we wait just a few minutes?" He opened the door for Carlos and Lori. Once inside, he caught Catarina's eye. "Perhaps Lori and I could make everyone some coffee, while you and Carlos rest from your labors."

She knew what he was doing. Carlos probably knew, too. In addition to grieving the loss of his friend, he was carrying misplaced guilt—survivor's guilt—for not having taken Martim's disappearance more seriously.

The water made a loud rumble while Lori let the pipes clear. Close beside her, Anton measured coffee into the French press basket and whispered to her, "He looks terrible. Is he alright to fly?"

Her tone was more defensive than she intended. "He wouldn't fly if he wasn't." She filled the pot but left the water running. "He wishes he'd started looking for Martim sooner."

"We'll know more later today, but I don't see that would have made a difference."

Catarina had taught Lori well. "That doesn't change how he feels."

Catarina had taught her husband well, too, and he nodded to agree.

"Carlos is going to talk to Martim's parents. I'm going, too."

"Would you like me to come?"

"It's not needed. You're busy with two investigations now."

"What would really help is if I put certain tasks in your hands. Talk to the Sousas again. Talk to his friends. Talk to his fiancée and her family. See if anyone had a reason to want Martim dead—anger, revenge, competition. I'll have the local police send us Martim's record and anything else they might have on both families."

"Maybe we can find a connection between Martim and the boy...Ángelo."

He filled four cups, knowing full well that none of them would take more than a single sip. "One more thing. If you can locate Martim's car at the marina, we'd know he made it that far."

As they carried the coffee to where Carlos and Catarina sat deep in conversation, Anton added, "Remember, Lori, you are now doing this as a representative of the Central Government. You're free to back up anything you want by saying that."

The door to the Sousa home was opened by an older woman who motioned Lori and Carlos inside without saying a word. Lori handed her the flowers they'd brought, wrapped in paper and already going limp. She'd run through what she could say. *We thought daisies were cheerful. We hope these brighten the house.* More than insincere, everything she thought of seemed cruel. So she said nothing.

Lori thought the place felt emptier than the last time she'd been there, as though no one had lived there for a long time. She had no explanation for why. The plants weren't wilting. No dust had accumulated on surfaces. There were no stale smells in the air. It just felt emptier in some way.

Martim's father, Joca, was there but only physically, sunk in a sofa as though he'd grown roots into the cushion. On the table beside him was a corkscrew and a bottle of wine, three quarters empty. Rafe, now his only son, stood up as though a man twice his age. Beatriz was beyond making the effort. They all wore the clothes they'd slept in.

Before anyone had a chance to settle back, the older woman returned with three small mugs, each with a spoon in it. Behind her, Alicia carried a carafe of coffee and a bowl heaped with sugar lumps.

They sat in silence for much of first twenty minutes, sipping coffee, interrupted by the sounds of the house settling as the sun warmed it and by clinks of cups on saucers that seemed very loud. Any conversation was strained; it began with a comment or question from Carlos and was answered with a few polite words.

"He loved taking pictures," Carlos remembered.

"Yes," Rafe said.

"He did," said Beatriz.

Lori thought, *The last thing he said to me was that he was going to take pictures.*

"When will they return Martim to us?" Beatriz asked Carlos, as though he held information that was denied the family. His mother's shoulders slumped. His father shook his head as though trying to dislodge the image of his son, dead.

"I will find out for you," he said. The response was typical of the men she loved, Carlos and Anton. Not *I don't know*. Not *As soon as possible. I will find out for you.* And he would.

Alicia spoke. "Would you like some cookies?"

Carlos was about to decline when Lori accepted. "Let me help you get them." She could hear Catarina saying that a distraction, even if a chore, was a kindness at times like these. She followed Alicia into the kitchen. There was a balding spot at the back of her head, where her hair had been crushed out of the way and not brushed back into place.

With the exception of some unopened mail and a bunch of overripe bananas, the counters were filled with containers of food. Alicia lifted the tops of a three before finding one she wanted. "Cookies?" she asked in English.

Lori thanked her and took one.

"My children gave me pills to relax me, but they do nothing," she confided with a wry smile.

Again, Catarina's words came to Lori. Sometimes the greatest kindness is to simply be there. She chewed slowly and waited.

"It is not an American tradition, I think, but my sons planned to live at home until they married." She looked like she wanted a favor when she asked, "Would you like to see his room?"

Lori expected that it would be different from the rest of the house, which was the province of his mother, but it was much the same. The furniture was his from childhood. A single bed was made up with a smoothed cover and two pillows were aligned at the head. A quilt was folded neatly at the foot. The mirror attached to the heavy walnut bureau was tilted so Lori could see just the top of her face. Martim had been quite tall.

He'd added a few touches of his own. The top of the old bureau held several nicely framed pictures of Martim and Carlos, Martim and Rafe, Martim and Natalia, Martim and his new plane. A postcard from Portofino was tucked into the mirror frame. On the back, someone had written. *You'll love this place!* A calendar on the wall was marked with his appointments for the month. In the square for the night he'd died, he'd printed *Carlos and Lori with Natalia.* She thought it odd that he'd used an old-fashioned paper calendar rather than his phone—maybe he just liked looking at the days of his life decorated with reminders of good times.

Alicia reflexively smoothed a small wrinkle in the quilt, adjusted a picture hanging on the wall, picked a loose thread from the curtain.

"It's so tidy, especially for young bachelor," Lori commented. *Did it reveal his true self or hide it?*

"He kept it that way himself. He said he didn't like to think of his mother cleaning up after him. Even as a child, he said if he won the lottery, he would get me a maid. My other children said they would get me new cars or trips around the world, but he always said he would get me a maid."

Alicia lost herself in private thoughts for a moment. "I didn't come in often. I wanted to give him his space. It can be hard living at home as an adult."

"I'm sure he loved living at home."

"I think he did."

Her smile made Lori feel good.

"He said he wanted to stay here after the wedding, so he could save for a house."

Martim had wanted to stay in his small childhood home rather than in the de la Rosas large house or their guest house. *Was that his preference or Natalia's? Was staying at the de la Rosas even an option if the man Natalia married was Martim?*

An orderly array of photos covered one wall. All showed a sensitivity for small things that might have been lost in the bigger picture. A lone bee took center stage in a field of wildflowers that blurred as they receded around it. Drops of seawater decorated the break of a single wave in a vast ocean. The propeller of his new plane was reflected in his mother's eye.

"Did Martim take these?"

She nodded.

"Do you mind if I look?" Her visit to the Sousas had a dual purpose.

"Mind? No. I do not mind. I want someone to look. I want someone to care enough. Maybe there are answers somewhere here."

She looked so white, Lori was afraid she was about to pass out, so she took Alicia's hand and led her to the bed. At the sound of squeaking springs, a large black dog of some breed mix came in. He poked his white muzzle around the bed, sniffing but not for food.

"Urso has been Martim's dog since childhood. He keeps looking for him. He doesn't understand he isn't coming back." She looked like she was considering that certainty for the first time.

Urso got on the bed with Alicia, and the two snuggled and were soon asleep.

Lori felt a terrible sadness and a stab of anger that someone had taken so much from this family.

She did as Alicia wanted. She looked. She opened the small wardrobe and the bureau drawers. They were sparsely filled and most of the contents were well used. He was saving money. One drawer served as his desk, and Lori checked out his passport, his work ID, brochures on Italian vacations, and the deed for his plane, free of encumbrances. With the advent of electronic communication, people didn't leave much by way of paper correspondence. There were business cards and a few personal cards, one from aunt in California for his birthday two weeks ago and one from a woman named Lilia congratulating him on the purchase of his new plane. There were no love notes, perhaps because none had been written or perhaps because—like many men—he simply wasn't sentimental about keeping such things.

Lori took pictures of the calendar pages to get better idea of what Martim had been doing and who he'd been seeing in the last weeks of his life. Starting in April, almost every entry referenced Natalia, her name always written out in full. Perhaps doing that brought him pleasure. There were no entries after the square for October 10th, the date of his the wedding. Now the rest of those squares would remain blank.

She unfolded the quilt, lightly covered Martim's mother, and tiptoed away.

Carlos and Martim's brother were on their feet before she was two steps into the living room. "She's asleep. On Martim's bed."

"I told them that Anton is getting involved," Carlos let her know.

"He will find out what happened," she assured the family. It wasn't just to soothe them. She knew he would keep at it until there were answers.

Joca interrupted from his corner of the sofa, gruff with bravado, "Leave it be. Nothing will change what happened."

"I'm sorry. I didn't mean…"

Unexpectedly, he rested his elbows on his thighs, hid his face in his hands, and wept. "I let him die alone. I was sure there was nothing to worry about." Rafe sat beside him and cradled his father in his arms. The overt grief didn't last long. He wriggled out of Rafe's embrace and left looking beaten.

She was about to apologize again when Beatriz asked, "What can you do to find who…?" When Lori didn't respond immediately, she pressed, "Help us. Please," and Lori made a sincere promise to do that.

Beatrix had another request, "Would you ask the police when we can get his watch and camera back?" It turned out they were much loved by him, both presents from his parents, the watch for getting his pilot's license and the camera for his eighteenth birthday.

Lori saw the camera as more than a cherished memento. "Martim was taking pictures when we…when I…last heard from him. Those pictures might be important. They might let us know exactly where he was and who was near him. Could I take his laptop to see if they've been uploaded? And once his phone is released by the police, could I look through it?"

The answers to both were yes.

"There's one more thing, perhaps a difficult one to talk about." She glanced at Carlos to get a go-ahead to bring up what he'd told her. He nodded.

"Please tell me everything you know about the circumstances that sent Martim to prison." It was an important interview technique, asking an open-ended question, one that couldn't be answered with a short response, before retreating into silence. People generally filled the silence.

Which is what they did, one stepping in when another stopped because of failed memory or reluctance to say something. When Martim was eighteen, he'd been found passed out on the deck of a stolen boat. The boat had clipped the side of a private dock before running aground. Everything was against him: he had been drunk; the boat was stolen; a family of four had been on the dock, and a child had been badly injured.

The family of the child said Martim had been alone in the boat. (Beatrix shook her head *no*.) A man who was fishing nearby said he'd seen two people in the boat as it raced up and down the shore. (Rafe nodded his head *yes*.)

"Someone else must have come up with the idea of stealing the boat," Beatrix said. "Martim would never have done that on his own."

"Someone else must have encouraged him to drink so much," Rafe said, "Martim didn't do that even then."

In other words, they said what most family would say in such a situation.

Martim himself had said he remembered nothing of the incident. Waiting for trial and while in prison, he refused to talk about it. His family had different opinions about the reason. Beatrix thought Martim was ashamed of whatever part he'd played in the theft and the accident. Rafe thought was protecting someone.

Anton took advantage of every visit to the marina to pass slowly by the harbormaster's office and hold Branco's eyes with a disapproving stare. The thought of catching him arriving at work late even got Anton out of bed earlier in the morning. This morning, the office was still locked up when he peered through the window.

"Yesterday was his day off," Catarina reminded him.

Anton pursed his lips. "That's no excuse."

"It is not. It is only a reason why he might have slept late. Remember Luis said Branco has a history of drinking too much."

"That's still no excuse." He had wanted Catarina to size up Branco's reaction when he questioned him about the *Doura*, and he had wanted to do that before the ship returned to port. Now that would have to wait.

The *Iaso* was there, however, and occupying the best slip in the marina. Their experience aboard was very different from their experience with Captain Karlsson. To begin with, the *Iaso* looked very different from most people's conception of a yacht. While still white and large, it was sleek, its streamlined form low to the water like a missile gliding on the surface. Instead of heavy teak railings and picture windows, it was outfitted with steel trim and black-glass windows that tapered like a tiger's eyes.

The man who was stationed at the bottom of the gangplank was dressed in khakis and a white polo shirt, not overtly a uniform yet clearly the same dress as the man at the top of the gangplank. When he learned of their business, he called ahead, and from his end of the conversation it seemed the request to board was being passed up an established chain of command.

While they waited, birds pecked at crumbs left on the dock by early morning fishermen, which was enough to occupy Anton's impatient mind for about two minutes. After that, Catarina was needed to remind him to breath slowly. After twenty minutes, he told the guard—in the friendliest of ways—an entertaining story about an entire crew that had been held liable for passively hindering an investigation and kept in port for several weeks while the courts adjudicated the matter. Catarina saw the mask-like expression that the guard kept on his face while he worked through what Anton had said, and she saw him twitch when he finally got the message. He stiffened, then apologized for the delay, but his apology sounded like he had memorized it word for word.

A young woman sporting the same khaki-and-white outfit arrived to escort them on board. Walking fore, faint smells told them they were on a well-tended ship: the wax of deck polish, the ammonia of window cleaner, the aroma of freshly brewed coffee, and some sort of disinfectant that reminded Catarina of hospitals.

They were temporarily blinded when they moved from the deck to a small room off the saloon, as well appointed as every other space they had passed. Metal gleamed, glass sparkled, upholstery was crisp, art was large and abstract. Even the floral arrangements looked like they had just been put in place. It seemed like the sort of place where a battalion of people moved in to smooth every crease and vacuum away every stray dust mote the moment it was vacated. And judging by the silver-framed family pictures and mementoes on bookshelves, this was not a leased yacht; it was privately owned. The owner of the *Iaso* was beyond merely wealthy.

If that owner was evil, he didn't look it. White-haired, pink-cheeked, and blue-eyed, Stephen Fowler looked like a kindly professor. He gave them a warm smile when he greeted them, apologized profusely for keeping them waiting, and offered them refreshments that appeared about five seconds later. Catarina took him as educated and either American or Canadian.

"If I may ask, who is *Iaso* named for?" she asked, as much out of true interest as to start the conversation on a pleasant note.

"Iaso was one of the Greek goddesses of healing. I'm a doctor, you see."

"What is your specialty?" Anton asked for more than conversational reasons. The islands lacked doctors, and he was always on the lookout for possible settlers. On Santa Maria, Maria Rosa, their neighbor and a nurse had been filling in for Doctor Leal since he stopped practicing.

Catarina smiled to herself to think that her husband's love of his islands was so great, he imagined that someone with the tastes reflected in everything around them—and the money to satisfy them—would choose a country practice on Santa Maria.

"I'm retired now." Fowler thanked the young woman who had wheeled in a bar cart with Hermes china and a Jensen tea service, and dismissed her.

Catarina saw he didn't want to talk about his profession. An image of one of those women with swollen lips and stretched faces came to mind. Perhaps he had been one of those cosmetic surgeons who used their skills to accommodate people who equated their appearance with their happiness, and that had made him enough money to retire to a lifestyle like this.

She kept her mind on the job. "Could I ask where the *Iaso* was last Tuesday morning?"

His answer came quickly, "The day before, we'd dropped anchor off a charming cove on the north shore, past a lagoon with palm trees. Sadly, we had to leave later Tuesday morning."

It could have been Breakwater Cove—or one of several others on the north shore, past a lagoon with palm trees. "It would help us if you could pinpoint that for us."

"I'll ask the captain immediately," which he did in a brief phone. "He will text me the coordinated shortly."

"As far as you know, is everyone who should be aboard the *Iaso* accounted for?" she asked.

Fowler called the ship purser for the manifest, and the purser appeared with it almost as quickly as the refreshments had.

She didn't say so but looking at the manifest, Catarina was amazed at the number of people who worked on the *Iaso*, easily twice the number of guests. She was also amazed by the diversity of the guests, probably a reflection of the diverse society where Fowler made his home. There was a family from India, two couples with Arab surnames and London addresses, and others from Brazil, South Africa, and New York City.

"You have so many friends, Dr. Fowler," she said with admiration.

"Stephen, please. And, yes, I've been blessed in many ways. These voyages allow me to share one of those blessings with others."

The purser confirmed that all crew had reported for duty as expected both before and after Tuesday, and Fowler said he had seen all his guests at dinner every night. No one from the *Iaso* was missing.

The first picture he showed Fowler left the man shaking his head. "So sad to see a young life cut short." His clenched his jaw and held the picture of the tattoo up to the light, focusing for several seconds until he said that he only wished he could help them. Just as Anton was about to ask if he could show the pictures to others on board, Fowler said, "If I can keep these, I'll have my crew and passengers take a look."

"There is some urgency. Could we—"

Again, Fowler preempted him. "The morning crew ends its shift in an hour. That would be the best time to find both shifts on board. I'll have my purser make arrangements and send you an accounting immediately, if you would leave your contact information."

Anton was reluctant to press the matter. Good relations with visitors were important to maintain.

Just then, Fowler's phone pinged. He held it out for Anton and Catarina to see.

Anton took a picture of the coordinates on the screen. He shook his head to let Catarina know: not Breakwater Cove.

Escorted by the same young woman who had seen them to the owner, Anton and Catarina left through the saloon. In unspoken agreement, Catarina tried to engage the woman in conversation so that Anton could fall back and peek into areas that were roped off. "The *Iaso* is easily the cleanest ship I have been on," she gave a half-turn to smile at a young man sponging down the deck behind them.

The response was, "Thank you," but no more.

Talk about the weather and the Azores and the woman's favorite destinations also met with little success. She simply slowed her steps to accommodate Anton's pace and kept her eyes on both of them, and they stepped off the gangplank with the same sense they'd carried since starting their investigation: no forward movement.

"So," Anton summed up once they were out of earshot, "no one is missing, and no one recognizes Ángelo."

"So far." Catarina knew he was discouraged. Her husband was not a man who waited patiently for what he wanted, especially when what he wanted involved the safety of his islands. "Do you know what I would like?"

The thought of doing something to make his wife happy put a smile on his face. He wrapped his arm around her and waited.

"I would like to walk back to our hotel and have lunch in the courtyard."

The walk started well enough, sunny and a bit breezy, but those breezes carried in threatening clouds and the air grew colder with every step. Such was weather on the islands, generally mild, occasionally and suddenly stormy.

By the time they reached the hotel lobby, fat drops were splashing their shoulders.

"At least we enjoyed the walk, but it will be an indoor lunch for us," Catarina sighed.

"It still might be chilly. Would you mind getting our sweaters from the room?" Anton asked.

When she returned, a young waitress met her in the lobby. "Please follow me, senhora Vanderhye," and she escorted her to the courtyard. She took an umbrella from the urn by the door and with as pretty a smile as possible, she opened it for Catarina and escorted her to the far corner, where a small fireplace glowed warmly and Anton sat under an umbrella dripping water in a circle around a perfectly dry table.

Catarina thought what she had thought many times before, what she and Anton had in fact talked over many times. Their young lives may have been hard, but that had brought them to each other and neither would have traded a single moment they had had together since then for anything they had faced before then.

By the time Anton's espresso arrived, they were ready to talk over their visit to the *Iaso*.

He floated an idea, "We could ask to speak to the guests."

"As accommodating as Fowler was, I don't see him welcoming any more intrusion on his yacht."

"True, and the last thing we need right now is publicity about the difficulties of cruising in the Azores."

"In any case, would he not be within his right to refuse?"

Anton took a moment to consider. "We'd need a search warrant and for that we need probable cause, which we don't have and which Borges would certainly block."

It was at this point in an investigation that Anton's mind began reaching for any and all anomalies he could find in what he had seen and what he had been told. This wasn't in itself a bad thing. Although there is merit to the aphorism about thinking horses—not zebras—are approaching when you hear hoofbeats, there is the possibility, however slim, that there are indeed zebras coming up behind you.

And so he began. "Why, on a private yacht, were certain areas roped off?"

Without strong evidence to the contrary, Catarina's steady mind still believed that the hoofbeats were unlikely to be made by zebras. "We rope off areas of Casa do Mar to protect friends and guests from tripping over Beto's construction debris."

He moved on to the next observation that he hoped would give him some traction. "Did you see how closely we were guarded? That woman didn't leave our side."

She smiled indulgently. "I don't know that I would call it being guarded. We were strangers. The wealthy often are wary of being taken advantage of and have well-trained security. She could just have been doing her job well."

He was still thinking of zebras. "Fowler took a long time to say he hadn't seen the tattoo."

"He might have been trying hard to remember but…"

"But?"

"I will give you a little credit for that one. It is also true that a person can take a long time to answer because they are running through possible answers in their head."

He gave a gotcha, "Aha!"

"No *aha*, Anton. That is a less likely scenario, and one that usually requires a longer pause than Fowler had." Now Catarina was hearing zebra hoofbeats herself. "He did clench his jaw before he answered, although that could have been because he was concentrating and not to steady himself while he lied."

Another gotcha sound, this time a long *hmmm*.

Catarina laughed. "Look what you are doing to me. I have just thought of one more thing he said. 'In fact, we left later Tuesday morning.'"

"Why would that be odd?"

"You asked where he had been on Tuesday morning. He said he left *later* Tuesday morning. It could have been just a turn of phrase, as in *later in the morning*. But it could have meant later than something else."

Later than what? they wondered.

On his way to see Dr. Nunes, the Coast Guard alerted Anton. Thanks to a network of trusted boat owners, the *São Pedro* had been spotted fishing and tracked on its way to a small harbor on the eastern shore, far from the Devil's Hands.

Anton picked up Catarina and drove off at his customary hair-raising speed. From a distance, it was easy to see: this was not the Ponta Delgada marina. Here, they would find no restaurants with prix fixe menus or shops selling sunhats, no whale watching boats or dive boats, and certainly no yachts. Though not strong enough to be unpleasant, the smell of wrack and rust and fish oil was a reminder that this was the province of men who made their living from the ocean.

They stood side by side on boards chewed by the marks of hand saws and watched the *São Pedro* come in hard and fast. Close to the dock, the fisherman turned the key in the ignition. The whine of the outboard motor faded, and he coasted the last few yards. What had once been a trim boat painted a cheerful yellow was now sad-looking, its paint grayed and flaking, its trim corroded by salt air. Lobster traps, fish hoppers, and heaps of wet netting took up most of a stained deck that hadn't been cleaned in years.

When he took note of them, an expression of wariness crossed the fisherman's face. It was too late for him to head back out to sea, at least not without raising the suspicions of everyone watching, so he elected to jump off the boat, tie off quickly, and walk away even more quickly, pretending not to hear Anton's calls to stop.

A man as large as Anton, though twenty years younger, put himself in the fisherman's path and did that twice more as he tried to sidestep his way around to avoid whatever might be coming his way. Anton and Catarina caught up in time to hear the large man say, "I thought you might want to know that someone is trying to get your attention." The tone was helpful, kindly even, but the sly smile said he knew the man had been trying to get away. Catarina thanked him with a warm smile of her own.

The shenanigans of dashing off the boat and making as if he hadn't heard them had left Anton in no mood to be pleasant with the fisherman. "Your name?" he asked sternly.

He lifted a leathered face permanently etched with frown lines but kept his eyes at half-mast. "Fredi."

"Sit," he said, pointing to the pilings, and he flashed his government identification in his face.

Fredi hunched over a high bulging stomach that made him look about ready to give birth. He wasn't the most pleasant person to sit close to. The smell of alcohol and a faint odor of vomit came from his clothes. Catarina was glad the wind was onshore.

"Were you off Breakwater Cove last Tuesday?"

"Might have been. I'm not familiar with the names of these waters."

Playing the good-cop role, Catarina stepped in and described the Devil's Hands.

"That rings a bell. I might have tried those waters last week. Monday or Tuesday."

According to Frau Meickle, he'd been there every day since she arrived. Anton hardened his jaw. "What were you doing there?"

Fredi's Adam's apple moved up and down. "Can't a man fish his dinner from the sea anymore without the government getting involved?" He looked sideways at Anton's very large hands, which were tightening, and reconsidered his response. "Fishing."

"In unfamiliar waters? Where do you usually fish?"

"Here and there."

Anton thought he knew what Fredi was up to. "Commercially?"

"For myself."

Catarina knew, as well. "I could eat fresh fish every day." That wasn't true, but she needed to catch him in a lie to get his cooperation.

He looked relieved. "That's why I go out every day, you see, so it's fresh."

"Does your family like fish, too?"

"I'm a bachelor…" his voice trailed off; he looked at the *São Pedro* and realized he'd painted himself into a corner.

Azoreans have a long history of fishing, and fish—including *bacalhau*, the dried and salted cod that helped their ancestors survive before the advent of refrigeration—are a staple of their diet. While industrial fishing boats far off the coast haul enormous catches, they make up a small fraction of the fishing fleet. Small, locally owned boats still bring in most of the catch. Either way, the crustacea, hake, octopus, sardines, tuna, and mackerel in Azorean waters are species of high commercial value.

The waters were being fished out. So a stringent licensing system with species quotas for individual boats was instituted. Violations resulted in heavy fines. Or worse: a boat could be tied up to a Coast Guard pier for a month.

Fishing for one's family was exempt.

But Anton and Catarina had remembered that the harbor patrolwoman had seen Fredi loading his boat with a lot of netting, and they'd seen the mounds of wet netting on the deck. The *São Pedro* had been after far more than the largest family could eat in a day or a week, probably unloading his catches at a series of marinas or even directly into the holds of long-distance haulers waiting offshore.

Catarina wanted to put Fredi's mind at ease. "We are only focusing on anything you may have seen near Breakwater Cove last Tuesday." Curiously, he didn't seem entirely reassured by her words. She took out her pad of paper and pencil and nodded to Anton.

"Did you see any boats in the area of the Devil's Hands on Tuesday morning?" Anton asked.

In the prolonged silence that followed, Catarina saw Anton's anger rise, and she gave a him a warning glance.

Anton waited until Fredi grudgingly admitted, "A yacht. It anchors just off the north shore a lot." His eyes popped open; he knew he'd just admitted to fishing there frequently. He wasn't about to say anything else that got him in trouble, and he clamped his lips shut.

Catarina heard Anton's angry sigh and gave her husband another warning glance.

When no one reacted to what he'd said, Fredi went on, "There was a boat taking tourists to look for whales and such.

Vieira. And a blue diving boat anchored near the crater. *Costa Diving.*"

"Did you see anyone on the vessels?"

"On the yacht, there was just this woman being pushed around the deck in a wheelchair by someone in one of those uniforms that crew always wears. On the whale watching boat, the usual collection of pale tourists taking pictures of nothing. The divers were already under when I looked up. There was just a kid who fancies himself a movie star showing off his muscles to the world."

There was nothing new in what Fredi had said—about the boats or about the people on them—but Catarina wrote an important note to herself. He'd given up more than he realized.

Anton took out his phone and found the picture he wanted to show Fredi. "Do you recognize this boy?"

The picture shouldn't have been disturbing—Dr. Nunes had seen to that—but Fredi's eyes snapped shut after barely a glance. "No."

Anton swiped to a closeup of the boy's tattoo. "What about this?"

He moved close to the screen and stared. "No," he said slowly. "I've never seen that."

They got nothing more from Fredi but from the relief on his face when they said their goodbyes, Catarina thought there was a question he'd been dreading—and they hadn't asked.

"Other than the obvious business with illegal commercial fishing, what do you think?"

"Fredi is hiding something," Catarina said. "I wonder why—almost a week later—he has such a clear memory of all the boats off Breakwater Cover. Clearly, it's a place he's been many times."

"Probably one of many places he fishes in for several days at a time, until he catches someone's attention and moves on."

"When a person is occupied with a task," she explained, "especially a repetitive one, the details of the background tend to be lost. It's called *the wallpaper effect.* So, if Fredi was fishing or hauling traps, it is unlikely he would remember all the boats that were in Breakwater Cover on that one particular morning, let alone their names and the time they were there."

"Yet, he did." Anton wrinkled his brow.

"Unless your brain is actively trying to commit such details to memory, it usually takes a significant event—something out of the ordinary—to fix that single time in your mind. You probably remember the sweater you wore the afternoon the hurricane hit Terceira and you found Dawn but nothing about what you wore the previous day or all the subsequent days on Terceira."

"So Fredi might have seen something or done something he wants to keep from us."

In itself, that was interesting enough to Anton, but what Catarina said next really intrigued him. "There is more. Fredi said, 'The divers were already under when I looked up.' There was a moment when he looked up from something, and that moment fixed everything he saw in his mind."

"What did you make of his reaction to seeing Ángelo?"

"It disturbed him."

"And he asked no questions about who the boy was or what had happened to him."

"Yet, he looked closely at the tattoo. Perhaps he'd already seen Ángelo's face, knew who he was, but the tattoo was new to him. Yes, Fredi is hiding something."

Anton and Catarina had arrived at the same conclusion using their different talents—she by knowing how people's minds work; he by spotting the anomalies in their actions.

Anton suggested that Catarina shop for new art supplies while he talked to Dr. Nunes. She knew why.

He ran into Nunes on the steps outside the police station. Neither was anxious to leave the sunshine behind so for twenty minutes or so, they sat in comfortable silence on a bench in the adjacent gardens. On some unspoken signal, both men got up, sighed, and made the dreary trip downstairs to the morgue.

Nunes washed up before walking to a gurney with a plastic-sheeted figure that seemed to be too slight to have been a man as robust as Martim.

"Has his identity been confirmed?"

Nunes didn't have the heart to scold Anton about breaking protocol by asking questions before he'd presented his findings. One murder on their islands was discouraging enough. Two was mind-numbing. "Initially with visual identification by a friend who is also a police officer and subsequently by fingerprints on record."

Anton felt very sad. "Where was he found?" He already knew what the text had said; he also knew he would appreciate Nunes's detailed response.

"An islander who had been home sick for three days found the body in his boat on the western side of Pier 3 at the marina. The body had been loosely covered by tarp, so it hadn't been immediately visible by passersby."

"When did he die?"

As expected, at this point Nunes's answer was qualified several times over. "I am not writing this down until further test results come in but I will tell you tentatively, based on ambient temperature and larval stages only, indications are that he probably—probably—died early last Tuesday evening. In line with this evidence, his watch dial is broken at 7:15."

Soon after his brief conversation with Lori.

Anton pictured Pier 3 and a steep drop off a slippery edge and into a boat filled with metal hoppers and grappling. "Could it have been alcohol?" It wouldn't have been the first time an inebriated islander had fallen to his death from a pier.

"It was not alcohol," Nunes said definitively.

"Is there any chance his death was accidental?"

He lifted up the sheet on one side of Martim's head and pointed to a shaved, flattened patch. "This was sufficient to crush his skull, perhaps even to prove fatal eventually, and it may have been the result of him hitting the deck hard from such a height. But unless he accidentally covered himself with tarps after he fell—"

"He couldn't have—?

Nunes held a palm out to stop Anton. "Pending further evidence, I will rule this death a homicide. I have sent samples to the lab for analysis. The results may prove informative."

"Did you find any connection to the boy?"

"Seriously? You expect more?"

Anton pleaded with Nunes's eyes.

"There was perimortem bruising."

"In the same way as the boy?" He wanted to pull his words back before he'd finished his question; he'd seen Nunes's tighten his lips.

Nunes exhaled a long breath. "No. This was very different. To begin with, there was no restraint. But the real story is here," he lifted up the sheet on the right side and then the left to show Martim's arms. The skin was marked with tear-shaped gapes. "Twenty-four defensive wounds. I'd say he put up a fight, faltering as he became disoriented from the head trauma and loss of blood from the knife wounds his assailant or assailants were landing."

Nunes folded down the sheeting that covered Martim's face. So much time had passed since his death that Anton saw little relation to the pictures Lori had showed him.

Despite his reservations and in spite of his training, the doctor gave Anton a definitive answer. "This is the cause of death." The wound spoke for itself, a dark slice deep into Martim's neck.

7

When the three of them returned to Casa do Mar, Toni and Nuno were kicking a football across the wide green field outside the Casa do Mar barn, and Liliana was sitting on a fallen log, deep in a book. They waved and smiled, but there were none of the running feet and tight hugs and high-pitched shrieks of delight that used to welcome them home. Catarina felt another one of those pangs that she had been feeling more and more recently. Yes, her babies were growing up. And far from being overjoyed at the thought of all the time that would be gained and the worries that would be shed—as she knew other mothers were—she was sad about everything that would inevitably be lost.

Maria Rosa's young children were playing beside her. She, however, was fast asleep in the rocking chair—they always referred to it as Catarina's chair—outside the kitchen door. Her sandy blond hair was pulled into a tight knot, and she wore baggy green scrubs that didn't flatter her short, plump figure. It was the way she dressed even when not serving the medical needs of the islanders and visitors.

The impression she gave was of being capable and serious woman (and she was indeed very capable and very serious about her responsibilities.) But there was another side to her, a side that she showed when she was stirred up by dramas ranging from those in the celebrity newsfeeds she followed to those even more exciting ones that involved people she knew. And the investigations Anton, Catarina, and Lori were brought into were her favorites.

At the sight of Maria Rosa in the rocking chair, Lori gave a soft groan. Anton's groan wasn't quite as soft. And they braced themselves for a long session of Maria Rosa's breathless delivery of recent island news and her equally breathless inquisition about what they had learned about the deaths on São Miguel.

Catarina cleared her throat to remind them—as she had in the past—that in most people what they deplored as gossip was a small failing and could have its value. In small communities, such people were the ones who noticed the stranger who was acting suspicious, saw the child who was in danger, knew the neighbor who was depressed and needed help. She moved two steps ahead the them and prepared to deliver a monologue of her own before Maria Rosa could start one. *Thank you for taking care of Liliana and Toni. I hope they were of some help to you. We've brought you some apple preserves. How are your own children? It's nice that they will be attending school with me soon.*

Nothing like that actually happened. When Catarina touched Maria Rosa's shoulder, the woman bolted out of the rocking chair with a long, loud scream and clenched fists, one of which held a small cylinder of pepper spray.

It took the young nurse a moment to take where she was and who she was there with. "Sorry. Sorry. Just a nightmare," she lied, and she slipped the pepper spray into a pocket.

Maria Rosa had arrived on Santa Maria six years earlier, with an infant, a toddler, and no husband. There'd been many attempts to find out about her origins and the father of her children but—despite her own fondness for information-gathering—Maria Rosa had deflected every question, so no one had broached the subjects in years. The only clue had been in a picture Catarina once saw on a shelf in her bedroom, a younger Maria Rosa with a handsome man who she'd said was, "the man I married but not the man I left." Catarina knew there was great pain behind those words and had never taken it any further.

Anton looked out over his island. There could be no better place on this earth, and he had had the fortune to be born here, to live here, by an endless ocean. He felt nestled by the green hills dotted here and there with the houses of his neighbors. He felt settled by rithe orderly basalt terraces built by his ancestors, cheered by their tiers of vineyards and colorful hydrangeas.

He was sad for people who did not live surrounded by this beauty, nourished by this community, and for those who had it but lived life too quickly to appreciate it, frantically searching for more and better when they had all this. He would have been such a person if not for a gift of fate when he was fifteen years old and had seen a redhaired girl stepping into a rowboat in the marina.

This place is ours, he thought, ours to love, ours to protect.

At that same moment, Catarina was standing by the barn, looking out over Casa do Mar and thinking much the same thoughts about the bright green fields in front of her and the deep green mountains behind her.

At the age of sixteen, she had been a brilliant student, serious, obedient, and destined to make her mark. Her parents had been firm about that. She was left to herself quite a bit when her father was posted to a military base on Santa Maria, and she wandered the island, sketching and reading. Her dream (not her parent's dream for her) had been to run a school. She had carefully considered its philosophy and goals. She had thought about everything from the books in the library to the plants in the playground. She had looked forward to nurturing her students. She knew she could make a difference in their lives.

Then she met fifteen-year-old Anton, and it was love at first sight for both of them. To her parents, he was beneath her in background, academic ability, appearance, and accomplishments. When she refused to attend the university they had chosen for her, so she could be near him in Lisbon, they denied her financial support and distanced themselves from then on. Anton and Catarina had had to work to put themselves through school and were in their late twenties when they finally graduated. They'd agreed: they would put other dreams on hold so they could start a family.

They had been happy with their roles as spouses, as parents, and as respected community leaders. Then, life turned again. Anton learned the elementary school principal was leaving, and he thought Catarina would be perfect for the position.

In the kitchen, Lori was looking at the watercolors of Casa do Mar that Catarina took great pleasure in painting. They were Catarina's vision of what their home could become—the plants that would fill their gardens, the outbuildings that would be remodeled as guest cottages, the barn that would become their family home.

When she'd first seen the paintings, Lori had been at a low point in her life. The synchronized swimming she'd taken up as a ten-year-old had become a metaphor for her life. On the surface, everything was in harmony. She was strong and in control. Hidden under that surface, she was working frenetically and fighting for every breath.

Born to older parents who'd happily shared the life of a childfree couple before her surprise arrival, Lori had not been a wanted child. Both busy and lonely as an adult, every year in New York City had taken her further from the life she wanted. Until, as an up-and-coming young executive, she was fired for exposing a scheme that would have cost hundreds of jobs solely to line the pockets of a few at the top of the company. She was escorted from her desk with the threat that she would never work in public relations—perhaps anywhere—again.

Then she saw an ad—more a plea than an ad and anything but sleek—for a short public relations gig on an island she'd never heard of. It was to have been an easy way to have a vacation before settling for a life that would be far less than she'd thought it would be. She didn't know it at the time, but it would remake her life into so much more than she'd ever known it could be.

Anton and Catarina wanted Casa do Mar to be both a rural hotel where their family could grow together and a model to attract grants for the living heritage trust that had been their passion since they were newlyweds. They needed help getting the word out and bringing the guests in.

The task proved to be more challenging than Lori had expected. Anton and Catarina had emptied their banks accounts to buy Casa do Mar, and Casa do Mar was nearly derelict.

They'd come a long way since their early days. With Anton's vision, Catarina's sense of style, and Lori's marketing savvy, they had transformed the old dairy. They had cleared away decayed bales of hay, rusted tools, rotting carts, and two centuries' worth of cobwebs and caked dirt. Beto, the tyrant-contractor who shared Anton's determination to preserve the traditions of the

Azores, had removed black basalt stones and oak beams, installed electricity and plumbing, and returned most of what he'd removed to its original place. The local craftspeople on his crew had rebuilt the spaces in the way their ancestors would have, keeping as much of the original stonework and carpentry as possible. A carriage house had become Casa das Flores; a shed had become Casa do Bosque.

Lori's expertise in public relations had worked wonders. Casa do Mar regularly had guests, and she'd added a lucrative side business. Since many visitors were the descendants of emigrants from the islands, she offered personalized experiences with visits to ancestral villages, meetings with distant relatives, and the opportunity to fund small parts of the preserve in the names of the people who'd made the difficult decision to leave their homeland behind. It was genius.

Now the old dairy's milkhouse, where milk had been cooled until the cream rose and where butter and cheese had been made, was to become Casa de Leite. Or it would be when the three of them matched its interior to the vision in Catarina's watercolors.

It had to be. They would need the income from Casa de Leite. Sixteen months ago, Lori had helped her new friends to apply for a grant from the Gillis Foundation to develop the living heritage preserve. They hadn't gotten it, but Meghan Gillis had been enchanted with their vision for Casa do Mar—so much so that she'd wanted to see what could be made of their plans. She'd arranged for a loan to renovate the old dairy's outbuildings, and the first payment was coming up fast.

Together, they walked to third guest cottage, nearing completion.

"The busy season is starting," Anton said what they all knew—but it was nice to be reminded.

"It's going to be busier than ever," Lori said cheerfully. "We're fully booked for four weeks in a row, starting in September." Thanks to her efforts, a genealogy website had profiled Casa do Mar and a magazine article was expected out next month. "Liliana and I will be long-term roommates." The two shared a bedroom when Casa do Bosque was booked.

"Have you thought about what will happen when I start as principal?" For her part, Catarina had thought about it every day for weeks. *Perhaps to take the job had been selfish. Who would tend to the guests? Who would care for the children?*

"Not a problem. Anton has a plan!" They'd heard those very words many times from him. "I've asked Gabriela if she would like to help us run the rural hotel." At the Terceira police department, where they'd met her, she'd been a master of planning and organization, matched only by Catarina herself.

"And I," declared Lori, "will help with the children. It may mean the occasional cold cereal for breakfast or a wrinkled uniform for football practice, but we'll do it."

Beto was getting ready to go home for his lunch and afternoon nap. He thwacked his pants and shirt, sending clouds of dust into the air around him.

"Better to leave the dirt here than at home," he chuckled with Anton. "My wife is threatening to leave me. No worries. She says that same thing every time I'm on a job. Then when I'm finished, she yells at me for sitting around so much."

He stared at a hacksaw that had been left on the ground. "Huh. Old age is playing with me. Again."

Old age? Anton did not like hearing those words from a man who was a year younger than he was. "Again?"

Beto reached around his waist to knead a sore spot on his back. "Yesterday, I searched my toolbox three times for a certain screwdriver. Then, one of my men—one of my *young* men— looked for it, and there it was, in the toolbox right where it was supposed to be. Now today, I thought I'd oiled this hacksaw and put it on the truck already, but here it is. Old age."

Anton helped him to load the remaining tools into his truck, feeling doubly old because much the same thing had happened to him with his lost-and-then-found football whistle and because he felt the strain of lifting Beto's heavy toolbox.

When they opened the front door to Casa de Leite, Lori said, "Gorgeous," Catarina said, "Perfect," and Anton drew his lips up in that expression that he hadn't worn in a while, the one that made him look like a genie had made his wish come true. Beto had broken through a crumbling stone wall across from the entry to install a window that flooded the cottage with light and gave sweeping views of endless ocean and green hills.

They got to work clearing construction dust, cleaning windows, putting the furniture in place, and unpacking what Catarina had ordered. They plugged in lamps and screwed in bulbs, they hung drapes, they put out binoculars to watch the beauty of the island and good books to read after the sun went down. Just before guests arrived, they would add finishing touches: a basket of fruit and one of Catarina's freshly baked loaves of *massa sovada*, sweet bread.

The physical labor had done them all good.

As they closed up, Lori said, "I'm going to set up some excursions ahead of time. In September, the cottage is booked by a marine-biologist couple."

That reminded Anton of something that had slipped his mind. "I have heard from Ethan."

Hearing the name of Anton's American nephew stirred up tumultuous emotions in Lori. They had met almost a year before, and there'd been more than a little attraction. Then the marine biologist had suddenly left for a position as naturalist on a project off the coast of Turkey. They'd corresponded quite a bit since then, and they'd found themselves in synch about so many things—just not about when or even where each might want to settle down. Ethan was happy to travel the world looking for what he wanted. Lori had found what she wanted—or at least very close to it.

"He's returning to the Azores," Anton said, and he closely watched Lori's face for a reaction.

Despite the welcome normalcy of the day, none of them slept well. Catarina had been thinking through the start of the school year. Lori had been trying to increase Casa do Mar's social media presence. Anton had been dealing with grant applications for the living heritage site. The truth was that they were doing anything to take their minds off Ángelo and Martim.

It was time to confront what they knew. Anton took a deep breath and went first. "A Coast Guard specialist looked at the coordinates Lori got together and assessed the water currents around the Devil's Hands. She confirms Ángelo could only have come from the waters in Breakwater Cove."

He referred to an email that had come in late last night. "Harbor Patrol is keeping an eye on the three yachts but, of course, only when they're in our territorial waters. They also sent background information on all three, with as much as is known about where they were last week."

Lori laughed, "You don't trust Branco's log?"

"The Judicial Police is coordinating with harbor authorities to do its own investigation of Branco. Incompetent, certainly. There may be more, perhaps in the gray area between ethical and unethical, perhaps deep in the middle of black crime."

Catarina tried to get them back on track. "Shall we start with the *Sirena*?"

"Captain Karlsson was hiding at least one thing. Not surprisingly, his so-called guests are paying clients. And he doesn't have business license. Again, not unexpected. Neither the local police nor Luis's people could find anyone who owned up to being hired—and not paying income taxes—as day crew for the *Sirena*, so that's a dead end for the moment, and we're waiting to hear about the four men who were supposedly aboard last Tuesday."

Catarina gave her impression of Lars Karlsson. "He has fallen on hard times. Looking around the *Sirena*, it is clear that he has postponed making needed repairs and is using less expensive alternatives—part-time crew, less expensive berthing, even takeout meals—whenever he can. He is a proud man of a certain age. To be in the position of asking for money from others is hard for him. He prefers to be thought of as *having guests*, leaving out that they are *paying* guests. He is stretching the truth because he is embarrassed he has not achieved his dream."

"Stretching the truth is far from killing a boy." Anton was ready to move Karlsson to the bottom of the list of suspects.

Catarina thought. "Men like Captain Karlsson, who have long-held dreams that are tied to their sense of worth, can do more than get embarrassed and stretch the truth if those dreams are thwarted. They may feel justified in doing anything they must to protect that dream."

"The question would then be," Lori mused, "how could Ángelo have threatened that dream?"

"Do we have anything on the *Doura*?" Catarina moved them along to the second of the three yachts.

Anton referred to the email from Harbor Patrol. "It's a slippery vessel, never where it's expected to be, always turning up where it's least expected."

"A tourist vessel?" asked Lori.

"It's registered to travel between the Moroccan and Iberian coasts and to the islands. At the moment, it's en route to Lisbon, supposedly returning next week. Immigration says it does bring in E.U. travelers and some residents, but few of either."

She caught the drift. "Too few to make the run profitable?"

"I'll have one of Luis's agents talk with the captain about passengers and fees."

"Try checking those against tax records." Stories were legion about criminals who were caught simply because records didn't jibe.

In her tiny, neat print, Catarina made a few notes next to *Doura*.

"Are you planning to visit the *Sirena* and the *Iaso* again?" asked Lori. Then she said, "All yachts are not the same."

It was like the train of thought that we all have from time to time, one unexpressed idea leading to another, until what is finally said seems to bear no relation to the original subject. In Lori's case, she'd thought that if Anton and Catarina were returning to those yachts, it would be convenient for them to fly to São Miguel together, when she went to talk to Natalia. She was planning to pick up the new Casa do Mar brochures at the printers at the same time. That formed a mental picture of showing them the brochures when they left the yachts. But she couldn't picture the yachts—because all yachts are not the same.

"All yachts are not the same," she repeated. "Did we ever show Frau Meickle pictures of the yacht she saw?"

Their expressions gave the answer and a minute later, Lori had sent pictures of all three to Luis. "We should know soon." That might limit the work that had to be done but not by enough to relieve anyone.

Catarina tapped her pencil on a line in her notebook. "Fabiano Deníz," she said. "He gave us nothing more than a vague impression that other boats were in the cove. In a way, that is good for him. If he were trying to cover up something, it would be more likely for him to construct a detailed memory for us."

The local police had looked into Fabi for them. They'd confirmed his earnings at the Costa dive shop and as a waiter at a couple of marina restaurants. He was making good money for a young man on São Miguel, especially when his side business was taken into account, but you wouldn't know it from the way he lived. It certainly hadn't gone for a newer car—his barely looked like it would make it out of the parking lot—or better clothes—his uniform of jeans and tee shirts was worn. His address was in the poorer part of town and with his parents. The local police had no reports of him hanging out at bars or gambling.

"So, where is his money going?" Anton asked the group.

It wasn't a hard question for Catarina. "A girl? A loved one? A cause?" she suggested.

Anton opened another attachment on his screen. "Fabi may not have been able to give a useful description of the two passengers he took out without the Costas' knowledge, but the Judicial Police did visit the café where he said he'd picked them up, and they managed to find them. They're still at Hotel do Ouvidor, and they say nothing caught their eyes as unusual. Like Fabi, they were only marginally aware of other boats in the area and as far as they knew, Fabi was left alone on the boat while everyone else was diving together."

Catarina was still concerned. "Preening as Fabiano does is a natural behavior in young men who feel uncertain about their worth, but I believe in his case it is also a well-tended mechanism to bring in the largest tips. I am not concerned on that account.

That being said, I saw in him a determination not to reveal something significant. I'd like to look into him."

She made a notation on her notepad. "Do we have more on the last of the five boats?"

Anton scanned his screen again. "According to Harbor Patrol, after we talked to Fredi, the *São Pedro* vanished. It hasn't been seen in any of its usual spots, offshore or at the marina, but they're on the alert and will let us know as soon as it's spotted."

It was in this easygoing back-and-forth that accompanied these reports that collectively they worked their way through everything that might be relevant, flagged what didn't fit the expected pattern, and decided on next steps.

Anton knew what they had to tackle next. He suggested a short break. Lori sat on the front steps with Catarina, lifting her face to the sun. Anton made himself an espresso to wake his brain and steady his spirits.

When they returned, he filled them in on the latest from Dr. Nunes.

"Martim died soon after he talked to Lori."

Lori could still hear his voice. "I'm interested in why Natalia was going to be late, and I'll ask her tomorrow."

She was ready to move on when she remember her conversation with Martim's family. "Anton, when will his camera and watch be returned to his family? They were presents from his parents, the camera for his eighteenth birthday and the watch when he got his pilot's license. They were his fondest possessions next to his plane."

Anton was mystified. He'd read the report. "Dr. Nunes was called as soon as Ángelo was found by the police. He went to the crime scene himself." He could picture the plastic bag on the medical examiner's counter. He remembered a cell phone. He remembered a watch. But there'd been no camera. He checked Nunes's report, and checked it again. Nunes never made mistakes. He'd even had the waters around the boat checked for evidence. "There was no camera on the boat or anywhere in the area."

"But he was taking pictures just before he died."

"Is his family certain he was using that camera?" Catarina asked. "These days, everyone takes pictures with a phone."

"Martim's camera was a professional model used by photographers. Apparently, that's what he always used."

"Killed for the camera, a used one at that, and when the cell phone and the watch were left behind?" Anton found the idea barely believable.

"With any luck, the pictures have been uploaded; that would be standard these days. I'll ask about passwords tomorrow."

Lori told them about the boat theft that had cost Martim his career and asked for a copy of Martim's police record. "The aftermath also cost Martim his closest friend, Natalia's brother, and left bad blood between the families. On the day of the trial, Gustavo and Rafe got in a fight on the steps of the Judicial Building because Gustavo refused to testify on Martim's behalf. It was so bad that even Rafe couldn't testify, and no one stood up for Martim."

They looked at each other, not certain of the significance of what Lori had said, and for a few minutes, they aimlessly shuffled papers and stared at screens.

Until Anton spoke. "Ángelo is the key." He felt a squeeze on his heart just saying the name that almost certainly wasn't the boy's name. "He died first and many things about his death are odd. Where did he come from? No one has reported a missing person, not the boats that were nearby, not hotels or Immigration, not islanders or police departments."

He was fairly certain it was the truth when he added, "He had a long history of abuse and neglect; he wasn't one of ours."

Lori and Catarina nodded to agree. It was conceivable, barely, that someone could have been so maltreated in one of their own close-knit communities. But it was farfetched to believe that no one would have noticed and no one would have reported it in all the years the boy had suffered.

"He came in illegally, then?" Lori tried to clarify.

"Perhaps he was aware he was coming in illegally. Perhaps he was not. But someone is covering up his entry, doctoring crew records, lying about who remains on board, something."

"Or he could have been a stowaway," Lori reminded him.

"True." Anton chewed the inside of his cheek. "But he was naked. That just doesn't jibe with being a stowaway."

"Why were his clothes removed? To prevent identification?" Lori wondered.

Their responses came almost at the same time.

"No attempt to alter his dentition," said Anton.

"His fingerprints were intact," said Catarina.

"His tattoo wasn't removed," said Lori. "So why else would he have been naked when he was killed?"

"Sleeping?" suggested Anton.

"Showering?" suggested Catarina.

"Swimming?" suggested Lori.

They were all feeling the frustration of too many questions and not enough answers. Rather than restoring their sense of purpose, they had been drained of energy.

8

Lori and Carlos started at the airfield that served the company Martim had worked for until his last flight on the day he died. He had been well liked. When his friends were told why they'd come, they offered information and speculation, and more than one of them offered a strong arm and a clenched fist once his killer was found.

They didn't have the combination for the padlock on his locker, but no one objected when they asked if they could break it open, and bolt cutters were brought from a tool bench. Unfortunately, the steel was too hard for them to cut through. The airfield administrator was suggesting that they cut through the metal locker itself when the janitor passed by, reached on top of the locker, and peeled off a sticky note. "He wrote down the combination in case he forgot."

Inside, they found what one would expect: a picture of Natalia, an extra pair of sunglasses, a clean shirt, the registration papers to his new plane, a second set of keys to his car. Carlos pocketed the car keys, and Lori took everything else to bring to Martim's family.

They also checked out his new plane, *O Sonho*—The Dream. The inside was pristine, with not so much as a fallen hair to be seen.

Carlos ran a hand along the body. "I hope it goes to someone who will appreciate it."

"Will you be able to arrange that for the Sousas?"

"Yes. It's almost new. They'll get a nice amount for it."

Neither said what both were thinking: That wouldn't help one bit.

Next on their list of sad tasks was finding Martim's car at the marina. Along the way, Lori read from the pictures of the calendar hanging in Martim's bedroom. One by one, they dismissed every entry as mundane: a cleaning at a dentist Carlos knew well; lunch with Beatrix that she confirmed; dates with Natalia. Everything ordinary, ordinary, ordinary.

Since the first time he'd been involved in one of Lori's cases—limited to the most peripheral of roles—Carlos had wanted to know what it was like to investigate. He'd pictured the excitement of discovering clues, motives, and secrets, and the ultimate triumph of putting it all together. That was before. Now it was just a miserable responsibility.

They did what they had to do. At the marina, they walked up one row of parked cars and down the next, looking for Martim's car. When they found it, Carlos took the parking ticket from the dashboard. "Just after 7:00, as we'd thought," he said with no joy.

They went to Pier 3. The mooring for the boat where Martim's body had been found was empty, the boat owner presumably out enjoying a beautiful day.

Lori tried to picture the scene. "The sun would have been setting in that direction, but Martim could have been taking pictures anywhere around here." *Around here* included a long arc of coastline, the shops and cafés of the new marina, and the boats lined up between them. There was too much to point to any one place where he might have seen something that led to his murder.

She was thinking aloud, her thoughts bouncing from one place to another, her feet pacing back and forth across the dock. "We'll need to talk to the Sousas about possible passwords. Hopefully, the pictures will be on the cloud. It'll be awkward to do it directly, but we'll have to find a way to ask where each one of them was on Tuesday evening." She went on, to herself, "We need to think about motives. Revenge and anger are possible, so we'll have the local police ask around. Maybe there was some dispute that attracted attention. Also, he might have been killed for something he knew. Or maybe he actually was killed for an old camera."

She took a breath and looked up.

Carlos was crying. "He was right here, waiting for us, when he died."

They drove west into the hills of The Green Island, past orchards and river valleys. The land was dotted with calderas, volcanic cones, and hot springs, their temperature moderated by ocean tides. Natural beauty was everywhere. Ahead was the Sete Cidades lagoon, two crater lakes connected by a narrow strait, one dazzling turquoise, the other enamel blue. Cryptomeria, evergreens found naturally only in Japan, China, and the Azores, towered well over 200 feet. Made possible by the combination of the island's location in the Gulf Stream and its volcanic past, the island hosted areas of lush tropical vegetation and the only tea plantations in Europe.

Lori had no plan. In itself, that made her feel uncomfortable. She'd scaffolded her life on plans, to-do lists, action points. That had given her some semblance of control in the uncertain days of her childhood. Now, her only thought was to spend time with Carlos, time away from the sad business they'd spent the day on, time to appreciate what was around them, time to simply be together. For miles, they were lost in their own thoughts, his about Martim and all the *ifs* that plague survivors, hers about him.

"I'm fine, Lori. You don't have to do this."

"What does it tell you that I don't have to do this?" He didn't know. "It should tell you that I *want* to do this." She may not have known exactly what *this* was, but she would stay by his side until she figured it out. He was her friend—or as someone like him is often called, "more than a friend." In the past few months, it had become more difficult for her to define precisely how she thought of Carlos. She knew she felt a tenderness that she'd felt for no one other than her small Casa do Mar family. And she knew that sometimes she felt a longing to have him near that projected into an indeterminate future.

"It will do me good to be in the sky," Carlos was saying, "showing our islands."

She found herself worried about his safety. "Let's spend a little more time together."

As the drone of the car's engine filled her ears, her mind took her to a place with hazy images of a home and children and a man. To her surprise, the man's face flickered, sometimes Carlos, sometimes Ethan.

After dropping Carlos off at the airfield, Lori drove past the de la Rosa house, crossed two intersections, turned the car around and pulled over. From that vantage point, she had a good view of the driveway, behind it the harbor and the rest of the old town. She waited. Twenty minutes later, a late model Mercedes pulled out, two figures in the front seat, and the gates swung closed. She got out and walked downhill close to flowering shrubbery that bordered some of the best houses in town.

The front windows of the de la Rosa house revealed little; the drapes were drawn. Boldly, Lori walked across the cobbled patio and knocked.

Natalia opened the door herself, her wide eyes and pouty lips fully made up. "My father isn't home," she said, half-hidden behind the door.

"I want to talk to you not your father."

She looked in back of her and into the rooms on either side of the hall. "Alright."

They settled in the same furniture-packed, lavender-scented sitting room where Lori had met her father and brother. Lori wasted no time. "I want to go back to what you told me about being worried about Martim the day he died. Why were you worried?"

She gave a look to say she had no answer. Lori didn't have a clue whether that meant the reason wasn't in her memory or she didn't want to say. There was, she realized, a third option. It was possible Natalia didn't care enough to try to remember. Was she that type known as a poor little rich girl? Had Martim been a convenient way to leave her father's house? Even worse, could her engagement simply have been a threat to hold over her father's head in order to get what she wanted?

Lori repeated her question slowly, "Why were you worried?"

"He didn't answer his phone."

"When was that?"

"Early. About noon? All afternoon, actually."

The explanation should have been simple. He'd been flying his last chartered flight. "Couldn't he have been busy?"

"I thought something had happened to him."

"Why would you think that?"

"Someone from his past could have killed him."

That had been her father's thought—and before Martim's body had even been found.

"But then you talked to him and said you were going to be late for dinner. Why were you going to be late?"

"I…" Her eyes went to the front hall. "I found out I had to wait for something."

Lori was getting impatient and a little irritated. "Natalia! This is serious. Someone killed your fiancé, the man you were supposed to love."

"I did love him!" A rivulet of black mascara snaked down each cheek.

"What did you have to wait for?"

She had a cautious expression, like she'd been in this situation before and was deciding the best way to proceed. "You don't understand. It's different here. It's different for me. I have responsibilities."

"To your father?"

Her nod was more an upward tick of her chin.

It didn't come easily, but Lori did her best to imitate Catarina's even, sympathetic tone. "What did you find out that would make you late meeting Martim?"

"My father came home. He said he was going out at 7:30. If I waited… It would just be…easier to wait." Her eyes wandered to the front hall again. "Then he changed his mind about leaving. My phone… I didn't have my phone… I tried…"

She rubbed red-rimmed eyes, and her makeup smeared into clownish ovals. "And now Martim is gone," she wailed, "and everything we'd planned is gone. No fresh start. No Lisbon. No little apartment with a balcony. No walks on city streets. No anything."

Her words, her delivery, even the dramatic raking of her hair seemed so stereotyped, Lori was having doubts about Natalia. Did she lack genuine feelings for Martim or was she a somewhat naïve young woman who hadn't yet grown into adulthood?

She saw Natalia's reaction before she heard Henrique de la Rosa turn the knob—as though somehow his daughter had smelled his looming presence through the front door. He went directly into the sitting room. A few paces behind him, Gustavo stood in the shadows, looking uncomfortable.

"How dare you come into my house uninvited," he glared at Lori.

Lori was not one to be cowed. "I hardly broke in. I wanted to talk with Natalia. I thought she lives here, too."

"Don't be disrespectful. You have been given all the information you are entitled to. My daughter hadn't seen the Sousa man since the Saturday before he died. The relationship was going nowhere anyway."

"I'll be leaving then." She tucked Carlos's car keys behind a sofa cushion as she got up. "I just..." she looked around, "need to find..." she moved the cushion aside a bit, "my car keys."

"Marta," de la Rosa yelled for his maid, Fabi's mother.

She was there in an instant, as intimated and as tired-looking as she'd been the last time Lori saw her.

"Find this woman's keys."

As soon as his back was to them, Lori whispered in Natalia's ear, "Anton Cardosa, Central Government," then brightly said, "Here they are."

She said a curt goodbye and walked out of the room.

Henrique himself pulled the front door open. "Goodbye."

And she was left on the other side of the closed door, thinking hard.

Judging by the way the pousada doorman quirked his head in the direction of the chair, Fabi had been waiting in the lobby quite a while. Even from a distance, it was clear his posture was no longer confrontational. He was nervous. Anton knew enough to slow his steps and let Catarina take the lead.

Fabi stood. His expression was intended to show that the meeting was entirely coincidental, but he must have gone out of his way to find out where they were staying. "Is the investigator staying here?" He asked the question of Catarina not Anton.

"Please sit, Fabi," she said, and she took the chair opposite him. "Anton, could you please ask for coffee to be sent for us?"

Fabi's eyes followed Anton to the front desk. He cleared his throat and wiped his palms on the legs of neatly pressed pants. A long pause. "Everything good for you?" he smiled such an awkward smile it was hard to connect him to the swaggering young man she'd met three days ago.

"Yes. Thank you."

"Have you found anything helpful about that boy, the one whose picture you showed me?"

"We are making progress."

He gave a short hum, and his eyes darted here and there as he searched for something to say. "Let's say I knew...I remembered something. That would be helpful, right?"

"It could be." Anton was heading back. She caught his eye and shook her head slightly. He turned back.

"Well, I was thinking. Your...him..." he looked in the direction Anton had gone, "he's going to tell the Costas, you know, about the extra divers."

"I believe he said—"

"Tomorrow. He would really do that?"

She nodded.

"Why? I'm not hurting anyone."

"Putting aside that you are hurting the Costa brothers' profits, the Minister is a man of his word." That was true.

She knew he was hiding something and that it could be important to their investigation, and she knew he wanted to trade information for Anton's silence. "Why don't you just tell me why you are here, and we can take it from there?"

He looked defeated. "Either way I will lose my job."

"If that happens, there are other jobs you can get."

"I need *this* job. I need what I make from…you know…from the divers who pay me directly."

"The pay from your other jobs is not enough?"

He shook his head miserably.

"You cannot live more simply?"

"I live simply!" At the sound of Fabi's angry voice, Anton stomped in their direction. Once again, Catarina warned him off, but this time he stayed very close.

"Tell me about your life, Fabiano," she said in her gentle Catarina voice.

The outburst had relieved something he'd been holding in. Punctuated by quiet sobs and roughly brushed away tears, he did tell her, the first time he had unburdened himself to anyone.

The story was unexpected and at the same time one of those stories that is typical of many people who live with the difficulties life has given them, quietly coping with no end in sight. When he was a child, Fabi's younger brother contracted a fever that left him with the mental age of a five-year-old. Ever since then, Fabi had been responsible for his brother whenever he wasn't in school, tending to his physical needs while his parents worked every hour they could. Even with E.U. medical coverage, there were steep expenses associated with keeping his brother at home and providing him with just a few extras to make his life more comfortable. The mere suggestion of a government care facility, an *institution* as his mother called it, made her cry and his father lecture Fabi about being a man and living up to his responsibilities.

Fabi had accepted all this, not because of his mother's distress, not because his father told him to, not for any reason he told Catarina about. But she knew from the words he chose. *The disease got him not me. I wish there was something I could have done. When I'm away, all he can do is sit there.* As was true for Carlos, survivor guilt is a terrible curse.

Everyone took turns caring for Fabi's brother and working, his mother for Henrique de la Rosa, his father on a fishing boat, and Fabi at three part-time jobs, the best ones he could get with an education that had been limited by circumstance. Money had been tight, but they had managed—until his father's stroke a year ago. And overnight, he'd became the responsible adult of the family.

Just twenty-two, he was left with the chores of lifting two grown men out of bed each morning, tending to their toilet needs, and dressing them before dropping his mother off at the de la Rosas and going to the first of his jobs at Costa Brothers.

Fabi wasn't working shorter hours and calling in for time off because—as Alberto Costa assumed—he was lazy and self-centered but because he was needed at home to do what he had been doing since he was twelve years old, taking care of his family.

Catarina knew. Our judgement of others is limited by what we know of their circumstances and by how deeply we can feel what they feel. Now that she'd had a closer look—and a more attentive listen—to Fabi, she recharacterized his behavior on the diving boat. His posturing and anger had been fear of losing his job and letting down his family.

She held his hand, "Everything will be fine, Fabiano," and she signaled Anton.

"Fabiano has kindly come to help us," she said after she told him to take the seat next to her not Fabi. (His size could be intimidating.)

"How is it you can help?" His voice, so kind at other times, tended to be gruff when he was in his role as investigator, and particularly when someone—a child, no less—had suffered.

Catarina saw Fabi shutting down. "We hope you will give him some consideration because of his effort to come here." Her words stood somewhere between a statement and a question.

"Tell me what you think will help us." His voice had gentled a bit.

"That morning...Tuesday...I was there in Breakwater Cove...and..."

Anton nodded, as Catarina had taught him, and waited.

Fabi glanced at Catarina. "I saw him…the kid…I saw him at the rail of the ship just before he jumped."

To himself, Anton screamed, "He jumped?"

"He caught my attention because of the way he was dressed, skimpy white trunks worn high up. Then he just sort of fell overboard."

"No one pushed him? He jumped?"

"I had a clear view. I couldn't take my eyes off him, just a kid, you know. He was alone. He looked port. He looked down. He looked port again. And he just let himself go to the sea without even reaching out for the rail."

They couldn't believe what they'd heard. Did Ángelo fall overboard accidently? Had he committed suicide?

Anton controlled his urge to pepper Fabi with questions. In a measured tone, he asked, "Which boat did he fall from?"

"It was one of those yachts that have been hanging around our waters."

"Which one?"

"I don't know." He looked miserable. He looked like he was still hiding something. Unexpectedly, he stood and took a step toward the lobby door.

Quickly, Catarina was by his side. "I understand, Fabiano, that we all sometimes do things that we do not want others to know about. Those are not always terrible things, are they?"

She'd struck a chord. "Maybe."

"We all regret things we have done."

He was quiet but his body language told her he was relaxing a bit.

"What is it you want to tell us?"

"I can't…" but there was little force to his words. "I saw him." Pause. "My divers were surfacing." Another pause. "I saw the sharks." A deep breath. "By the time I got the divers out of the water, I'd lost sight of him and of the sharks. I didn't go back to look for the kid."

"If it helps, Fabiano, the boy was not killed by sharks."

He shuddered and bit his lip. "Is that enough…?" he looked to Catarina.

Anton opened a picture of Martim and held his phone out. "Have you seen this tattoo?"

Fabi was still wary. "No. Look, I've got to get back to work. Is there anything else?"

"Is there anything else you think will help us?"

He shook his head and made a hasty exit, having forgotten to ask if Anton was still planning to tell the Costas about his side business.

They walked from the marina in light fog. It would thicken overnight, as fog that moved in from the west usually did, but for now it just gave a gauzy glow to the large white building ahead. The building was both in keeping with the island's colonial architecture and functional. On the second story, there were only two large windows, below them a double door that was wider than it was tall, presumably to allow vehicles access to the interior courtyard. They entered through a small door in the right panel. On the other side, the smell of cigarettes was suspended in the fog. Smoking was still almost as common on the islands as it had been a hundred years ago and even more common in a place such as this where apathy and restlessness lived.

There were almost twice as many people inside as usual. The dayshift was preparing to leave, while the nightshift was just arriving. You could tell them apart by their uniforms, some wrinkled and some crisply pressed, and by how much stubble was on their chins.

They passed a lineup of rooms along a long corridor with shiny linoleum floors. In one, posters advised securing all nonessential items in lockers and washing hands well before going home. On a long, worn counter, there were sign-in sheets and a pencil tethered to a nail, two coffee makers, a row of stained mugs, a box of disposable gloves and another of tissues. The next room was set up with a fingerprinting scanner and a camera, both digitized these days, and shelves stacked with blue jumpsuits. Further on, in another room, a young man was slumped in a chair facing a much older man, a guard, who was staring him down.

It all looked orderly, neat, clean. Framed posters gave regulations for visits and listed prisoners' rights. Unlike other such places, Anton and Catarina hadn't been searched, hadn't even been asked if they carried anything that could be used as a weapon or a means of escape. No one had looked into the pastry box Anton carried. Some of the people they passed—guards and prisoners alike—looked hardened by life but none were confrontational, and Catarina had the impression—a correct one—that violence was rare.

As they walked, Anton asked the warden, "Do you know anything about a Martim Sousa that might not be in the records? A young man. He would have been released about six years ago."

"I do," he said slowly as he recovered his memory. "I can't tell you much for a couple of reasons. First, it was closer to eight years ago. I'd just arrived as administrator. Second, he doesn't stand out in my mind. The difficult ones usually do."

"How is Manuel doing?" asked Catarina.

They had both been to visit Manuel more than once, and the warden was aware they had been—still were—friends. "He takes comfort in helping the padre and caring for our chapel. He grows the flowers for the altar, you know. I trust him to return to his cell from the garden when he is ready.

"He's become the confidant of many of the younger prisoners, advising them, scolding them when needed. It isn't mine to say but if it were up to me, he…" He left it hanging.

He opened the door to a spacious visiting room. During the day, its windows gave a sweeping view of the Atlantic. Now that the sun had set, they were black mirrors, reflecting a bank of modern light fixtures overhead. The room was furnished in sleek-lined furniture that was more upscale than one would expect in a prison—the recent gift of an inmate's family—but for a man who'd lived a life surrounded by the warm wood bar his great-great grandfather had carved and by a collection Water's Edge memorabilia collected over many years, that was little consolation.

"I hope this isn't a bad time for you, Manuel," Anton said as he hugged the man he'd arrested for the murder of Isabella's abusive husband.

He gave a wry laugh, shared by a man of similar age who was wiping down the tables and chairs. "I don't have a lot of social engagements at any time."

Catarina hugged Manuel and handed him the pastries, and he bestowed two kisses on her cheeks. "How are the children?" he asked, although they all knew that he would have heard if there was anything amiss on Santa Maria.

"They're with Maria Rosa."

"She's a good woman. After all she's been through, she deserves happiness in life." Manuel was the sort of person who blended into the background, quiet and observant, and he likely knew more than Catarina did about someone who, despite being her close friend, never mentioned her past.

They let Manuel ask his own questions first, about Isabella, about Matias, about little Paolo who stood to inherit it all: Water's Edge, the stretches of land earmarked for Anton's heritage trust, the legacy of six generations of Dekkers and Costas.

Catarina took his hand. "Everyone misses you, Manuel."

These visits were always difficult for Anton. He lived with the choice he had made to arrest his friend for a crime he might have committed himself given similar circumstances. "I wish you could be with us and not here."

"There are many worse things." He was thinking of what Isabella had endured. "We are treated well enough, better than many in the world. In fact, some of us support an orphanage in Ghana."

From past visits, during normal visiting hours, Anton and Catarina had seen the respect other inmates gave Manuel, perhaps because of what he had done, certainly because he was the man he was. One of the reasons they'd come that night was to ask if he'd heard anything about Martim or knew someone who'd been there at the same time as Martim.

Manuel scratched his forehead. "Of course, it was before my time here. If I remember, he was just a kid, reckless like you were when you were young, Anton. Before Catarina. He'd stolen a boat, and something went wrong. Someone…a child…was hurt…badly, I think."

Anton had been hoping for more than what was in the records Luis had sent him.

Manuel waved at his fellow prisoner, now mopping the floor at the far end of the room. "That's Duo. When he works in the kitchen, he makes a pasta—not as great as Isabella's—but great. He's been here a lot longer. He might know more."

He did. But they had to wait a while for Duo to get to what they didn't already know. "Martim was a model prisoner from the moment he arrived. He was friendly, more with us old-timers than with the kids closer to his own age. But even with us, he didn't talk much. His mother and sister came every week, his father and brother less often. Oh, that sister made an amazing cherry pie." He eyed the glossy white pastry box and swallowed. "In the beginning, another man visited a few times, but the visits were short and cool. You know how you can tell, without hearing words or even seeing them move their lips?"

"Could it have been his lawyer?" Anton asked.

"I'm pretty sure he was defended by the court, and he looked too young to be a lawyer anyway."

He thought some more. "I'll tell you something else. He didn't get much by way of mail, but there were days when it was like he knew something was coming. He'd work his way to the front of us guys who were waiting and when his name was called, he'd grab the envelope and go off by himself."

"You have no idea what it was he got?"

"Not a clue, sir. We all teased him it must have been a love letter, but he'd just fold it into his pocket and work his way back through whoever was still waiting for mail and disappear."

Anton and Catarina were watching Duo leave when he turned around and said, "One thing. Once, he said something—and don't ask me what because I've tried remembering and never could—made me think he had a grudge against someone and a plan for getting even once he was out."

The goodbye hugs they gave Manuel were always long, and Catarina made a point of cupping his cheeks gently when she kissed him. It was one of the greater hardships for a man like him to face in prison, they had said to each other once, not to have the comfort of being held by someone who cares about you.

They were left to walk down the long hallway to the exit on their own. Security didn't seem like a major issue. Then again, as the president had said, they were on an island surrounded by thousands of miles of open ocean. Perhaps more important, people knew each other and looked out for one another and strangers.

Walking away, the prison loomed over them, an intimidating face with a gaping mouth formed by the wide door and two glowing eyes where the windows had been.

Anton's cheery nature couldn't help but being dampened by memories of the last time he'd climbed the grand staircase to Luis's office. The Judicial Police in Ponta Delgado occupied one wing of the same colonial palace where he'd met the new president and where the tenuous nature of his Azores heritage project had been pointed out.

In a small conference room, once a colonial governor's dressing room, Lori and Catarina waited. Catarina had already laid out a series of folders down the center of the large oak table, also a legacy of the past with enough dents and gouges to obscure what had once been a delicately incised border of the flowers of the Azores. Laptops were open. Phones were out. There was a lot to work through.

Anton emptied his pockets of scraps of paper, the usual assortment of thoughts that he'd worried could be pushed aside by more pressing issues. Catarina took a small notepad from her bag, and Lori projected her laptop screen to a large monitor she'd set up.

"If Fabi is to be believed—and Catarina thinks he is—Ángelo fell from a yacht in broad daylight," Anton started.

"Any word from Frau Meickle on the pictures of the yachts?" Lori had sent pictures of the *Sirena* and the *Iaso* to Luis.

"Two agents went over yesterday, but no one answered the door. It doesn't matter as much now." He tried to keep a deadpan face as he slowly spooled out the information. "They have contacted the four men who were playing cards aboard the *Sirena*. They are from Lisbon. They entered São Miguel four days earlier and left for the mainland on Thursday."

He cleared his throat. "The local police visited each one at home, and each one said they didn't recognize Ángelo or the tattoo."

His lip twitched up on one side. "All are well known to the police there because," he let it out with a chuckle, "they are highly decorated police officers."

"Why come all the way to the islands to hole up on a boat and play cards?" asked Lori.

"They were taking a vacation from their wives complaining about their gambling."

"And now they're in big trouble with their wives!"

"The only useful information we got from them is that at least one of them was awake through Monday night and into Tuesday morning. Nothing was heard or seen, and the *Sirena* is pretty small for a yacht. Not conclusive but it's beginning to seem like we can focus on the *Iaso* and the *Doura*.

"We've already heard from the *Iaso* purser," Lori took over. The purser's response had come as quickly as the refreshments and register had appeared when they were on board. "He says that he's shown the pictures we gave him, and no one recognized either."

She showed a four-page spreadsheet of names, each with *NO* under both *Man's Face* and *Tattoo*. "I'll give them credit for organization."

"It was just that way on board," Catarina remembered.

"There are a lot of people for a pleasure cruise," Anton said, squinting at the list.

Lori was familiar with life aboard a luxury yacht from her days with Matthew Cunningham, her last employer. "Most would be support staff." She highlighted the last three pages of the document. "Column H shows two or three sharing the same accommodation; yet, their home addresses in Column D are all different. It's unlikely that any of them are connected to one another except through their employment aboard the *Iaso*."

"And so they're less likely be lying about the same thing," Anton came to the same conclusion Lori had. "I've also had the names checked with Immigration. Most are registered as entering the islands aboard the *Iaso*; a few—guests, I presume—flew in and joined the cruise here in São Miguel."

"Can we go back to look around, perhaps ask more questions?"

"We're not at a point where that's advisable." He was thinking of more than the president's wishes; demanding to board would have ramifications for the islands' reputation as a haven for transatlantic voyages and could damage tourism. "I'll have the local police keep an eye on all of our boats."

"Could there be a limitation to this information?" Catarina raised a possibility they hadn't thought of. "The people listed might simply not have seen Ángelo."

"I thought we'd discounted his being a stowaway because of how he was found," Lori said.

"I am thinking of another limitation. Could someone on that list have known he was on-board but is now lying to us for some reason?"

This was the way the three of them worked, challenging each other's ideas until they arrived at a reasonable conclusion.

Anton consulted an email. "Fredi has been suspected of fishing without a license, perhaps even stealing from other traps and nets, in more than one jurisdiction. He was taken into custody twice but couldn't be held. Insufficient evidence. I think we can assume he was illegally fishing in Breakwater Cove last Tuesday."

Catarina spoke almost to herself, "I do think he is hiding something that disturbs him more than a charge he has easily evaded before."

"Maybe he didn't kill Ángelo," suggested Lori. "Maybe he knows who did."

Anton grumbled. "His boat is among the missing again, but I'm going to have the Coast Guard find him…again…and bring him in. A little intimidation is in order."

It was a good time to take a break before moving on to what they knew of Martim's murder. They were opening the door to the conference room when—within seconds of one another—two of Anton's phones pinged. He looked, raised those eyebrows with upturned commas at the ends, and groaned. "The *Doura* turned around mid-voyage between Morocco and São Miguel. It's headed for deeper waters."

"As you said: *slippery*," Catarina noted.

"The Portuguese Coast Guard has had it on their watchlist, suspected of transporting aliens—and that could tie in with the boy's death."

"Ângelo," she whispered to herself.

He drummed his fingers in frustration. "Right now, we will assume that the *Doura* is working outside the law."

Lori was conspicuous by her silence. Finally, she asked, "Why did the *Doura* suddenly turn around? What were they told? Who told them?"

It was something to consider, Anton nodded.

The second text was from the local police. As much as possible, the alibis of the Sousa family and the de la Rocha family had been verified—but by family members, which gave small reassurance. Family and friends would and often did lie for a loved one they thought was innocent—and for one they suspected was guilty.

"Do we really think someone in his own family or his fiancée would kill him?" The question came from Lori, who knew perfectly well it was a possibility.

"Almost everyone has a trigger or breaking point," mused Catarina. "Alcohol or drugs may have played a role in Martim's murder. It may have been unintentional. It may have grown from displaced anger at someone else, another family member or even a stranger."

"According to his daughter, Henrique de la Rosa suggested Martim might not be returning her calls because someone from his past had harmed him. One more thing: she and Martim were planning to move to Portugal after they were married—a fresh start, she called it."

"That would have meant leaving her father," said Catarina. "His bravado when he threw you out may be an illusion. He may be a frightened man—frightened of aging, frightened of being on his own—feelings not unknown to most humans, but some parents are willing to sacrifice their children for relief from that fear. They see their children only as extensions of themselves. They cannot accept that a child's life does not belong to the parents. Henrique de la Rosa strikes me as such a man."

"Consider this: It's a stretch but without Martim, Natalia would have probably stayed at home, and her brother would have been free to live his own life as he pleased."

Anton shook his head. "So, despite all our work, we still have every one of the suspects we started with."

Lori typed a list of names as she spoke, "Not if we look at probabilities. I'd put the entire Sousa family on the low end, followed by Natalia, who really seemed to at least want the marriage, if only to escape her father's house. So we're left with Henrique and Gustavo de la Rosa."

Anton sighed, "And unknowns with unknown motives."

"Carlos did ask Martim's family about those letters that Duo said he was getting. None of them sent them. So who did and why were they so important to him?"

The conjecture went on and on with no progress. *Could they have actually been love letters, either from Natalia or from someone else? Could they have been part of an appeals process? Could he have been expecting something regularly, like grades from one of the online courses he took or bills for something he'd bought on time? Could the envelopes have hidden contraband?*

Texts and calls flew out, and the answers returned. Martim and Natalia were barely friends when they were younger. His family knew of no special girl in his life. His lawyer said there had been no appeal or indeed no contact after he'd been sentenced. The courses he took posted grades online. He had no bills. And, they decided, any contraband would have to have been very small.

At last, a frustrated Anton got up and asked, "Any other lines of inquiry we've forgotten?"

His mind was tangled with a jumble of thoughts, all of them negative. He worried that Ángelo's killer was still a danger.

He wondered if Martim would have died if he'd been able to stop Ángelo's killer in time. He considered turning the investigation over to Luis and his trained agents, because, as he told himself, he was getting nowhere.

Catarina eyes found his. "There is only so much you can do."

The investigation was wearing on them in more ways than one. Anton had been pulled from his work as Minister of Heritage, which he felt was his primary responsibility. Catarina had no time to think through everything that needed to be done before the new school year began. Lori felt bad about not spending more time with Carlos after the death of his best friend. And all three shared worries about the future of the living heritage preserve, its fate now in the hands of a president who didn't appreciate its value, and their rural hotel, now in no one's hands and losing money by the hour.

But this was no time to shift priorities; both the good will of the president and the success of Casa do Mar depended on their solving the mysteries around the deaths of Ángelo and Martim.

Leaving Lori to spend a little time with Carlos, Anton and Catarina returned to the marina yet again, this time to put some pressure on Fredi.

It was not to be. When they reached the *São Pedro*, Fredi was slumped over the aft bench. He didn't wake when Anton stepped aboard or when Anton called out in a loud voice. He didn't stir when he banged on a metal gas can with the end of a wrench. Anton looked closely. Fredi was breathing—alcohol fumes. A wave slapped the side of the boat sending a bottle of vodka rolling across the deck. It was empty. Anton was sure he knew where the contents were.

Fredi gave two loud snores and without warning, he retched over the side of the boat.

"Get up!" Anton bellowed.

Fredi looked up unconcerned, perhaps uncomprehending, and raked a hand through unkempt hair.

Catarina's thoughts about their previous visit with Fredi had steeped in Anton's brain for two days now, and they were on the verge of coalescing into some important revelation. Fredi hadn't been reassured by knowing that they weren't interested in his illegal fishing activities. If anything, he'd seemed more defensive, "still hiding something," as Catarina had put it. While what he was hiding could be one of a number of other things, Fredi's clear memory of every detail about the boats in Breakwater Cove, despite what Catarina had called *the wallpaper effect*, made Anton certain that the fisherman had seen or done something connected with Ángelo's death.

Anton stood over Fredi—very close. "I will have what I need to charge you by tomorrow morning." He neglected to say that would be for illegal fishing, something far from Fredi's mind by then. "You have until you're brought in to tell me what I want to know and not a minute longer. And Fredi…" Fredi's red eyes looked up, "if it's at police headquarters, I'll make sure you receive no mercy."

Fredi collapsed on a pile of rags and couldn't be roused. They wouldn't get anything from him today.

Anton decided to put his frustrations behind him with his first espresso of the afternoon, perhaps accompanied by one of the chef's cannoli's. "Let's go back to Convento Real and sit for a while."

It was not to be.

Catarina squinted into the sun and said, "I think that's Fabi over there."

She waved at him.

He narrowed his eyes at her and turned to hoist a wooden crate off the Costa diving boat.

"Perhaps he didn't see you," Anton said, and he gave a long, loud whistle to catch his attention.

Fabi looked in their direction and turned away again.

"He looks angry," Catarina said.

She was already crossing the dock. Anton caught up with his wife in time to hear her say, "Fabiano! How are you?"

"How do you think I am?"

Catarina saw the bitterness in the young man's eyes. "Has something happened?"

"What do you think?" He turned his eyes on Anton. "Your wife was wrong about you. Some 'man of honor' you are. Or maybe she just isn't a woman of honor."

Catarina didn't have to look to know how angry that had made Anton, and he didn't have to look to know how pleased she was that he'd said nothing.

"Fabiano, please tell us what has happened."

"The Costas just gave me one hour to get my things off their boat," he lifted the crate high in front of their faces, "so here they are."

The man who could look intimidating just by standing there now wore a hurt expression. "I said nothing," Anton told him. The truth was that after Catarina filled him in on how Fabi was dealing with the circumstances life had put him in, he'd felt a bit ashamed of having assumed the worst of him. So he'd put off saying anything to the Costas, hoping to find a way to both do the right thing and help a young man who was trying the best he could.

He didn't have a chance to explain this to Fabi. He was already storming off.

Anton didn't think the day could get much worse. He was wrong.

It was a warm evening. The fragrance of flowers carried into the pousada lobby from the park. From a distance, Catarina watched Anton come down the stairs, large and graceful at the same time. Halfway, he stopped and patted one pocket and then another, his hands performing a dance she was familiar with as he tried to determine which of his three phones was softly vibrating.

His face lit up when he heard what someone had called to tell him. He found her eyes and held them while he quickly stepped down to meet her. "That was Beto." He kissed her cheek. "The outdoor lighting fixtures for Casa de Leite have finally arrived."

"You will pick them up now?"

"Do you mind?"

She didn't. They would both enjoy the evening they'd planned more knowing Beto could finish that last task tomorrow. "I will walk in the park until you return."

He kissed her again. On his way to the parking lot, he passed a street vendor who was closing down for the night, loading buckets of roses, irises, and freesia into the back of his truck, and he bought an extravagant bunch of white freesia for Catarina—not that they weren't surrounded by flowers at Casa do Mar, but it put him in mind of their student days in Lisbon, when as much as they wanted, such luxuries were out of reach. It would remind her of the same thing.

Catarina's eyes followed Anton as he squeezed into the small Fiat and drove down the main boulevard no more carefully than when he was driving the back roads of Santa Maria. As much as she trusted in his abilities to keep himself safe, a small part of her lived in torment whenever he was gone.

Dimming light filtered through the treetops. The last children were hustled away by parents. The last office workers made their way to cafés or homes. The last birds nested safely in the leaves overhead. Catarina was alone in the park. She walked the perimeter path, inhaling the smell of kahili ginger and red cedar and enjoying the memories they brought back.

In a snug spot between two hydrangeas, she settled on a bench. That was where she got the sense that despite appearing to be deserted, someone else was in the park with her. Such feelings, Catarina knew, were not to be discounted without consideration. They originate deep in our primitive brain, which subconsciously processes the environment at all times. And when that primitive brain finds something threatening, it tickles your conscious mind with warnings. The system alerted our ancestors to poisonous snakes at their feet while they watched distant grasses for saber-toothed tigers.

Perhaps my uneasiness comes from this terrible business we have become involved in, she told herself, or perhaps it is simply the thought of Anton racing around in an unfamiliar car.

A sound, more human than animal to her mind, prickled her skin. She listened closely. There were faraway sounds from the boulevard: the purr of car engine, the rattle of trucks, the occasional bleat of a horn, a voice carried on the wind. Nothing more. She felt foolish when she spotted a young couple walking arm in arm not too far off. Having someone else in the park does not mean that person is a threat, she scolded herself. You are in one of the safest places on Earth.

Close by, she heard the soft, slow crunching of footsteps on the wood mulch of flower beds next to the path. An image of Ángelo inserted itself in front of the bench. Then one of Martim.

She got up and started to walk back towards the buttery rectangles of light from the pousada's windows.

Again, she felt foolish. She saw the pousada doorman cutting across the park, still in uniform. Shifts must be ending about this time, she realized, and some people will take shortcuts across the grass and even through the mulched flower beds.

She heard the footsteps again, from somewhere in back of her.

She turned and called out, "Is someone there?"

There was no reply. Now the footsteps came from behind the bushes to her left.

"Hello. Is someone there?" she said more loudly.

It was the lack of a response that worried her. She picked up her pace, shadows catching her peripheral vision and disappearing when she looked at them. Her subconscious brain took over, her eyes widening, her nostrils sampling the air, ready to fight, ready to flee. And she started to run.

It was the wrong thing to do.

9

When she awoke in her Casa do Mar bedroom, Catarina was happy to hear Anton snoring. The sound that was infamous for marital discord did not bother her. Her husband's soft snorts, much like those of a beloved dog's, had always been a soothing reminder that she was not alone. Indeed, he hadn't left her side since he saw her in the pousada lobby, even fitting himself into the back seat of Carlos's plane for the short flight back home, and she had snuggled against him the entire time, holding the bouquet of white freesia between them.

She hadn't chided herself for the fear she'd felt in the park, or for letting that fear distract her from the vine she'd tripped over before hitting the ground so hard. Someone had been watching her in the park, waiting for her to be alone. She knew who it was, and she had a pretty good idea why. But to tell Anton now would work against him.

As usual, Anton awoke to find himself alone. This morning, however, he felt so much more alone than usual. He hadn't let Catarina out of his sight since he'd seen her in the pousada lobby, limping and holding a throbbing wrist against her chest. When she told him what had happened, he wished he'd been able to shield her from the fear, protect her from the fall, save her from the scrapes and bruises. Even when she soaked in one of the bubble baths she enjoyed, he'd insisted that she leave the door open, and he'd listened for sounds of some calamity he couldn't put into words.

He hadn't allowed Catarina to dissuade him when he called Carlos to fly her home to Casa do Mar that night, that hour. Later, after she'd fallen asleep, he'd run his hand over the scratches on her leg and, yes, he'd silently let two tears run down his cheek. To think that his Catarina had been so frightened.

He pulled on his at-home pants, softly worn and warm, and went to look for her. Overnight fog was moving out of the channel quickly on swift air currents. The ocean was stippled with whitecaps. He turned to let the salted air wind rake his face, hoping it would carry off some of the heaviness in his heart. Maybe Beto had been right. Maybe age was playing with him. Optimism and good cheer had been woven into his character so much so that even as a grown man, he'd been teased about being too happy, not serious enough. That quality had always been able to screen the challenges that life put in his path. But yesterday he'd let his frustration with the investigations get to him. Then, in the way that happens to people, he'd been reminded of how much worse life could be—and of how much good fortune he still had to counterweigh any bad fortune that came his way.

He'd wanted Catarina to have a late, slow start to her day, even planned to brew a large pot of coffee the way she liked it, with plenty of steamed milk and sugar, and to pour it for her while she sat in her favorite chair overlooking Casa do Mar's green hill. (Neither much liked eating in bed.) He'd pictured them sitting in silence and giving themselves over to warm breezes that carried the scents of brine and roses and the cinnamon from their morning pastries.

Instead, he found her taking laundry off the line. In the morning light, he saw the bruise rising purple and blue under her left eye, and he winced. "Does it hurt, my redhaired girl?" he asked, and he ran a finger very lightly over the mark.

"It is a bit tender," she kissed his fingers, "but your touch soothes it." Her face radiated calm and confidence—in him and in herself.

Lori saw them through the Casa do Bosque window, his arm around her waist, her head nuzzled against his chest. Back in New York, she'd carried with her a haze of discontent, so mild it was elusive, a consciousness that she wanted something different for her life—but she didn't know what. She'd known for many months now: she wanted what Anton and Catarina had.

Her thoughts wandered to Ethan, who was due to arrive that afternoon, and to Carlos, who'd been a constant presence in her life for over a year. The two men could not have been more different. Ethan with his interest in the big issues of politics, climate change, and philosophy, and his plans to experience so much. Her place in those dreams would be smaller but the dreams would be so much bigger. Carlos, on the other hand, was content with his world. He wanted for little and appreciated a lot. His dreams were of family and simpler pleasures.

What, she asked herself, were her dreams?

They were about to start final walkthroughs of the cottages, opening shutters, watering flower pots, making up beds—all the usual things they did to help their guests remember their time on the Azores as a wonderful experience—when Liliana appeared.

"What's the word, hummingbird?" Lori asked. The first time Liliana had heard Lori say *See you later, alligator!* and suggest its rhyming response *In a while crocodile!* she'd broken out in giggles. Since then, Lori had taken great pleasure finding as many such rhymes as she could, and each time she was rewarded with the same bubbles of laughter.

"I finished my book," she said in a voice that said she was bored and wanted something fun to do.

Toni appeared next to her and said in a similar voice, "We finished our game." Beside him, Nuno put on his best pathetic look. "We're bored."

Catarina eyed them. "Boredom does not mean you *have* nothing to do; it means you have not found something you *want* to do. As the French say, *je m'ennuie*, I bore myself."

Her children were familiar with this speech, and there were a few moments of horror when she went on, "If you cannot think of anything you want to do, I have something for you to do." It was not what they wanted to hear.

She handed Toni a bucket. "It's heavy," he groaned.

She handed Nuno a sponge. "I don't know how to use it," he looked up pitiably.

She handed Liliana a bottle of disinfectant. "I don't like that smell," she wrinkled her nose.

"It's just disinfectant. Follow me. I'll show you what to do." She waited for what she knew would come next: the sudden remembering of all sorts of things they did in fact want to do.

In retrospect, it had been too easy. The children dispersed, and they heard nothing more from them for the next three hours, until Liliana reappeared and said, "I think we need help."

They smelled the cookies before they saw the chaos. The kitchen table was covered with flour, the sink was filled with bowls, spoons, and measuring cups, and there were stacks of cookies on cooling racks.

The bakers had done their taste testing. Toni's mouth was ringed in chocolate and Nuno was licking his fingers.

"They're to sell for our football team," Toni said proudly. "If we make it to the championship, we need to have money to buy souvenirs."

"We have two problems here," Anton used his serious voice.

The boys held their breaths.

"First, it is not *if* we make it to the championship, it is *when* we make it to the championship."

They raised their eyebrows, eyes still waiting for the punishment to come.

"Second," Anton's face looked grim, "I don't know if these are good enough to sell." He sampled a cookie. "I'm not sure you put in enough sugar. Lori would you try?"

She took a bite and chewed slowly. "Mine might have a bit too much sugar. Catarina?"

Catarina considered. "If the dough was not mixed properly, some cookies will have too little sugar and others will have too much. We will have to taste each one."

They divided the cookies—even the burnt, underdone, tiny, and oversize ones—among themselves, brushed the crumbs from three chairs, poured three glasses of milk, and sat down.

The children were confused. They opened their mouths to protest but couldn't come up with the words.

Then they saw Anton's grin break through and Lori laugh out loud and Catarina take out the plastic containers she used to take cookies to bake sales.

The silliness had felt good. That was something they shared, joy in being childlike. Perhaps it was because each one had had childhood taken from them. It had changed them in different ways, though. Anton had laid claim to his right to remain a carefree child. Catarina had become an adult long before she should have. Lori had denied her loss altogether.

With twelve hands, it didn't take long to clean up, but as Anton scrubbed the kitchen sink, a thought niggled at him, just out of reach. He'd been reminded of something relevant to their investigation.

Lori recognized the tall, loose-limbed figure walking barefoot across the damp grass.

They both picked up their pace and met close to the fig tree outside Casa do Bosque. The hug—and then the kiss— seemed natural despite the four-month separation. The last time they'd been this close, they'd been dancing, and it had been romantic in every way she could think of.

Close up, she saw his hair was shorter, standing up in blond spikes, and he'd gained weight. The planes of his face had softened, his jaw was rounder. That first hug confirmed one thing was the same: he still had a well-muscled athlete's body under the sports shirt and jeans.

"What brings you here?" she could feel the nerves in her voice.

"One answer would be *a grant*." He kissed her lightly on the cheek. "A better answer might be *being closer to you*." He kissed her again.

She didn't know how she felt about either his answer or his kisses, and it must have shown on her face, because he quickly added, "The grant work is interesting, exploring the underwater craters around Fayal and Terceira. The scientist in him was carried away, "Imagine what could be there—not just gold and silver from ships that went down during the Age of Exploration but the detritus." He spoke of what others deemed ocean trash with as much reverence as the gold and silver. "Picture it, a world of explorers and thinkers and pirates, shrouded by water, waiting to be brought back."

Lori had heard the same excitement when he talked about his previous jobs, the most recent one unearthing underwater ruins for the Turkish government and the one before that as an advisor to the Obama administration on the exploration of Hawaiian coastal waters.

The moment he pulled into the Casa do Mar driveway, Carlos spotted Ethan, and he hurried down the hill to meet him. It wasn't a matter of wanting to insert himself between Ethan and Lori; the two men showed no apparent competition for Lori's attention and in fact liked each other's company. Both were adventurers, although in different realms. Carlos (whose poor eyesight had nearly kept him from a pilot's license) flew the skies. Ethan (so nearsighted he had special scuba goggles made to see underwater) swam the seas. Both worked hard and enjoyed the times when they weren't working.

Some of the differences between the two men were external. While Carlos took pride in the way he dressed, Ethan generally threw on what was close at hand—today, wrinkled khakis, an old sweater, mismatched socks—and still looked good. Carlos's hair was always neatly trimmed and combed. Ethan had run his fingers through longish hair after his morning shower and hadn't touched it since. Carlos was closely shaven and smooth-cheeked; his friend was not.

The way in which they had come to see Lori's future was shaping up to be another difference between them, and that became apparent soon after she left them to check the Casa do Mar bookings.

"I think she's enjoyed this time away from the life she lived in New York," Ethan was saying.

"She does love our islands," said Carlos.

"I wonder how much longer she'll be here."

His words flicked at Carlos's heart. "She has no need to leave."

"Perhaps there's no need to leave right now, but a woman like her isn't going to be happy on a quiet, isolated island after years of flying around the globe to parasail and dive and climb mountains."

"You can do all those things here." To himself, he added, "And I can fly her anywhere she wants to go."

Ethan gave a laugh, not a meanspirited one but one that indicated he thought it was funny to compare what he saw as Lori's future with the life Carlos was talking about. What's more, the laugh was a collegial one that said he thought they were sharing the same funny thought.

They reached the top of the hill and the family group settling in on the patio.

Ethan stretched in his chair and linked his curled fingers on top his head. The gesture caught Anton's attention—and his heart. He flashed back to his own mother, sitting outside his boyhood home and relaxing in that same way. Such a gesture must have come from Ethan's own mother, the older sister he'd barely known before she emigrated to America. What came to his mind was the realization of how easily such traits could be passed down, and he wondered what of him would be found in Liliana and Toni, and perhaps in their children. He made a mental note to always show the best of himself to them.

Carlos and Ethan had taken seats on either side of Lori, although each was occupied with people other than her. For Carlos, it was Anton and Toni and two of Toni's friends, and the talk was all about football. The Santa Maria tournament was coming up, and the winning boys' team would play the other islands' teams to claim the championship. Toni and his friends hung on Carlos's every word; not only was he tall and flew his own plane, he'd been on the championship team when he was their age.

On the other side of Lori, Ethan had his own followers. Liliana and her friends, having become (at least in their own minds) almost grown women, were having a conversation (in their minds, an adult conversation) with Ethan, raptly listening to every story about his recent diving adventures in Turkey (and drooling over the good-looking stranger just a bit.)

And Anton sat there, weighing a marriage that would officialize Lori as a member of his family against a marriage that promised to keep her geographically close.

It was an evening to stay at home. Fog had become drizzle and then small raindrops, and by the time Estela came to pick up her son, large ones were spattering the kitchen window.

Nuno was at the table, playing video games with Toni.

"He's been spending more time here than at his own house," she said to Catarina.

"They have been happily busy all day." After the cookie making—and the cookie-making cleanup—they had gone off for outside play before settling in for yet more inside play.

The two boys looked at each other, accomplices in boyhood pranks and adventures, just like Anton.

Catarina noticed tension on her young friend's face that went beyond the usual strains of being a single mother who was both working and trying to get her teaching certificate. "Shall we give the boys a few minutes to finished their game?"

That was met with enthusiastic whoops from both boys.

"In Toni's room," she said firmly, "so we can enjoy a quiet cup of coffee." She gave Anton the shortest of glances, and he retreated with them. After so many years together, words were seldom needed.

She poured a cup of coffee for Estela. "Are you excited for the start of the school year?"

Estela's mouth relaxed just a bit.

"Just think, you will get your degree at the same time as you finish one year as kindergarten aide. Soon you will have your own classroom."

A small smile came to Estela's face. Whatever was worrying her, it was not her upcoming job.

"I like your new haircut," Catarina said. Rather than her usual sleek ponytail, recently Estela's head had been topped with a mass of frothy curls. With the new haircut had come a new color and more makeup than usual, and until today Estela had been wearing a half-smile that never left her face. Catarina had a hunch—and Catarina's hunches usually proved true—that her friend was in love.

She knew that Estela had been seeing Rufo, the mechanic in a nearby village who kept the family's Volvo running despite the abuse heaped on it by Anton. All signs had been that the relationship was a happy one, and Estela had been seen taking long walks on the beach with him and sharing meals with him at nearly every restaurant on the island.

"Do I remember that you ate in the new Italian restaurant in São Pedro?" Catarina asked.

That was when Estela's lips tightened again. "Yes."

She let the silence build as what Estela was holding in slowly rose. "Rufo is moving to Portugal."

It was a common enough story. "How do you feel about that?"

"He wants us to marry." There was no energy in her voice.

Catarina waited. A proposal was not usually cause for such turmoil.

Sombra, so attuned human emotions, came close and laid a warm chin on Estela's legs. She wiggled her fingers in the dog's dark fur. "Nuno and I have a life here. After his father left us, it was hard for him. Now he's settled, and I have a chance to be a teacher. I know people here. I have friends here."

"Could you postpone making a decision until Rufo is settled, and you have your certificate?"

The response—no—came quickly. "I'm pregnant." The tears she had been holding in sheeted down her cheeks when Catarina embraced her. "If we go, how will Nuno feel? If we stay, how will the new baby feel? What if he insists we join him? What if he doesn't want us to join him?"

There could be no right or wrong answers, Catarina told her, because we never know the future. We can only take the path we think is best at the time. And the paths we choose not to take will be left behind.

Outside, thunder rolled and Casa do Mar blinked into view with every flash of lightening. Even with Estela and Nuno gone, it was a tight squeeze in the kitchen. Carlos arrived with dripping wet hair, still looking perfectly groomed. Ethan raced over from Casa do Bosque—vacated by Lori for his visit—barefoot and wearing a UMass tee-shirt. Sombra scratched at the door but with one look at the wet world outside, she turned around and retreated to a corner of the warm, dry kitchen. The children occupied another corner, dividing their attention between their bowls and a deck of cards. The adults sat in a tight ring around the table, enjoying Catarina's fish stew, which was one of Anton's favorites. (Then again, nearly everything she made was one of his favorites.)

Start to finish, the day had been…so normal. It's what they'd needed. They were ready to carry on with what had to be done.

They may have been ready to carry on with what had to be done, but others were not. By the next morning, word had spread: the island's trio of detectives (who undoubtedly were more talented than any specially trained detectives elsewhere) were investigating a suspicious death. Naturally, that had attracted people, and Casa do Mar was buzzing with close friends and bare acquaintances, all wanting insider information on the investigation.

There were also those who wanted access to Anton and Catarina for other reasons. Leon Machado, a local businessman with political aspirations, was pushing for development. Matias Cabral wanted to discuss ideas for the living heritage trust. And now that it was known she would head the island's elementary school, Catarina had a stream of well-wishers, advice-givers, and favor-askers. Most were supporters (who were thrilled to have such a well-trained academic and one they liked) and a couple were subtle detractors (who had wanted to see the position filled by someone with a longer history on the island.) "We'll come by to help decorate the classrooms next week," more than one said. It would be both to show community spirit and to keep an eye on the new principal.

It wasn't until afternoon that Anton was able to share his news. Like that crackling of ice just before a thaw, it gave them hope things would soon change.

To begin with, Luis had texted. "Frau Meickle is certain that the *Sirena* is too small and, as she put it, 'much too boxy' to have been the yacht she saw in Breakwater Cove last Tuesday morning, so that confirms what our gambling policemen from Lisbon said. But she couldn't say whether it looked more like the *Iaso* or the *Doura*."

They compared pictures of the two boats. Both had the latest profiles for yachts: bullet-sleek and hard-edged. It was hard to see the differences.

"If Fabi is to be believed, Ángelo fell from one of these." Anton's tone said that he was not convinced of Fabi's veracity. He just couldn't picture such a frail young man climbing over a railing and falling to his death.

"The *Iaso* is set to leave the islands tomorrow. Without a compelling reason, it will be out of our jurisdiction by noon. The president has refused to have it held." As Anton said it, he saw the president's point of view. The evidence wasn't just slim; there was no evidence. To make the matter worse, the *Iaso* was part of a close-knit community of vessels that paid premium prices to stop in the Azores.

The news on the *Doura* was both bad and very bad. For the past few months, it had been monitored by a consortium of Mediterranean countries and was suspected of trafficking in refugees from African territories suffering from war, from drought, from famine. "We're waiting for more from that group but right now, the ship is nowhere to be found."

Dr. Nunes also had news for them. He'd received Ángelo's DNA profile. As with every report he delivered, both what he'd posted and what he'd told Anton in a brief call were accompanied by his usual caveats, including *This only reflects probabilities.* and *Nothing is final.* All that being said, the lab found a curious mix of ancestry in Ángelo's DNA: Spanish and Maya that might reflect Central American ancestry, along with threads most commonly found in isolated Dutch and Russian groups.

As soon as she saw it, Lori knew it was the clue to Ángelo's origin that they'd been waiting for. She did a quick search for any populations that showed that unusual combination of Maya-Spanish and Dutch-Russian. As it turned out, only two countries in Central America had any appreciable population of Russian Mennonites, a persecuted diasporic population with both Dutch and Russian ancestry. Mexico and Belize.

In his official capacity, Anton sent queries to the authorities—every authority they could come up with, from the federal police of both countries to their consulates to Interpol. Each query was accompanied by Dr. Nunes's report and a picture of Ángelo's tattoo, and each ended with the same plea: Please help us to find his home.

"In connection to some medical waste that's been found washing up on nearby beaches, including Breakwater Cove," Anton went on, "Dr. Nunes picked up on something else. He did a toxicology screen on traces left in one of the syringes. It was the same sedative he found in Ángelo." All three of them knew that was important. They just couldn't figure out why.

They moved on to Martim's murder. "Police weren't able to turn up a single lead on a motive—no one who might have wanted revenge, no one Martim owed, no one who could have benefitted from his death, and nothing of interest from Martim's time in prison."

"I feel like we're narrowing the possibilities with Ángelo's death but not getting anywhere with Martim's," Lori said, discouraged.

"Ah, but I have saved the most promising news for last."

After a complete forensic sweep, the police had returned the boat where Martim died to its owner. Just as happens when someone spots a minor change in a familiar place, a crooked curtain fold, a door left ajar, a dropped flower petal, the boat's owner immediately saw what had been missed. In the crevice between two deck planks, he found a memory card.

Lori peered at the picture Luis had sent. "It looks like a match for one I saw in Martim's room."

"I'll have Luis send you the memory card this afternoon."

"I'd just as soon go to São Miguel myself. I'll hitch a ride with Carlos in an hour."

"And we will join you later." It would be for Martim's funeral.

Lori rushed off to throw a few things in an overnight bag and meet Carlos at the airfield.

By the time Lori was airborne, the work day several time zones to the west had started. Anton's plea to Interpol and twenty or so police agencies in Mexico and Belize had been read and replies were coming in. One after another said there was no record of a missing boy matching Ángelo's description. One of the Belizean authorities said otherwise.

Captain Jesús Rodriguez sent a picture of the crest of the Sociedad por los Niños Perdidos, The Society for Lost Children, SNP. It was a dead ringer for Ángelo's tattoo. The only thing missing were the numbers: *311*. SNP was a quasi-religious group with an estate on the coast in Corozal Town. It had been taking in children since the 1950s, first orphans and more recently *orphans of poverty* whose parents were too poor to care for them and had brought them to be cared for.

A young woman had filed a report with the local police three years ago. She claimed she'd been raised in SNP's isolated orphanage until the age of sixteen, when she walked away from the farm field she'd been working. 'Escaped' was the word she'd used. She was asking for help finding her brother, who had also been raised in the orphanage.

After a disclaimer that stood between defense and apology, the captain said they'd made a call to the orphanage sometime after the sister's fifth visit and had been told, as his sister had been told, that the boy had left. His whereabouts were unknown. Captain Rodriguez read from the report, "They use our facilities all the time, then they disappear." Given the boy's age of fifteen, the issue had been dropped.

Anton's parting statement also stood between opposing stances, understanding for the predicament of an understaffed police force and a threat to make their negligence an international issue.

Catarina scribbled a note for Anton, and he added one more thing: He would look favorably on efforts to locate the sister and try to match her DNA to that of the boy in Dr. Nunes's report.

"Back to the beginning. Back to the beginning," Anton muttered as he paced the grass outside the old barn, passing in front of Catarina's rocking chair, where she sat scratching Sombra's ear. "We started with what Frau Meickle said and the Vieiras confirmed: There were three boats in Breakwater Cove the morning that Ángelo died. If you believe Fabi is correct, he came from either the *Iaso* or the *Doura*."

At that point, Anton was thinking aloud. He wasn't looking at Catarina's face. He didn't see that she was beginning to doubt herself. She considered a connection between Fabiano's family and the de la Rosas: Marta, the woman Gustavo de la Rosa had somehow twisted his father's arm into hiring to take care of Natalia. If Natalia married, Marta might not be needed. Her job, the job that helped to keep the Deníz financial ship from sinking, would be in jeopardy. *What if Fabi had reason to lie? What if he was covering for someone? What if he had killed Martim himself?*

"Wait," she said. "If we confront the wrong person, it could alert whoever is really responsible."

That person has killed before, possibly twice, thought Anton, and he could again if cornered.

Time was running out. He called Luis for a small army of agents to help with surveillance, starting with the de la Rosa house. "I want eyes on every single person in that family."

Catarina sadly mouthed another name.

"And locate Fabiano Deníz. Keep him under surveillance, too. And his mother..." He lifted his head, trying to remember.

"Marta," whispered Catarina.

"Has Fredi been brought in?" He hung his head. "Let me know as soon as he's been found. Any news on the *Doura*?"

It was the only piece of news that he could rest a little easier about. The *Doura* had crossed into Italian waters and been boarded by the Italian Coast Guard, its human cargo locked in the hold. It had been confirmed as off the coast of Portugal on the morning of Ángelo's murder and crossing into international waters when Martim died. The possibilities were narrowing.

The remaining hours of the day wore on with calls they forced themselves to answer, half-hearted attempts to make plans for the next few weeks, and a quiet family dinner. When Toni asked for a cookie before going to bed, something tickled Anton's brain for a fleeting second. He knew it was important but, as happens when your conscious mind chases a dream, his thought evaporated before he could latch on to just why it was so important.

For Catarina, one of the exciting things about her new job would be spending her days close to a library. She liked the physical presence of books, seeing the lineup of colors and titles on the spines, catching the dry, dusty smell they picked up in their time on the shelves, feeling the velvety pages under her fingers. Her own books had been in boxes for almost three years. Even if she unpacked them, there was nowhere for them to go until a home was carved out of the cavernous Casa do Mar barn. So she had resisted, borrowing books from the Portuguese-only collection at the local library and giving into e-books.

She fell asleep to thoughts of opening a box or two and filling the bookshelves in her new office with a few of her favorites—the poetry of Frost, Chekov's short stories, Austen's novels. She could almost smell them. She could almost feel them. And it made her so happy that Anton, tiptoeing into the bedroom after his late-night routine of keeping in touch with people he knew (and snacking on leftovers from dinner) could still see the smile on her sleeping face.

He had just pulled the covers up high and opened his latest thriller, when Catarina's phone trilled. He reached over her and touched the green button, ready to blast whoever was disturbing his wife's sleep after her disturbing experience on São Miguel.

Before he could say a word, he heard a breathless Maria Rosa whisper, "Catarina! Catarina are you there?"

"It's Anton. What wrong?" His first thought was of her children.

"Come. Can you come? There's someone here."

By then, Catarina was awake. "Stay here," he said in that tone his voice took on when he was taking charge of a situation. "Maria Rosa says there's someone over there. Probably just an animal or a neighbor taking a shortcut home." But he couldn't imagine why such an unexcitable, capable person had reacted as she had on an island so safe that people hadn't replaced front-door keys that had been lost generations before.

"No. Maria Rosa has been worried…frightened…about something for a while now. I am coming."

They could just make out the house across the road, dark and screened by tall, slender trees. Anton tried the front door knob. It rattled, but it was locked. "Maria Rosa," he pounded. "Open the door."

A small shuffling sound. A click. The door swung open, and Anton was across the small living room and in the back hall within three seconds. He swung his phone flashlight in wide arcs, across two faces with closed eyes, across a bed with covers thrown off, behind a shower curtain and into closets, into the room that served as ancillary clinic and home office.

"I don't see anyone, Maria Rosa."

Huddled by the front door with Catarina, she pointed through a window. "Outside. Maybe. I'm sorry. I overreacted. There's no one."

"Tell me what frightened you," Catarina squeezed her friend's arm.

"I'm sorry," she repeated.

Some people have to be convinced to unburden themselves. They feel that kindnesses are offered out of social obligation, and so the offer must be made several times, beyond the norms of social obligation. Such was the case with Maria Rosa.

After a few minutes, she admitted, "I know someone's been around the house recently. There've been little things no one else might notice. A branch I kicked aside on my way out wasn't there when I returned. The end of the potato vine I'm growing on the back patio was crushed. I keep pulling shut the door to that little shed in back, but it's open again in the morning."

Anton was going to point out that there were many explanations other than someone skulking around, intent on doing her harm, when she said it herself. "On their own, none of them mean much, I know. It could be an animal or a child or my faulty memory. But together they made me worry...overreact."

Before leaving, Anton checked the grounds. "I'll call Felipe when I get home. He will look into this." With regret for the implications, he added, "Lock the door until Felipe gets back to you." He, too, had a feeling that something wasn't quite right.

10

While Carlos was flying a group of businessmen to Fayal, Lori was sitting in a cliffside park in Ponta Delgado, working her mind through the mysterious paths of the cyberworld to a place where Martim's pictures lay. The memory card was her last chance to reach that place, her last chance to get some indication of what Martim was doing in his last minutes alive.

His phone had been returned by the police, and his family had immediately turned it over to her, along with the password. But it had proved as much of a dead end as his laptop. Yes, there were thousands of pictures and, yes, they were backed up to the cloud, but the most recent ones had been taken five days before his death.

Martim's camera was old, a gift for his eighteenth birthday. The memory card very old, practically obsolete compared to current USB drives that store 128 gigs and more. That wasn't the problem. As in isolated communities of any culture, from American prairies to Alpine villages, the people of São Miguel tended to hold onto all sorts of things. You never knew when they might prove useful. It had taken just two phone calls for one of Luis's agents to borrow the necessary reader from a baker in a neighboring village.

The edge of the card had been bent, either when it was ejected from the camera or when it was extracted from between the deck planks. That wasn't the problem, either. Lori had gently pressed it flat and slipped it into the reader.

The problem was that—as old as it was—the card was password protected and, unlike the phone or the laptop, there was no repository for the password and no link to a remote server.

Hacking or court orders would get her nowhere. Lori knew she could make endless attempts to enter a password—or just a single one before everything was wiped clean.

She hoped a solution was out there and took herself for a walk to clear her head. There was nothing like the salt air that blew over islands in the middle of a vast ocean. The ocean swam in front of her watery eyes. She inhaled deeply, and her flesh rose into goosebumps. Unlike the hardier Catarina and the almost famously hardy Anton, she felt the cold that could suddenly come over the islands when winds shifted.

She considered the passwords Martim might have chosen. At the top of her list was the name of his plane, *No Céo*. Then there were the usual birthdates and childhood pets and favorite teachers that Rafe had been happy to provide her with. Or it might simply be the one he'd used for his phone and laptop. The list was long.

Thank goodness for *Keychain*, thought Lori. No more decorating desktops and computers with sticky notes that displayed your passwords to the world. At least Martim had stored all his other log-ins in *Keychain*, in case he forgot them. She slowed her steps. Not *all*. He'd been worried enough that he might forget the simple combination to his locker that he wrote it down. Perhaps he'd done the same sort of thing with other combinations that weren't stored in *Keychain*, like his plane door and car door...and camera. Perhaps he'd stored them in some other way.

She ran the last few steps to the apartment, pushed opened the door and didn't bother to close it. The phone and laptop were still on the age-darkened table that belonged to the landlady, the memory card still in the large bowl Carlos had bought to hold fruit.

It took less than two minutes to find the folder on Martim's laptop. *To Remember*. The notations were personal but hardly cryptic. *No Céo com Martim*, his plane's name, and eight digits. *Airfield Locker* and the padlock combination they'd used. *Camera* and 8-5-2006, his eighteenth birthday, the day his parents had given him the camera.

She reached for the reader. *Here goes nothing*. She gently pushed the card against the slot. The previously bent edge caught for a moment, then clicked into place. She whispered what she hoped was the password three times. Holding her breath, she entered it. The screen flickered. Isolated pixels appeared and disappeared. A menu popped up showing a long list of dates. *Yes!*

The triumph of victory was short lived. The most recent date was seven years ago.

Lori got up and stretched. She texted Anton and Catarina the bad news: the memory card wasn't the one Martim had been using the night he died but an old one that had somehow been tossed out into the boat that night. She went to close the front door, but stopped halfway there and smiled.

And she ran back inside.

She could see Martim in all his eighteen-year-old excitement, rushing out to take pictures with his new camera, not stopping to change the factory settings. Made before such devices updated themselves automatically, his camera had never shown the correct date and time.

The pictures may have been time-stamped seven years ago, but they clearly had been taken more recently. The last set showed what had indeed shaped up to be a beautiful sunset at the marina, a fiery sky reflected in the water and clouds and off the hulls of luxury yachts and humble fishing boats.

Is there something Martim saw, something I'm missing? Lori squinted at picture after picture. She enlarged them until they dissolved into incoherent pixels. She saw nothing unusual, nothing that could have cost Martim his life.

Her only hope now was Matthew Cunningham. The owner of a successful multinational corporation, he'd been a suspect in the first crime they'd investigated. Since then he'd saved Casa do Mar from financial ruin, become Anton's closest long-distance buddy, rescued her career with a job, and been more than understanding when she left that career to follow her heart back to the Azores.

With Matthew's ties to the tech world, he might have a lead to someone who could enhance the pictures and tell her why someone had taken an old camera when they killed Martim.

Martim's funeral began in a Vila do Porto church that dated to 1702, and it was as traditional as expected, a ritual virtually indistinguishable from those two hundred years ago.

There were many more people there than someone unfamiliar with the Azores would expect. Older women dabbed at their eyes with handkerchiefs. A contingent of former classmates had come from as far away as Madeira. All of the pilots who flew with Martim were there with their families. The Sousas sat quietly in the front pew, Rafe and Joca tightly flanking Alicia. The only member of the de la Rosa family who came was Natalia, who sobbed quietly in the back row, a pile of discarded tissues beside her.

Carlos was there, of course, and beside him an empty space waited for Lori.

The casket in front of altar was open. Martim had said he wanted to be cremated, but this was for his mother, and he would have understood. Prayers were said. Hymns were sung. Eulogies were given. The padre tried to offer solace and hope for an afterlife when people would see their friend, their brother, their son again. The space next to Carlos remained empty the entire time.

Once, twice, three times, Catarina looked at Anton and mouthed, "Lori?"

On the way to the cemetery, Anton texted Lori. There was no response. Carlos would know more, but he was one of the pall bearers, so they had to wait until after Martim's coffin had been lowered into his grave and the mourners had left for a late lunch at the Sousas.

It was hard to find parking anywhere near the small house. People filled the driveway and the front lawn. They sat on the front porch and on the front steps. A slow stream moved into the house to offer condolences to the family and back out again, holding paper napkins and glasses of wine and plates of food, all provided by women in the neighborhood who kept bringing platters and bottles from nearby houses.

Anton and Catarina scanned the scene until they spotted Carlos in the living room. "She was gone when I woke up," he said at the same time Catarina said, "We thought she would be with you."

Further discussion was ended when Rafe joined them and introduced his family. They said the words people do when they want to offer comfort, even though everyone knew there were no words that could soften the loss.

Alicia grabbed Anton's sleeve. "You will find who did this to my son?"

"We're working on it right now and will continue without stopping," Anton told the family. It crossed his mind that perhaps that was what Lori was doing. "Lori did look at the pictures on the memory card the police found." There was no need to remind them where it had been found. "Unfortunately, it was an old one."

The animosity between the Sousas and the de la Rosas exploded in rapid-fire questions from Rafe. "Have you questioned de la Rosa? Do you know what he's capable of? Do you know what he did to our family? Do you know what he did to Martim?"

His father warned him, "Enough."

"No. Not enough. He destroyed Martim's life, just like he destroyed his children's lives."

"I called," Rafe said as though trying to exonerate himself from not having done something more to save his brother's life. He looked at Catarina, then at Lori. "Remember, I told you?" He bobbed his head up and down, asking them to confirm that, which they did. To Anton, he said again, "I called Natalia's cell and the house number."

Catarina could see Henrique de la Rosa ignoring any call that came in from Martim's family.

"He did it, you know he did it, or he got Gustavo to do it for him."

His mother's weary voice broke in, "You don't know that."

Anton tried to reassure him, "I've had his alibi checked. He was with his family."

"Then they're lying!"

"I promise to check it again."

Alicia's weary voice broke in, "Don't bother. I was watching the house that night. I knew Martim was meeting Natalia, and I wanted to talk to her father. I saw her leave the house. And I saw Henrique drag her out of her car."

"Then Gustavo did it!" Rafe's voice crescendoed.

"No, my love, Gustavo was standing in the doorway, watching, not doing a thing to help his sister, not saying a word to protest what his father was doing."

"I stayed until long after dark, long after... None of them left the house."

Joca's jaw had fallen. Everyone else followed his gaze, which was fixed on the doorway where Natalia and Gustavo de la Rosa stood.

Rafe's muscles tensed. He crossed the room in three steps and, inches from his former friend's face, he muttered, "You're not welcome here."

"Rafe," Gustavo pleaded.

"Leave."

"We should hear what Gustavo has to say," Alicia said, but her words sounded far from kind.

In agreement about something, the de la Rosa siblings nodded to each other.

"My father has thrown his weight around for the last time," Natalia said for everyone in the room to hear, and quite a few had packed in. "Gustavo?"

Words poured out of his mouth on a single breath. "Martim was not alone when he took... I was the one who took the boat." He swallowed hard. "I was the one who ran it into the dock. I went into the water to get the child. Everyone assumed I'd come from the shore."

Alicia took Joca's hand.

Having begun the confession, Gustavo seemed relieved to finish it. "Martim was... We'd been drinking. He didn't remember it was entirely my fault," he let out a deep sigh with the secret. "My father convinced... No, it was me. Martim was still passed out in the boat, the child was in the ambulance, and the police were questioning people. I walked a few meters away to call my father." He held the gaze of the Sousa family. "I swear to God, I was calling to ask about how I should talk to the police. My father... I allowed my father to convince me to let Martim take the entire blame."

From the moment Gustavo made that call, every action his father cornered him into led to another darker corner, from denying he was in the boat to refusing to testify on Martim's behalf.

Natalia looked vindictive. "In exchange for not saying Gustavo was also in the boat, our father offered Martim money."

Until that moment, no one—not Anton, not Catarina, not Carlos, not even Martim's family—had given a second thought to how a young man of such modest means could afford a plane of his own, one *free of encumbrances* according to the paperwork.

"How could you, Gustavo?" Beatriz asked her childhood friend.

Again, the siblings' eyes met, and Natalia nodded for Gustavo to continue.

This was the hardest part. You could see it on his face. "My father does not approve of the way I want to live my life, the way I will live my life. He threatened to tell everyone," he drew himself up, "that I am homosexual." The almost outdated term came out awkwardly, probably the first time he'd said it aloud. "If I said anything about having been there, he said he would make sure I got nothing except being laughed off my island."

"The bastard." That had come from Beatrix.

Rafe was not placated. "So your father—you, Gustavo— took four years of my brother's life—took his chance to join the Air Force!—so you wouldn't be embarrassed about something that embarrasses no one anymore?"

"It was more..." but Gustavo couldn't go on. Because he still didn't know what it really was.

Catarina did. Any child raised with a domineering parent who holds and makes a point of promoting certain beliefs finds it difficult to accept the contrary. The children of survivalists truly believe their world will come under attack. The children of polygamists truly believe God ordains plural marriages. The children of men like de la Rosa truly believe that they are so flawed by their sexual orientation that they will lose not only their family's approval but the approval of their entire community. Gustavo feared being left with no one.

"We must remember that people do not always behave in a way that is logical to us," Catarina said. "It is true that Gustavo committed a crime. It is true that he was not honorable after—"

Rafe interrupted, "Not honorable? Is that all it was?"

Natalia came to her brother's defense. "Gustavo tried. Gustavo has always tried. When we were younger, he traded his chance to go away to school for my chance to have Marta—"

Again Rafe interrupted, this time explosively, "He traded my brother's life for an inheritance!"

Gustavo only hung his head.

None of players knew how much of what Gustavo had done was altruistic and how much was selfish, or how much harder he could have fought his father's influence. Not even Gustavo knew.

Alicia's voice came out on gasps of air. "You let my poor son believe he was to blame for causing that family such pain." To Anton, she said, "I want Gustavo charged for what he did."

"I'm sorry to say it is too late." He left her to think it was because too much time had passed. The truth was that her son was dead, so there was no longer an aggrieved party. "But people know now," he looked around a room of people who had hung on every word.

"My father will not get everything he wants. Job or no job, I'm leaving him. I have friends in Lisbon and will start there."

Gustavo looked at the Sousas. "I will stay and if you allow me, I will try to make this up to you in some small way."

To Martim's family, it was as though the words had not been spoken. They turned away to talk to others in the room.

Lori shared Anton's inability to let go of a problem, although for her it wasn't limited to those few-and-far-between times when they were scrambling to keep their world right. When her phone had pinged with a text from Matthew Cunningham at 3 a.m., she hadn't fully fallen asleep yet.

Check email. And take care of yourself.

She'd made sure that Carlos hadn't been woken up and had slipped out from under the covers slowly to keep him in the cocoon of their body warmth. Her thumbs were on the screen before she'd taken a step away from the bed.

10K THANKS!

The email was from the head of Matthew's IT department and with it came the link to a program he thought could clear up the images from Martim's camera. She ran the image files through the new program.

The sequence of sunset pictures had become so familiar she could see them with her eyes closed. The harbor. The lights appearing on the far shore. The pleasure craft returning. The yacht hulls gleaming as the waterfront opened up for a night of dining. And at the center, a honeyed sun oozing into the Atlantic, coloring the sky with fiery reds and vibrant corals.

But no. The sunset wasn't at the center of every shot. Toward the end, Martim's attention had shifted. He'd taken several pictures of wine being uncorked by a group of middle-aged people watching the sunset from the end of a dock. It took her half an hour to determine that not a single one of their faces came close to looking like any of their suspects.

There were a few more pictures of cigarette smoke rings being blown into the darkening sky by a lone figure on a fishing boat. Did his tattoo look like the one Ángelo had? She spent twenty minutes on that before realizing it was only a St. Peter's cross.

Then Martim had turned his attention back to the sunset, but this time to the smears of a colorful sky reflected off the hulls and windows of nearby boats. She could see the *Iaso*, with a few people on the foredeck. One held a closed book it had probably gotten too dark to read. A steward brought a cushion to another. A couple napped next to a table with empty wine glasses. More of Lori's time was eaten up checking every frame carefully.

The *Sirena* was in the background, berthed in its new, less expensive slip, still and dark and seemingly deserted. Captain Karlsson, however, was at the crossroads of pedestrian traffic in the west marina. Wearing his full glittery uniform, he sat next to an A-frame board advertising cruises. Lori spent more fruitless time examining everyone who accepted a flyer from him, then everyone around him. Not one of them looked familiar.

By the time Martim took his last ten pictures, the sun's show of colors and shapes had for the most part ended. He was framing a sailboat, the *Rosalinda*, against a silvered sky. Not his best pictures, she thought. She looked more critically. It was more than that the sunset light had paled; to her eyes, his composition had become sloppy and his horizon line had tilted. Was that an artistic statement she just couldn't grasp, or was she missing something?

The new program had revealed nothing relevant.

The living room had brightened with the sun. Resigned, Lori had closed her laptop and stretched out the stiffness in her neck. The sleepless night had left her wide awake, and she'd decided to dress and bring Carlos some fresh-from-the-bakery-oven rolls.

On her way out, the coffee maker had come to life with a blue light that was reflected on the curve of a nearby mug as a shiny streak. And that blue streak had sent her back to her laptop with a thudding heart.

She saw. In those last ten pictures, Martim hadn't been focusing on the whole of the *Rosalinda* but on a patch of its hull daubed with diffuse light that had been stretched into unrecognizable shapes by the curve of its hull. It hadn't been difficult to compress those pixels into a truer reflection of what they were a reflection of, but no amount of time and fiddling brought out enough detail to be of use.

She had opened the compressed pixels with the program Matthew's IT head had sent, and they had resolved into shapes that were at least comprehensible. In the first three shots, an attenuated blurred figure moved steadily in one direction, followed by two other figures, equally blurred but much larger. At that point, they were more the suggestion of human figures than clear images, almost like the patterns people find in clouds or Rorschach splotches. But they were definitely at the center of Martim's attention.

She had run the files through the program again, adjusting filters and kerning. It had happened very quickly. In the fourth shot, taken when the small figure had moved into a shadow, the face of a young girl resolved. She was wearing pajamas of some sort. Her eyes were wide, the tendons of her neck stood out, her mouth gaped, lips stretched against teeth. She was terrified.

In the next shot, the girl was cowering behind a chairback. High on the her arm was a dark mark. It was just a smudge, but the general shape and size had reminded Lori of something. She had lightened the area, but the exposure only washed out the mark. She had fiddled with saturation, and the mark blended into the girl's skin. When she sharpened the image and further filtered it, she had made out a few disconnected lines. Then, in the same way a human mind fills in the gaps of partial images to perceive them as complete ones, her mind had pulled those lines together into *SNP* and a cross of some sort.

It was the worst position to be in: Lori was missing, likely in danger, and everything Anton could think of doing had been done.

Catarina was about to suggest one more possibility when the call came in. Fredi's fishing boat had been spotted, and the Coast Guard had carried out Anton's order to impound it. That had had the desired effect on Fredi. He had exploded in an angry tirade of threats against the officers, for which he had been taken into custody. He was being held at the jail four blocks from the pousada.

That led to some conflict between the couple. When Catarina heard that Anton intended to question Fredi, she insisted on accompanying him. And he resisted. And she insisted.

Anton hadn't wanted her to see the interrogation because his intention was to make things very uncomfortable for Fredi—not because he had been fishing illegally, although that was taking its toll on his islands, and not because he was a drunk, although he saw that as a scourge on civilized society, but because Catarina had been certain he was hiding something relevant to their investigation.

Catarina had her own reason for wanting to talk to Fredi.

Under orders from Anton, Fredi had been taken in handcuffs to the smallest room in the police station, windowless and outfitted with a single metal table and two chairs. The two officers who were guarding Fredi had made sure he overheard tales of how vindictive Anton could be.

Although a faint odor of alcohol still came through his pores, Fredi certainly looked more alert than he'd been the last time they saw him. He'd even showered and put on clean clothes.

Anton ignored him. "We may be asking for hair analysis and a DNA profile," he said to one of the guards, "so alert the medical examiner we may need samples taken."

Fredi's eyebrows went up. "Samples?"

"I'm getting a search warrant for the boat and home, so assign two officers to that," he said to the other guard.

Fredi opened his mouth to protest and closed it.

"And check with Warden Madruga about an intake this evening, when I'm done with…" He only quirked his head in Fredi's direction. And when the guards asked if they should wait to carry out their orders until Anton was finished questioning Fredi, Anton stood close to Fredi, looked down, and said with intent, "Go. I can handle this very well."

He pulled out the other chair for Catarina and continued to stand over Fredi. He got right to the point. "I want to know about Tuesday morning in Breakwater Cove."

"I already told you."

"Tell me again."

His eyes shifted, and he talked. Catarina heard him repeat what he'd told them twenty-four hours before. The same words. The same intonation. He had rehearsed it, she knew. Perhaps not a lie but obfuscation. "Now tell the minister the rest of the story," she said, and she said it in a way that made it seem she already knew the rest of the story.

Anton knew she was up to something. He cracked open a folder and pretended to be checking it, pointing to various places on the papers inside and making noncommittal *hmm*s.

"Could we have some water, Minister?" Catarina asked, and he reluctantly put his head out the door to ask.

She had long since put it all together. The shadows in the pousada park so soon after Anton mentioned returning to Convento Real in front of a drunk-but-not-quite-passed-out Fredi. Who else would have something to say but was too frightened to say it to Anton directly?

"What did you want to tell me?" she said in a whisper that she hoped would reassure him that her aim wasn't to expose him to the beast of a man who was just now turning his attention back to him.

Beads of sweat appeared on his forehead and with the sweat came more of the cheap wine that still lingered in his system.

Catarina thought Fredi was the sort who, for all his faults, draws a line between whatever bad he'd done and allowing the murderer of a child to escape. "Fredi, a child has died."

"I saw the body," he whimpered.

They held their breath.

"It was being carried to the base of the Devil's Hands." He looked at Anton's face. "He was already dead! I had nothing to do with that."

"Why did you not tell us?" Catarina knew the reason and was only trying to ease him into a state of simply telling the truth.

"I didn't want to get involved. The fishing license business. I'm not exactly loved by you people."

"And?"

His lips glued shut.

"Close your eyes, and tell me moment by moment what you saw."

He said nothing.

Three seconds of silence later, Anton tagged on to what she had said with a short growl of exasperation. Two seconds after that, Fredi closed his eyes and started talking.

"I saw him face down. I thought he was swimming. Wearing white trunks. There was something wrong about the trunks. I didn't know what, but I wasn't really even thinking about it when I went back to...you know...checking the traps. At some point, I realized he was being carried by the waves, not moving on his own. Then I realized that the white wasn't in the right place to be trunks."

His eye flew open. "I wasn't looking at him then, not even thinking about what I'd seen, and suddenly I knew. I can't explain it. I just knew he was dead."

Catarina could explain it. Most people have experienced it. Even when operating a notch below consciousness, your brain carries the sights and sounds it has picked up, and it continues to process them long after you've focused on other things. "This is good, Fredi. Go on."

He closed his eyes. "The body was caught in a current, and it drifted until it was caught by the Devil's Hands. I rowed over. I was just curious. Really."

"What did you see when you got there?"

"He was a kid. There was a bandage around his middle. You see? Not trunks. A thick white bandage, taped all around." His voice softened, "And some blood in the middle." His eyes opened, slowly this time. "When I saw the sharks, I had to get out of there, you know. I'm just a fisherman in a small boat." He eyed each of them in turn. "Are we good, then?"

They said nothing.

"I was worried you'd come after me, you know, think I'd done it. But I didn't! Hand to God."

Catarina stood quickly and told Anton the interrogation was over. It would not have been in anyone's best interest for him to catch on to what had happened in the park until he was far, far from Fredi.

Berthed where it was, the reflection on the *Rosalinda's* hull could have come from the restaurants and bars along the harbor or from any number of other places around the marina. Lori had toggled between last pictures Martim had taken and broader shots of the area, trying to figure out the origin of the reflection of the girl's face. She'd pulled up a Google image of the marina, and she'd marked the positions the *Rosalinda's* hull, the boats in the harbor, and every café light and lamppost she could find. She'd laced copy after copy with angles of incidence and angles of reflection. She'd gotten nowhere. There were too many variables to know where the terrified young girl had been.

She'd found the answer simply and in an unexpected way. In the last four pictures on the memory card, she'd seen more than the disturbing image of a terrified child. She'd seen what might have saved Martim's life if he had noticed. Off to the side in the last four shots, a man looked in Martim's direction and, shutter click by shutter click, he grew larger as he closed the distance between them.

The man was wearing khaki pants and a white polo shirt.

The *Iaso* was departing for open waters within the hour. Martim's pictures would be enough to hold it.

Thumbs twitching on her phone, she texted Anton and Catarina.

Hold the Iaso!

If only she'd noticed that the message failed to send before she flew out the door.

11

Anton was weighing the risk of bringing in everyone who might be holding Lori. Chances were slim that they all could be located and taken into custody at the same time, and he was in turmoil knowing that any such activity could drive a desperate person to desperate acts.

Catarina was on the phone with Liliana. "Do you want to say anything?"

Of course he did, and he pushed himself out of his chair and made his way across the room, loosening stiff muscles along the way.

"I miss you, Papa," Liliana said.

He let his eyelids drift over tired eyes and her words soothe him with talk of home.

"I saved some cookies for you, Papa."

His bloodshot eyes popped open. There it was again. There was something in what she'd said, something just out of reach. Something connected not to Casa do Mar in general but to the cookies. He tried to re-create the cookie disaster, just two days and so long ago. Connections flickered in brain and went dark. *What memory had she brought to the surface?*

"Are you listening, Papa?"

He hadn't been, but he forced himself to now. Liliana was trying to decide whether to join an international online group of coding girls or to continue with her island group of environmentally minded students. He gave her his full attention and his best advice.

As happens when your mind is taken away from the unproductive cycling and recycling of thoughts, something did surface. Just before all the fun they'd had after the cookie disaster, the children had complained of boredom. Catarina had given them a bucket and a sponge and a bottle of cleaning liquid.

He was so close to something important. *What? What?*

From a café on the dock, Lori kept an eye on the *Iaso,* waiting for Anton to show up. She imagined he'd put his phone on mute for Martim's funeral, but that would be ending soon; he'd get her text and bring in the troops.

It was just after lunchtime, so the dock was dead quiet—with the exception of the *Iaso,* where preparations were underway to depart: supplies were being delivered; crew members were busy; passengers were returning with last-minute souvenirs. As expected, there were guards patrolling the wharf-side deck, one walking aft to stern, the other walking stern to aft. The two, both female, sometimes exchanged a few words when their paths intersected near the top of the gangplank, but their focus was on their duties.

Lori heard the low rumble of the engine test. On Matthew Cunningham's yacht, that was done about an hour before releasing the lines and clearing the dock. Still no Anton.

She left the café, walking casually and loitering on the dock close to the bottom of the gangplank, as though waiting for someone. Still no Anton.

If she could just look around, find the child or even the slightest evidence of wrongdoing, she could raise the alarm herself—with crew members or passengers or Harbor Patrol. She rehearsed possible excuses for her presence on the yacht if she did make it past the guards. *I thought it was my friend's boat.* She looked around; there wasn't another boat close to the *Iaso* in size or shape. *I'm lost.* With GPS? *I'm just so interested in yachts.* The first time she said that one, she knew it was absurd. *I lost my cell phone; could I borrow yours?* Still absurd but…she muted her cell phone and stuffed it in her pocket.

From behind sunglasses, she watched the two guards, patrolling like automatons, and timed how long both had their backs to the gangplank. A slow count of seventeen. It didn't seem enough time.

A motor bike passed by, rattling the boards. That would give her own footsteps up the gangplank a bit of extra cover. Still not enough time.

The tall guard put a phone to her ear, then pocketed it after one crisp nod of her head. She picked up her pace, said something to the short one, and left. The short one kept up her patrol, aft to stern, stern to aft. Lori saw a tiny window of opportunity when the remaining guard rounded a bulwark. *Could she get up the gangplank and out of sight before the guard turned back to face her?* She counted again. *No.*

The guard was stopped by a passenger who asked for a light. It would be a few more seconds as the guard turned into the wind and cupped her hands over the cigarette.

So Lori had run.

To her left, the guard was pocketing her lighter. To her right, a shadow stretched across the aft deck, coming closer. Other than retreating down the gangplank, there was only one option: directly ahead into a stairwell. The two steps down to get out of the guard's line of sight turned into two more steps when a voice sounded from the deck and a few more steps just to be sure.

She took a deep breath and listened. She heard footsteps at the top of the stairs and turned into an adjacent hallway. Then she heard a door opening and turned another way. With each turn, sounds from the deck grew fainter. With each turn, the light grew dimmer. Until she could hear only the hum of boat's engines and see only doors outlined in faint yellow lines.

She'd become disoriented in the maze of underdeck corridors, and it was time to get out. *But which way had she come? And did she even want to go back in that direction?* She fought an urge to turn on her phone's flashlight; if she had to turn it off suddenly, she'd lose the advantage of having accustomed her eyes to the dark.

By that time, she was no longer rehearsing excuses to explain her presence. For one, she was too preoccupied to think about needing one. For another, any excuse would have sounded ludicrous at this point.

Sweating despite the cool dark, she turned towards a feeble greenish light coming off buzzing fluorescent tubes at the end of one broad hallway. A man in the khakis-and-white-polo uniform appeared out of nowhere. Only his focus on a keypad entry lock kept her from being seen. She took one long step to hide behind a folding partition set up across a recess in the hallway. Through the crack between the hinged partition panels, she watched him tap in a code and go into a room that was bright with light. The smell of outgassing plastic and disinfectant reached her nose.

Lens against the partition crack, she took a picture. Another person approached the locked door, this time of a middle-aged woman carrying a clipboard. Lori took another picture and, as the woman punched in her entry code, a video.

She had two choices: return to wandering through a confusion of dim hallways with no reasonable explanation for her presence or hope that the room ahead led to an exit.

At the same time, both of the people who'd entered the room left. Lori reasoned that since she hadn't heard any voices when the door opened, it was unlikely there'd be more than one person in the room and, if there were, they'd be occupied doing something that required their full attention. She came out from behind her screen and using the video as a guide, she tapped in an entry code. The light on the keypad blinked from red to green. She pushed against a heavy door and slipped inside. The door swung closed with a slow whoosh.

It was bright inside. And very quiet. And cool, almost cold. The whirring ventilation system did little to dispel the smell of disinfectant. She explored the space, first with her eyes and then by walking around, putting one foot and the other down softly on shiny linoleum. It wasn't as large a space as she'd thought. There was a low table at the center with two desk chairs neatly parked underneath and two computers on top, hardwired and locked into position by strong cables. There were no lamps, no phones, no papers, no office supplies.

A 360° scan told her what she didn't want to know: there was only a single exit, the door she'd come through. She knew she should get out. But curiosity got the better of her. Just a quick look around, she told herself.

She took every step quietly and walked the perimeter of the room. Four rooms opened off it, all with wire-netted windows set in their doors, one with double swinging doors and an entry push pad, the other three with both keyed and electronic locks. Inside the first of those rooms was a narrow bed, a night table bolted to the floor, a lamp screwed into the wall, and nothing more. It was locked. The same was true of the second room.

Her ears pricked to the sound of sneakers squeaking on the waxed floor, and she squeezed under the table in the middle of the room just in time to see two pairs of feet cross the room. They stood in front of a door. Lori heard the faint beeps of another keypad code being entered and both sets of squeaky footsteps moving inside.

On hands and knees, she inched backwards from under the table and into the room with the swinging doors. She was in a much larger space and much colder one. There were cabinets along one wall, some electronic equipment on carts, and two narrow beds at opposite ends of the room, all indistinct in the minimal light coming through the glass insets in the doors.

A bank of pull-down lighting fixtures. Carts with centrifuges, microscopes, tanks of compressed gases. Cabinet drawers labeled for tubing, bandaging and tape, needles and syringes, and medications. Two gurneys. Two tables. It was an operating room. *Was this a paranoid billionaire's way of handling medical emergencies while at sea? If so, what were those tiny rooms—and why were they locked?*

She got to her feet and risked peeking through one of the window insets. Outside, the two young women who'd been talking were outside the door to the one of the locked rooms. The door opened, and they were joined by a man, short but bulldog strong. Lori pressed herself against the wall.

Her peripheral vision caught movement at one end of the operating room. She whipped around, arm high over her head, and faced the source of the movement: her own image, reflected in a shiny stainless steel door. Her suppressed laugh did nothing to dampen her adrenaline-fueled fear.

She peeked again, this time to see all three people melting into the darkness of the hallway as the heavy door swung shut again.

At least I can take a few of pictures, she thought, and she did. When the flash came back to her from the stainless steel door, it startled her just as her own reflection had minutes earlier. She took another hurried shot and headed to the door to make her escape, still carrying a mental image of that stainless steel door. It had a handle, the type you might find on a refrigerator, and a lock. Another quick look through the window. All was quiet outside, so she went to the back wall and lifted the door's latch. She tugged. Nothing. It was locked. She pressed her hand against the door. It was cold but far colder than one would expect just by virtue of it being metal.

Lori's eyes widened as her brain put together the facts.

When she took out her phone to text Anton, her heart gave one solid thump. She tapped *Send* on the message she'd written hours earlier. And tapped again. And again. There was no service. No one knew she was there.

That was when leaving became an imperative.

She opened the operating room door just enough to slip out sideways.

She waited and listened. The heavy sound insulation worked both for and against her. It was hard for others to hear her, and it was hard for her to hear anyone coming.

Something by the desk at the center of the room caught her eye. She didn't know how she'd missed it. At the top of a chairback, a man's head swiveled. Hands appeared on the armrests and a pair of muscled arms lifted him up.

Lori glued herself to the wall and froze. It was too late. He turned. She ran, at first through that single way out and then, as she heard his breaths behind her, blindly through a maze of corridors.

This is where Anton excelled. He took the information he'd gathered, the images he'd seen, the words he'd heard, and he found a pattern.

The memory that had been nagging at him from the hidden recesses of his mind announced itself loudly:

"I don't like that smell," Liliana had said.

"It's just disinfectant." Catarina had told her. "The *Iaso* is easily the cleanest ship I have been on," she'd also said, after she'd smelled a disinfectant that reminded her of hospitals.

Iaso, one of the goddesses of healing, Dr. Fowler told them.

A sharp cut on Ángelo's abdomen, Guilherme Nunes had thought. And in the medical waste that had been washing up on shore, he'd found a syringe with traces of the same sedative in Ángelo's body.

And from Fredi, "A thick white bandage, taped all around...some blood in the middle."

All at once, everything fell into place.

Ángelo had been subjected to some medical procedure while on board the *Iaso*. He'd been desperate enough to get off the ship that he had fallen or jumped to his death.

It might not be enough to justify an order from the president, and there would be consequences if he was wrong, for Casa do Mar, for the heritage site, for his job, for the good name of the Azores.

But Lori was missing. And if she was on the *Iaso*, he was not going to let it out of the harbor.

Lori felt a heavy hand on her shoulder. She twisted loose and ran—only to find herself trapped in a dead-end corridor, the only way out blocked by a man whose strength and determination seemed beyond her. When he reached her, she grabbed a railing for leverage to kick out, but her sweaty palms slipped, and he took her head between his palms and slammed it against a doorframe. For a moment, there was nothing but speckles of light at the back of her eyes and the taste of her own blood.

There was only one option, a wild charge past him. She never made it. He grabbed her arm and dragged her to the surgical suite.

Pushed against a cart in the operating room, she reached back. Her hand found a scalpel sealed in plastic. She used it before she knew she had. One lunge sent the metal through the plastic and into flesh. A long slit on a forearm, too shallow to stop him but deep enough to spray his blood over her hand and the scalpel. She lost her grip, and it fell from her hand.

All she could think of was to throw herself over it, so he didn't get to it first. He lifted her up by the waist of her pants and kicked the scalpel away. Kicking out, her shoes met some part of her attacker. It was enough traction for her to twist her torso and reach out to where the scalpel lay, now with its tip wedged under a cabinet.

He swung her around. She screamed, a reflex more than anything else, and lashed out with shaking hands.

The force of the blood shocked her so much, she forgot to run as he crumpled to his knees and then flat on his face with enough force to make instruments on the cart tremble. He clutched his neck where she had sliced, his eyes wide with fear, his mouth contorted with pain.

Blood leaked between his fingers and pooled on the shiny clean linoleum floor. For an instant, she was torn between running and preventing him from bleeding out.

The decision was made for her. A khaki-and-polo-shirt guard was in the doorway and behind him, Dr. Fowler stood, as cold as ice.

Anton toppled outdoor chairs and parted crowds as he ran through the patio to the parking lot, followed by Catarina. He was starting the car minutes later. With one hand, he pulled onto the main road to the marina. With the other, he yelled into his government-issued cell phone.

There was no time to work his way through to the president's office and little hope that the president would give him the permission he'd already asked for and been denied twice. His call was directly to Luis. The line was busy.

He threw the phone into the cup holder and accelerated. "Text Luis. I need him."

They were pressed against the car doors and each other as Anton took the curves at an even higher than usual speed.

His phone rang. Catarina got to it before he did. She turned on the speaker. Just three short sentences from Anton. "I need backup at the marina. Hold the *Iaso*. The president has not been asked." Luis would either help or not.

There are only two traffic lights in the city. Anton managed to arrive at both intersections just as they were turning red. He didn't stop for either.

A guard stood beside Lori as Fowler stuck a hypodermic needle deep into a vial and filled a syringe.

She thought of Ángelo.

"Relax," Fowler said in the most soothing of voices. "It will all be fine. You'll be doing good."

He took Lori's wrist in an iron grip and nodded to the guard, who opened the stainless steel door to reveal a brightly lit refrigerated room with two large shelves against the back wall. A body, wrapped in plastic like a shiny mummy, lay on the lower one. He began to clear the upper one. For her.

Fowler held her arm down. She felt the stick of the needle. *I'm not going without a fight.*

She pulled out the hypodermic, wrenched free of Fowler's grasp, and threw herself against the refrigerator door to close it. Fowler had been taken by surprise but not for long. He pressed a wall intercom and yelled, "Surgery. Urgent." Before his hand had left the button, she swung a cart hard, sending it careening into him.

She pushed her way through the swinging doors, raced past the desk and through the exit. In the hall, she heard shoes slapping the linoleum floor of the hallway…coming fast…too many to fight off.

One last chance.

She ran full force towards them.

But the hypodermic was taking effect. The sound of voices started to echo in the narrow hallway. Her legs fought hard against gravity. Her heart resounded against her eardrums. She ran more slowly, then erratically.

Five full seconds after she crashed into a wall of people, she understood: the arms wrapping her tightly were Anton's.

12

It was a quick roundtrip to the hospital for Anton and Catarina. In the tiny ambulance, they sat on either side of Lori, who was deeply sedated by the time Anton carried her off the *Iaso*. Once in the emergency room, both had been turned away. The emergency room was gearing up to receive more patients than it usually accommodated in a month, and the two doctors on duty had instituted a no-visitors policy.

Anton's initial reaction was to use the power of his office to insist on preferential treatment, but that wasn't in his nature—and he knew he was needed back in the marina.

By the time he and Catarina returned to the dock, it had been closed off to all but the emergency vehicles that were lining up.

Luis and Anton stationed themselves at the bottom of the gangplank and directed everyone who disembarked to the correct place. The island's two ambulances made repeated trips to take sick passengers and eight captives to the hospital. Dr. Fowler, the captain, and medical personnel were taken away in separate cars. Further triage became Catarina's. A nod from her could confirm someone's statement that they knew nothing about what was going on below deck or not. Three buses were filled with *Iaso* staff, two going to local hotels and the third destined for the police station.

Dr. Nunes, deep in discussions with research facilities and transplant banks, oversaw the removal of the body and coolers from the refrigerator. Catarina did not allow herself to dwell on what was in those coolers.

A girl in her early teens broke loose from the harbor patrolwoman who was trying to help her into an ambulance. She ran screaming down the dock. A EMT caught her around the waist, and she flailed out, pummeling his chest, kicking out. When a second EMT arrived, she simply collapsed, unable to fight anymore. The top of her pajamas slipped off her shoulder. Catarina saw the tattoo, SNP with a stylized cross, and she saw numbers below it, 7-4-1. Of course, she went over and spent time reassuring her that she was safe now and would be cared for.

One of last passengers to be wheeled to an ambulance was a young boy. His mother waited beside him. His life would have meant the sacrifice of another child. The woman told Catarina she knew nothing more than that there was an opportunity to have her child's failing heart replaced with a healthy one. She said it was to have come from a child who was braindead.

"There were days when I considered driving my car off a cliff with him inside, to save him from the months and years of torment to come," the mother tried to explain.

Perhaps she did not know the truth, thought Catarina, but did she suspect somewhere deep inside? But there was no way to know what was so deep in a person's heart.

Catarina and Anton were keeping a vigil by Lori's bed. Dr. Nunes had located the syringe that Fowler had wanted to empty into Lori's arm, and he'd made sure the doctors knew both what was in it and how much had reached her bloodstream before she'd pulled the needle out.

The hospital was still busy but slowly emptying of critically ill patients. Carlos made a short detour to see Lori on his way to the airfield; he'd answered the call for pilots to fly patients to the mainland. He was not his usual self. It wasn't just the dark circles under his eyes. Clearly, he hadn't spent the same time—or any time—on grooming. His hair was uncombed, his face unshaven, and he wore the same wrinkled shirt that he'd worn to Martim's funeral.

In Lori's room, he let himself be held by Catarina for a long time. "I am worried about her," he said.

Anton laid a strong hand on his shoulder and squeezed. "Guilherme assured us she will be fine. The drug has almost cleared her system. She has a concussion and will suffer the headache and nausea that go with it."

"Will we take her home tonight?"

"Not tonight. She has to stay in the hospital another day, to be awakened every three hours."

"I must go," he said reluctantly.

"If you have a few minutes, Anton and I would like to get a coffee in the waiting room."

Anton was slow to catch on and said he'd wait with Lori while she got herself coffee.

"I'd like the company," Catarina said firmly, and she tugged him out of the room.

Carlos held Lori tenderly. Her eyes flickered open. Still groggy, she said, "You look terrible. I love you looking terrible." And she fell asleep again.

The next day brought moments of great satisfaction that seemed to right their tilted world and moments of great sadness that made it wobble again.

The email from Captain Jesús Rodriguez arrived while they were still at the pousada. The young woman who had gone to the police in Corozal Town had been located. Her DNA had confirmed that the boy they had named Ángelo was her brother.

"His name was Gabriel," Anton said, wide-eyed at the coincidence.

Catarina called the woman and told her that her brother had been found in the waters of a peaceful cove after having saved the life of a passenger on the yacht where he had been living. Perhaps not the full truth, but no one should have to carry the burden of knowing a truth like that.

She persuaded Dr. Nunes to give her a death certificate that similarly obfuscated the circumstances around Ángelo's death. The blow to the top of his head was enough for him to say that in all likelihood, he had died due to a fall from the deck of a ship. With the help of their friend, Padre Henriques, she found a grave for Gabriel in Corozal Town. With the help of the city's mortician, Anton's second cousin, she arranged to have his body flown to Belize in a coffin where his injuries were locked away. And Anton and Catarina would be at the airport with Gabriel when his flight home took off.

By that time, statements made by patients and their families and by *Iaso* staff would confirm the worst. For eight years Fowler had operated a lucrative business in the trade of human tissues, branching out to his own transplant surgery business in the past two years.

It wasn't uncommon. With almost one hundred thousand desperate people waiting for organ transplants worldwide, organ trafficking and transplant tourism have become widespread. An estimated 10% of all organ transplants are illegal, and the Internet raises that percentage every year. In India, one man did six hundred illegal transplants over fifteen years. In 2011, Brooklyn man was convicted of making $160,000 selling human kidneys that he got sometimes by inducing the poor and sometimes by putting a gun to someone's head. In 2014, a Mexican man was arrested for kidnapping children to use as organ sources, and transplant networks in other countries kidnap children to murder them and harvest their organs.

Between black market transplant surgeries and the legal, safe, and ethical use of human tissues is a large gray area. China not only sanctions the sale of human body parts, it is the largest seller, harvesting organs from the bodies of executed political and religious dissidents. Mortuaries and hospitals have been known to replace bones with plastic pipes and strip out ligaments before burial, knowing that neither is noticeable in the casket and both can be transplanted or used for biomedical research.

Even the Transplantation of Human Organs Act has loopholes. It allows a person to receive compensation for the harvesting their spouse's organs—so some people have married their victims before killing them.

Most legal donors who voluntarily sell their own body tissues are poor women from developing nations. The average cost of transplant surgery is $175,000, with most money going to the organ broker. Only between $1,000 and $5,000 goes to the donor, and often the cost of their hospital stay is deducted from what they get.

It was that gray area Fowler crossed in his journey from a legitimate surgeon to a man who bought human beings to fund his greed. In the months to come, he would never admit to wrongdoing, insisting that he was providing a valuable service, not just to those who could afford to bypass the ethical legal system but also to those he was "helping to a better life by giving them the opportunity to leave poverty behind." On the matter of paying the owners of the Sociedad por los Niños Perdidos for harvesting organs from Gabriel and other orphans of poverty, Fowler claimed he had been assured that parents had welcomed the opportunity and that children were to be returned healthy.

Anton went to the Costa brothers on a mission.

As expected, the visit started with a grumble from Alberto. "You have heard? That kid's been cheating us. I figure he owes us a thousand euros. More."

"It's not a thousand euros," Júlio came back at his brother. "It's money we wouldn't have had if he hadn't found the customers."

"What about that gas?"

"It would have been burned anyway," Júlio sighed.

"Air!" he said triumphantly. "Anton, You have to make him pay for the air!"

Anton rewound the conversation to the beginning, when one Fabi's off-the-books customers had walked in carrying the flyer he'd picked up in the café near his rental house and looking for a lost pair of sunglasses. That had tipped off the brothers to Fabi's deception. Alberto had fired him when he stepped into the shop an hour later. Since then, business had been rocky, with the brothers unable to decipher their online bookings, unable to take out divers themselves, unable to do routine maintenance on the boat. And that played right into Anton's mission.

Under the guise of a friendly chat, he started with a comment about how he was getting older—as they were. "I'm learning that there are certain things best left to younger men."

Anton complained about the noisy bar in town that had been forced to close and had been replaced with a noisier bar, then shook his head and said, "The devil one knows is usually preferable to the devil one doesn't know."

He had ended with a story about how a contribution to a church rummage sale had led to a woman reuniting with a long-lost relative. "Yes," he said almost to himself, "in my experience doing a good deed often brings unexpected rewards."

Júlio took it from there. "You know, Alberto, Fabi did attract the younger crowd."

His brother harrumphed but admitted, "They are more likely to go diving."

By the time Anton left, they were talking about how they could sit back and enjoy life if they brought Fabi in fulltime and groomed him to run the business.

The next stop was the marina.

After Lori raised the issue of why the *Doura* suddenly turned around on its return to the Azores, it hadn't taken long for Anton to find Branco's warning to its captain and to figure out the harbormaster's role in the trade of desperation and human greed. Branco had been taking bribes to look the other way when undocumented aliens were brought into port and transferred to other ships bound for countries thousands of miles away.

Branco nearly toppled over when he looked up from his chair at the harbormaster's office and saw Anton accompanied by three Coast Guard officers, all looking grim.

Branco's departure was followed closely by the arrival of a new *capitão do porto*. Not unexpectedly, she turned out to be a former neighbor of Anton's and a former classmate of Catarina. She would do very well.

There was one more stop they had to make, this a sad one.

Word had reached them about Ema. She had terminal cancer. When they stopped by the Vieira boat, the entire family was pitching in to put it in order for the evening and to prepare for another day of sharing the island's waters with visitors. Ema was watching Zeze, her sons were repairing a fuel line, her daughter was washing down the deck, and Vitor was supervising it all.

So it went—not just in the Vieira family but in the Deníz family, not just in villages but in most places. People stoically carried on. They cared for one another, without prompting, without praise. They were grateful for the good life had brought. Even the dying felt that way.

As aviãozinho lifted into the air, they didn't look at the beautiful Atlantic below them or at the green hills that sloped down to it. The full moon didn't claim their attention as the sky lost its color and the sun sank below the horizon. No one commented on how good it was to have this investigation behind them or how good it would be to see their home again. They had been too close to sadness.

"If only we had been able to save Ángelo," Anton said, reverting to the name they had given the boy.

Catarina felt his pain physically, as a squeeze in her chest, as though it were possible for words to reach inside, grab hold of a heart, and twist. "Sometimes the best you can do is bring evil to light."

"Again and again," sighed Anton.

Home. It was the only thought in Lori's head when, between Carlos and Anton, she walked the pitted, moss-stained stones to the Casa do Mar barn. Watched over by Ethan, the children burst out the kitchen door, then slowed themselves to approach her gently. She smiled. "Come here, dear reindeer." And she held open her arms for them and felt their hearts, beating like soft drums, soothing her bruised skin.

Steamy fumes perfumed by the lavender soap Liliana had given her swirled around Lori in the bathroom. She wiped the mirror and looked into her eyes. *It's over. You're fine. Put it behind you.* But before she finished talking to herself, the mirror fogged, and she felt like crying again.

In the wee hours of the morning, she awoke thinking she was in danger. She couldn't fall asleep again until the sun came up and the soundtrack of Casa do Mar began to play. Beto's crew hammering and sawing. Jardiniero and Jardiniera bleating. Sombra's paws clicking on the wooden floors. The distant voices of her family.

Catarina spent time with her, at first sitting beside her on Liliana's bed and then outside on the sunny hill. She reminded Lori that the emotional shock of a disturbing event can be experienced long after someone is safe. And she made Lori promise that she would keep that in mind and come to her if that happened.

The splitting headache cleared, as did the nausea, and the comfort food Catarina made for her actually began to comfort her again. The sense that she was in danger also faded as she recovered, although it did return without warning and sharply in images of plastic-wrapped bodies and the sensation of a needle piercing her skin.

It wasn't until she'd left the main house, where everyone had insisted she stay until she was better, and walked back to Casa do Bosque that she actually felt completely herself. The cheery space named for the small copse into which it was tucked looked like it had been waiting for her. The large, papery leaves of the fig tree outside caught ocean breezes and seemed to applaud her return.

There, on a wall just inside the front door was one of Catarina's paintings. It showed her Casa do Bosque and outside it, the tiny figures of Anton, Catarina, and their children. When Lori had first seen the watercolor, it had been a reminder of the family she lacked. Later, she saw: Catarina had included her as one of the family, looking out to sea with an expression of peace.

It was a quiet morning on the Casa do Mar patio.

Carlos was sitting on one side of Lori, when Ethan came over and took the narrow space on the other side. Anton looked up and gave all three his smile of contentment before returning to his newspaper, one of several that the islands were proud to still be printing.

Beside him, Catarina was admiring the first buds of the roses she and Lori had planted last spring. Anton's claim to participation was that he had directed the entire operation, although that had been from the comfort of his seat on a nearby stone wall. (To be fair, he'd also kept Sombra away from the holes they dug.)

They could all feel the last of summer being carried away on crisp southerly breezes. Soaking rains had left the hills a particularly vibrant green and against that backdrop, leaves were beginning to glow with sparkling reds and smoky purples. The birds had worked themselves into a frenzy, over a territorial dispute or mating season or the prospect of all the breakfast crumbs soon to be brushed off laps.

Felipe crossed the road, behind him Toni and Nuno. The boys had spent the night together at Casa do Mar. Everything about them said they would rather be doing almost anything than following him.

Felipe stopped several yards from the house and motioned the boys forward. "I've been keeping an eye on the area since you called," he said to Anton. (It was typical of Felipe to have taken on the task himself.) "Early this morning, I left my car behind the church, walked around the back of Maria Rosa's house, and waited. After she left, I saw…You tell everyone, boys."

Neither spoke.

Catarina bent down, putting her face at Toni's level. "Son, what did Chief Madruga see?"

"We're making a house just for the two of us."

Liliana appeared at the Dutch door to give an adult look of disapproval.

Catarina kept a gentle smile on her face and nodded. Toni and Nuno responded with torrents of excited words, breaking into each other's sentences, pointing, gesturing, crouching low to show how they'd dug up treasures under the dirt floor and stretching high to show how they'd patched the roof of Maria Rosa's run-down shed. Then they remembered what had brought them there, and they sealed their lips.

"It must have been exciting, and it is certainly a good thing to make something better of what you have. What was the problem with the way you did it?"

Toni was unsure. "I hurt my thumb with the hammer?" Looking at his parents faces, he knew that wasn't the right answer, so he tried again, "I didn't tell anyone?" That was better, but clearly they were waiting for more. He thought. "We sneaked out of the house at night?" He thought again. "We didn't ask for permission?"

They apologized and were forgiven for what they had done and for having made Maria Rosa worry that someone was outside her house, although Catarina didn't make a big deal of that. She didn't want children to worry unnecessarily.

There were hugs all around, promises to be good were made, and the boys ran off to play.

"Wait!" Anton bellowed after them. "What tools did you use?"

"We borrowed Beto's tools," Toni's face was pure innocence, because in fact he felt no guilt for using a tool and returning it. Anton's response was restrained, the boys were contrite, and apologies were made to Beto (who was relieved not to have reached an age when he forgot something as important as where he had put his tools.)

Later that day, after Maria Rosa had returned from the clinic, Catarina accompanied Toni and Nuno back across the road to apologize again. It was only after the boys left that Maria Rosa's relief manifested itself in tears she could not control.

"This time," Catarina said, holding her friend close, "it was two harmless boys. You will never be free of fear if you do not let us help you with what led to that fear."

When she did tell her story, it was dispassionately and concisely. She'd been widowed and left with a child when her young man died of cancer. Two years later, she'd met an older doctor at the hospital in Lisbon where she was finishing her training, and she'd moved in with him. The abuse started soon afterwards. She'd promptly left—him and the hospital. Pregnant with her second child, she got a job in Porto, only to find that he'd followed her to the same hospital, enraged that she'd planned to keep his child from him.

He was a brilliant actor. He stood before the magistrate looking and sounding like an aggrieved citizen—and making her look and sound like a woman on the edge, perhaps a woman who couldn't be trusted to keep her own children.

He was clever. Not once was he caught when following her home, confronting her in shops, appearing in her bedroom late at night, threatening to leave her children motherless.

She planned her escape to a small, isolated island. And for six years, she'd had peace. Until she received an email from a school friend. Her friend was now working in the federal department that renewed nursing licenses and was congratulating her on her move to Santa Maria.

Maria Rosa had never updated her address at the nursing bureau—or anywhere. Year after year, she'd paid for a post office box in Porto and had everything forwarded. Yet, someone had put a change of address through for her two weeks ago.

The new house was a pleasant twenty-minute walk from Casa do Mar, and seeing it was a family affair. Anton carried a bottle of wine, Catarina brought a basket of biscuits, and the children tagged behind with a bag of flower bulbs.

Having lived in apartments all of his adult life, Carlos was most delighted by the land at the back of his house. It was just a sliver, once a large vegetable garden, and it banked against the bottom of a cliff that rose, first steeply and then very steeply into a darkly forested ledge. The bottom of the cliff—where it was merely steep and not very steep—had been terraced and tiny patches were planted with grape vines that had been so neglected it was hard to tell them from the weeds that had taken over. At the side of the yard, there were a couple of fig trees and a small outbuilding with only two standing walls and half a roof that sagged against the rocky cliff.

While the children explored, Carlos got carried away with his plans for a porch and a garden. "We could remove whatever that was," he waved a hand in the direction of the flimsy structure to the side.

Anton had a good laugh. "The wind will remove it for you in the next month or two."

"Perhaps Beto can help, when you are ready," suggested Catarina.

There was no land in front of the house and that, too, delighted Carlos, because the door opened almost directly onto the road, and across that road was the ocean. The house itself was almost as small as one of Casa do Mar's guest cottages and almost as derelict as they had been when Anton and Catarina first saw them. There was just the one room on the ground floor, with a 1950s-style kitchenette at one end, a 1930s-style bathroom at the other, and a loft above. "Look," said Carlos, "I can cross from the front door to the back door in six steps." And he could. And that delighted him.

He opened the wine and poured it into tall glasses he'd brought from São Miguel.

"*Salud.*" Anton raised his glass. "May this house be filled with happiness...and children."

Sometimes, their investigations took them away from their home for long days, and it had become a tradition to have a party for family and friends when normalcy returned and they were able to put such things behind them.

This get-together was a small one compared to others at Casa do Mar. Guests danced to music played by Matias and two of the waiters at Water's Edge. (Anton and Catarina danced together many times, he feeling strong and healthy, she feeling young and limber, both feeling very much in love.) Dishes brought by friends competed for space on outside tables and filled the night air with tempting smells. Talk seesawed from the mundane to the exciting.

Anton announced the completion of Casa de Leite and the first recreation of an early settlement on the heritage preserve at the end of the month. He'd already invited representatives of the Gillis Foundation and had plans to make a second pitch for funds to continue developing the preserve. (The Azores's new president had declined an invitation to attend, citing a busy schedule.)

Luis made a surprise and very welcome appearance. He'd called every day since they got home, asking after Lori's condition and thanking Anton for everyone's work. (Neither he nor Anton had heard from the president about their success, and they didn't expect to.)

Padre Henriques, still the picture of health although well into his eighties, brought greens from his well-tended garden. He attracted the attention of the children, who had learned early how generous he was with the candy in the deep pockets of his cassock. He brought a picture of Gabriel's grave in a flower-speckled meadow and news that the Church had stepped in to take on responsibility for the SNP orphans.

Standing next to Padre Henriques, Catarina told Anton that Fredi had followed her in the park. Not surprising—to her, at least—he took the news well now that his world had righted (and Padre Henriques was listening.) Fredi would pay the price he deserved for illegal fishing but only that and not any more for how his bungled attempt to give Catarina information had frightened her.

Anton took aside Maria Rosa and let her know that her change of address was made by the island's own Dr. Leal when he made a report on the vaccinations she'd given last spring. As for the man she feared was stalking her, he hadn't left the mainland in two years.

He gave her shoulder a reassuring squeeze. "It is time to end the worry. You are safe on Santa Maria."

Catarina unveiled her latest watercolor showing Casa de Leite, ready to welcome guests next week. The path to its bright red front door was lined with milk cans that had been repurposed into planters, each filled with begonias in that same cheery shade of red. The painting would hang high up on the kitchen wall with the ones she had done of their other two cottages, symbols of what they had accomplished together.

With Nuno by her side, Estela let it be known that she was expecting a second child. And when offers of support and all sorts of the items needed for babies were made, she accepted gratefully, knowing she'd made the right decision to stay with her community.

One more joyous announcement was made by Felipe and Gabriela. They were getting married.

There was mischief on his face when Anton raised a glass to the engaged couple. "It is never too late to take a chance on love," he said, a moment before he slid his eyes over to where Lori sat between Carlos and Ethan.

Lori was watching. *Why not take a chance?*

After the last guest had said goodnight, Anton, Catarina, and Lori stood together at the top of the Casa do Mar cliff. There was a full moon, so bright the dapples of lunar craters were no longer visible, and silver-streaked breakers laced the beach below. Catarina released her hair from its bun and let it whirl around her face in the soft breezes. Anton filled his eyes with the sight of his island and his lungs with its perfume. Lori stared into the starry sky as though it held the answer to her question.

There is a tendency as people get older to look back to 'the good old days' with longing. Things were better then, they tell themselves. People were nicer. Fruit was sweeter. Air was fresher. Even the stars sparkled more brightly. Not so for these three friends. With every year that passed, they marveled at how much better life had become.

Printed in Great Britain
by Amazon

21534915R00129